ROCKY MOUNTAIN *MAYHEM*

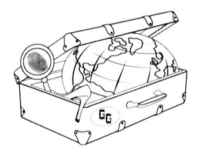

Joan Rylen

Also by Joan Rylen

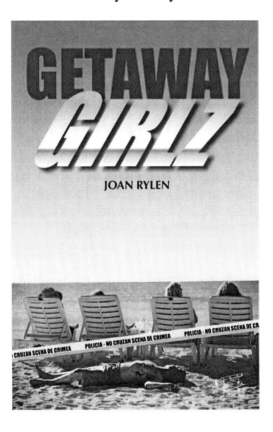

Named one of "20 recent releases, worthy of attention…"
— Maggie Galehouse, *Houston Chronicle*

To David, for your love and endless support.
Love, Robbyn

To Mom and Dad, thanks for always being there when I fall.
And even when I don't.
Love, Johnell

Prologue

Viv: hey there

B-Man: Hey lady! How goes it? Long time no talk.

Viv: been busy

B-Man: I hear ya. How are the kids?

Viv: good kid stuff all the time

B-Man: Right! They'll run you ragged!

B-Man: Wanna get together this weekend, or are you still dating that guy?

Viv: yeah we r in love he's great

B-Man: Love! Wasn't ready to hear that.

B-Man: How long you been dating him?

Viv: a few months but when you know you know

B-Man: Wow.

B-Man: I'm shocked.

Viv: proposal soon I hope

B-Man: I'm even more shocked but hope it all works out.

Viv: it will the kids love him too

B-Man: So what's on tap for tonight?

Viv: we r going to a play

B-Man: That's cool. Whatcha seeing?

Viv: shakespeare in the park

B-Man: I've been wanting to do that. What's onstage tonight?

Viv: othello

B-Man: Cool. You want to try to get together next weekend?

Viv: can't out of town

B-Man: Oh…romantic getaway?

Viv: friends

B-Man: Fun! Where are you heading?

Viv: colorado

Viv: im really going to miss craig i spend all my free time with him

B-Man: Yep, I understand. Well back to work for me. Take care Viv.

Viv: bye

***

Vivian Taylor drummed her fingers on the kitchen table. "Is there something you want to tell me?" She said to Craig and then laid her hand over an upside down sheet of paper.

"I don't know what you mean," Craig replied.

She looked at him, hoping he would come clean. "I've never given you any reason to think I've been unfaithful. So do you have something to say, because I'm giving you one chance."

He shook his head. "Noooo."

Vivian turned over the page. "Does this look familiar?"

Craig looked at it for a long moment, the color rising in his cheeks. "No."

"Listen, Craig, I understand you had a crap marriage. Your wife cheated on you. Whatever. But that's not me. So I'm giving you this one chance to tell me the truth."

Craig looked at the paper again, then back at her. "I don't know what you're talking about."

Vivian shoved the Facebook transcript at him. "I know this was you. I know you were the person typing this. Not me."

Craig pushed back from the table. "I don't know what this crap is."

"Craig, I fed Brandon these questions. He called me at work and told me someone was pretending to be me online. He knew it wasn't me. I'm the one who told him to ask what I was doing tonight. You're the only person who knew we were supposed to be going to a play."

Craig crumpled the paper and chunked it across the kitchen. "This is bullshit. Come on, get your purse, we're going to be late."

"I'm not going. I've put your things in a box by the front door. Please leave. I never want to hear from you again."

"Vivian, I didn't do this." He gestured to the paper now across the room.

"Craig, I have no doubt. It was you. Please leave."

Craig walked toward her slowly, backing her into a kitchen corner. "Forget about this. It's bullshit."

"If you don't leave, I'm going to call the cops." She glanced out of the corner of her eye at the phone hanging a few feet to her right.

Craig got in her face, gritting his teeth. "I didn't do this." His eyes flashed with anger.

Vivian's stomach lurched and her heart pounded. She reached for the phone but couldn't get to it. He leaned over, ripped the phone out of the wall and threw it across the room. The base thudded against the couch, and the handset shattered against the fireplace.

Before she could move, he was back in her face, sticking his finger between her eyes. "You're a total fucking whore, Vivian. You were a slut before I met you, and you're still one now."

"Craig, get out of my house." She pushed against his chest, but his 5-foot-10, stocky frame didn't budge.

He grabbed her wrists and held her arms out, slamming them against the wall. "You're going to regret this decision."

In full panic mode she kicked up her knee, narrowly missing his groin, but he released her arms. She took a step toward the counter and pulled a knife from the butcher block. She held it out in front of her and maneuvered around him. "Get the hell outta here, Craig." She reached her purse on the kitchen counter and dug around for her cell phone. "You're a crazy, sick bastard."

Craig grabbed a picture off the wall and threw it to the floor. He upended the kitchen table. A crystal vase with fresh flowers crashed to the floor, shards skittering everywhere.

Vivian ran to her bedroom clutching her cell, locked the door and dialed 9-1-1. She quickly explained the situation to the operator, as something else crashed on the other side of the door.

"The police are on their way," the operator said. "Are you in a safe location?"

Craig pounded on the door. "Vivian, get the fuck out here! We need to talk about this!"

"I don't think so. Please hurry." She looked around for an escape. *The window.* "I'm going to crawl out my bedroom window and into the backyard. I'm going to try to make it to my neighbor's."

Craig kicked the door and wood splintered.

"Oh crap, I'm getting out of here. He's trying to get through the door."

Vivian unlatched the window, kicked out the screen, threw her legs out and dropped to the ground. Her dog, Cooper, ran up, looking for attention. She took off sprinting toward the side of the house, and he matched her stride for stride. She threw open the gate and kept running expecting Cooper to follow, but instead heard him barking ferociously. She glanced back and saw him holding Craig inside the gate.

Good dog!

She ran to her neighbor's house and banged on the door, hearing sirens in the distance. "Angie, open up! It's Vivian!" She pounded on the door again. *Dammit!*

She ducked behind some bushes on the far side of the house. Sweat poured down her forehead and her heart raced. She put the phone back to her ear. "I'm hiding around the corner at my neighbor's house."

"The police are two minutes out," the operator said. "Stay put."

Just then Cooper popped out from around the bush and Vivian screamed. "You scared the bejeesus out of me!"

"Is everything all right?" the operator asked.

"Oh my god, yes. My dog found me."

Vivian heard Craig's truck start up, then tires screeching on the pavement.

1

Day 1

Audrey looked up at Vivian with curious blue eyes. "Where are you going, Mommy?"

"I'm going on a plane, remember? To the mountains." Vivian pushed a blonde curl from her 5-year-old daughter's face. Wound up it fell at her eyes, but pulled straight it reached her chin.

"Am I going?"

Vivian smiled. "No, sweetie, not this time. I promise I'll bring you back a special surprise."

Audrey pondered. "Who's going with you?"

"My very best friends I've known for a long, long time. One of them, since I was about your age." Vivian put a jacket in her suitcase, then stuffed everything down. "Do you remember their names?"

"I remember Miss Wendy. She always has candies in her purse. And Miss Lucy made me cookies for my birthday. Those were yummy." Audrey reached into the suitcase and pulled out Vivian's bra.

"Our room fits four people. Did you forget someone?" Vivian gently took her bra back and stuffed it into an outside pocket.

Audrey looked at her fingers and counted. "Mommy, Miss Lucy, Miss Wendy..." Her lip twitched to the side and she tapped her cheek as she thought about it.

"What about Miss Kate?" Vivian asked, tugging on the uncooperative zipper.

"Oh yeah! I wore a princess dress to her wedding. I remember."

"You're so smart!" Vivian scooped Audrey up and gave her a hug. "Nana will pick you up from Miss Margie's house later today."

7

Audrey clapped and squeezed her cheek next to Vivian's. "I love Nana!"

"I know you do, Sugar-pop, that's why I asked her to come. Y'all are going to have a fun week."

Three-year-old Lauren toddled into the bedroom from around the corner, dragging a pint-sized vacuum.

"There's my little helper!" Vivian put Audrey down and picked up Lauren. "Are you helping Mommy get the house all clean for Nana?"

Lauren shook her head, no.

"Well, it sure looks like you are."

Lauren looked at the floor, blue eyes mournful, lower lip sticking out, a contrast to the happy-colored small bows Vivian had put all around her hair, something Lauren loved.

"Are you sad Mommy is leaving?"

Lauren hugged Vivian's neck, still grasping the vacuum, which knocked against Vivian's back.

Vivian squeezed her for a moment, then drew her back and looked at her. "I'll bring you back a present from Colorado, okay? And Nana will be here. You're going to have a fun time. Promise. Plus, Nana can cook!"

Lauren gave a small smile, but Vivian couldn't help but feel bad. She put Lauren down and went to check on the twins, Ben and Olivia, who were playing with a large-piece puzzle in their room. They were almost a year and a half old and so cute. Ben had finally started growing straight, blonde hair and had giant rosy cheeks, and Olivia's light brown curls were already falling into small ringlets.

Ben saw Vivian watching, stood up and ran over. He never walked, went straight from crawling to running. And sweet little Olivia, she'd been a very careful walker, never wanting to fall. They were total opposites.

The last time Vivian left the kids had been several months ago when the four friends went to Mexico.

She had just turned 30, was in the midst of her divorce and really needed to get away, so the girls made quick arrangements and hustled her out of town. Their trip was filled with all sorts of fun: parasailing, barhopping, market shopping, sight-seeing. One problem though, Vivian had nearly been arrested for murder. She and her friends, Wendy, Kate and Lucy helped the local police solve the crime, and she was totally cleared. Since then her life had settled into a routine as a single mom of four young children. She smiled to herself.

It hadn't been easy and money was tight, but she managed. Fundraising for the hospital kept her busy during the day, and the kids filled in the rest of her life. Her friends and family were lifesavers. Everyone poured out to help after Rick left and the caught-you-red-handed (squeezing fake boobs) incident in the swimming pool. And post-divorce developments produced more shit than she could shake a stick at.

Vivian loaded up the car with kids and luggage, gave her dog, Cooper, a treat and then headed over to Miss Margie's house. She super-squeezed all the kids goodbye, then pointed the mommy-mobile to the airport.

She and her friends had decided on the Rocky Mountains based on the recommendation of their masseur friend in Playa del Carmen, Rodney. He had worked at a fancy resort near Vail and suggested going during "mud season" in late April/early May when the room rates were lower and most spas discounted. Lucy, living in Boulder, agreed, and having her vehicle handy helped save money.

The girls booked their flights and room months ago, making the trip über-affordable. Vivian called in her mom to keep the kids since Rick hadn't gotten permission from the SPS (swimming pool slut) to take the kids a little extra.

Whatever, Vivian thought as she followed the signs to the airport. *I managed, just like I always do, and I'll be up in the mountains soon enough.* She pulled into remote parking and pushed the button for a ticket. In no time she had parked, been picked up, gotten her boarding pass from a kiosk, checked her bag and made it through security.

Damn, I'm making good time. My life never goes this smoothly!

She grabbed a soda and bag of chips from the bookstore and stopped to peruse the titles. After a while she checked her phone and decided it was time to head to the gate. The plane was loading already, so she hopped into the back of the line.

Air travel is safer than riding in a car. She tried to keep herself calm as she took her seat, near the wing of the plane. It only partially worked.

Nervous and needing to occupy her mind, she picked up the inflight magazine and turned to the Mensa quiz. "The same name applies for a kitchen appliance and where cattle graze." *Stove, oven, refrigerator, microwave, mixer, blender, food processor, field, pasture, ranch.* Not wanting to look up the answer, she moved on. She skipped the Tom Swifty sentence, they're always stupid, and instead figured out how many Girl Scouts sold how many boxes of cookies. She allotted the other questions a minute each, gave up and flipped to the answers. Range was the kitchen appliance/cattle grazing. *Duh!* Vivian thought. *Who uses that word?*

She wasn't about to do the Sudoku puzzle so she grabbed her book, *Plum Spooky*, by Janet Evanovich, one of her favorite authors. She looked up from her book and caught the eye of a ruggedly gorgeous man walking toward the back of the plane to the tiny restroom. She felt an impulse to see if he'd like to join the mile-high club. *Was he wearing a ring?*

It was only a slight impulse, so she went back to reading about the mishaps of Stephanie, drinking her Coke and eating her chips. As he walked back to his seat, Vivian eyed him all the way, enjoying the view.

Before long she had given her trash to the flight attendant and put her tray table up. Then she was back on solid ground. *Thank you, Lord,* Vivian thought as the plane rattled and slowed. Once off the plane, she made a beeline for the restroom. She texted the girls while on the tram going from the concourse to baggage claim.

Good news! I'm not dead. We didn't crash. Baggage claim in a few!

She made her way through the crowd and saw Kate, Wendy and Lucy waiting for her by the carousel. Just like on the last trip, they surrounded her with open arms and giant hugs. Unlike the last trip, there were no tears. Instead, Vivian handed out trashy straw cowboy hats and stuck one on her own curly blonde head.

"Yeeeeeeeeeeeeee-hawwwww!" she yelled, drawing the attention of numerous bystanders, but she didn't care. The girls yee-hawed her back, holding their hats high in the air and waving them around.

"Nice. Where'd you get these?" Kate asked, sticking hers back on her straight brown hair. She was the stunning result of an American sailor and a Taiwanese mother. Tall and trim with almond-shaped brown eyes, she was a looker and smarter than most men who crossed her path. She met her match in Shaun, and they had been married just over a year.

"At a truck stop, of course!"

"You can take the girl outta the Get-Down, but you can't take the Get-Down outta the girl," Lucy said.

They all grew up together in Pasa-"Get-Down"-dena, Texas, a.k.a. Stinkadena, a suburb southeast of Houston. The city was mainly blue collar with roughnecks working in the refineries and industrial plants along

Highway 225. The air had an aroma of rotten eggs and a color the twinge of funk. In the Get-Down, you never knew when the next refinery was going to blow; you just had to be prepared to hunker down. The girls laughed about making it out alive and without any weird medical issues, though they were only 30. Guess time would tell.

Vivian had known Wendy the longest, technically since kindergarten, but they couldn't remember each other until first grade. That was a long way back to remember. They grew up a few streets apart, and their parents still lived in the same houses. People tended not to leave the area once they settled in. The funky air must have seeped into their brains and programmed them not to leave, kinda like "Hotel California." They had been in the same activities K-12 — Brownies, Girl Scouts, dance, band, flags, all-around getting into trouble.

The time they drove to Galveston when Vivian's car overheated was classic. They were determined to go to the beach, so they stopped every few miles to pour water into the coolant reservoir, and they ran the heater trying to pull heat off the engine. It was mid-July. Not the smartest thing to do, but they were determined. Indian Beach awaited. And boys.

Vivian had known Lucy since sixth grade where they met in band. They were band dorks but cool band dorks, or at least that's what they told themselves. Lucy and Vivian hit it off instantly and have had some kind of cosmic connection ever since. They could finish each other's sentences, knew what the other was thinking, and shared all the same interests; well, except Lucy was a neat-freak and Vivian was not. As roommates at the University of Texas at Austin they got along great, never had typical roommate issues. Vivian kept the living room as neat and tidy as her messy brain could. Lucy accepted it, didn't go into Vivian's bathroom, and it worked.

Vivian met Kate in the ninth grade, also in band. Though a complete brainiac, she was lots of fun and that was Vivian's style. She, too, went to UT Austin, and they would see each other from time to time, usually at parties or on Sixth Street.

The girls waited for Vivian's bag to emerge from the chute and laughed about Lucy wearing her high-heeled, sling-back slutty shoes that were way too much for an airport outing.

Lucy looked at Vivian and said, "This coming from Ms. Naturalizer slip-on clogs."

"I'm traveling, my feet swell, and I can easily get these off at security. Besides, they're comfortable, and I can walk in them without fear of breaking an ankle. Or my neck."

Lucy harrumphed and grabbed Vivian's giant burnt-orange bag off the conveyor belt, almost losing her balance on her stilettos.

Wendy, Kate and Vivian couldn't help but laugh. At least she didn't fall on the floor like she had at the Purple Peacock in Playa del Carmen.

"Damn, girl," Vivian said to Lucy. "You're looking even better than you did a few months ago. And I'm lovin' the hair."

"Thanks, I've been training for a triathlon, and the Colorado air does wonders for my curls." Lucy fluffed the auburn curls that cascaded over her shoulders and down her back. Her flawless, fair skin made her green eyes pop, and her muscular physique turned heads.

The girls stilettoed, clogged, tennis-shoed and flip-flopped out to Lucy's four-wheel drive SUV and loaded their stuff in the back. Vivian's grandiose bag went in first. Everything fit except the cooler, which they put in the back seat between Wendy and Kate, who were dubbed the "Back Seat Bar Babes."

Getting in the passenger seat, Vivian thought, *Nothing's gonna go wrong on this trip. I just know it!*

2

Vivian took her shoes off and put her feet up on the dash as Lucy drove away from the airport, toward I-70. Living in Boulder the past three years, Lucy made regular treks into Denver for work and into the mountains to hike, bike and ski. She was designated navigator on this trip, and all were glad they had Lucy's SUV and not a P.O.S. rent car like they did in Mexico.

Turning in her seat, Vivian tapped on the cooler lid, and her green eyes flashed with anticipation. "Whatcha got back there?"

"Let's see." Wendy opened the lid. Her long, silky brown hair fell across her face. "I can tell Lucy packed this and I appreciate the organization, but it looks like an assortment of *cerveza*, soda, water and...what's this?" She pulled out a bottle and read the label. "Fancy shmancy champagne."

"That's to celebrate with at the hotel," Lucy said. "We have to toast to our second girls' getaway. Don't you mess up my perfectly packed cooler, there's a system."

"Aye, aye, cap'n."

"Check out the seat-back pocket in front of you, Wendy."

Wendy stuck her hand in the pocket and pulled out their four "Life's a beach" koozies they had used in Playa.

"Woo-hoo!" Wendy squealed and handed them out. "I'm all about the koozie!"

Vivian examined hers. "Boy, this is looking ratty. It still has lime grime and sand stuck on it."

"I thought we needed a remembrance and didn't wash them," Lucy said.

"Aw, that was a great trip," Kate said. "Except for the Jon dying and you being accused of murder thing, Viv."

"I'll cheers to that," Wendy said and laughed. "So what'll it be for now?"

"Beer me," Vivian said. "Wait!"

"What?"

"Are there limes?"

"Hello!" Lucy said. "You're dealing with an expert here. They're cut up and in a baggie, ready to go." Since Lucy had the conveniences of home, she had run to the store and bought an assortment of snacks and beverages for the trip and cut up limes for Vivian's Dos Equis.

"I never should have doubted you."

A look of satisfaction crossed Lucy's face. "No, you shouldn't have." She then added, "Bottle of water for me, please!"

"You got it," Wendy replied as she got herself a beer. "And Kate, what are you having?"

"I'll stick with water for now, too."

"What?" Vivian said. "You pregnant?"

"I don't know, I could be," Kate replied. "We've been working on it. Hard."

This brought on laughter and woo-hoos.

Vivian offered a toast. "Here's to working it hard!"

More woo-hoos as they squished their koozied beer and water bottles together.

"So how's the separation… reversal?" Vivian asked Lucy. "It's been, what, a month now since you moved back in?"

"Viv!" Wendy laughed. "You make it sound like a vasectomy reversal."

"I didn't know what to call it."

"Well, I moved back in. We got back together."

"And?"

Lucy sighed. "No sex."

Groans all around.

"I'm working up the courage to, um…"

"To what, Lucy?" Vivian asked. "Why go back if there's no intimacy? Isn't that one of the main reasons why y'all separated in the first place?"

"Yeah, but there are good things in our relationship, and I just want to get settled back in before I push the issue."

"Well I think I'd push that. Hard." Vivian giggled. The girls in the back uh-hummed.

Salt-N-Pepa's "Push It" sprung into Vivian's head, and she sang a few lines.

Changing the subject, Vivian turned to Kate. "So y'all are working hard on a baby. How's everything else going?"

"We've settled into a good rhythm, ha ha, and everything else is good. Work is fine, busy, building a children's museum in San Antonio. Y'all should come down for the opening in a couple of months."

"How's your brother, Horny Huey?"

"Hugh's fine. Still single." Kate nudged Vivian's arm.

"Oh, no. Negatory. It'd be like having sex with you, and although I love you, I don't 'love' you."

"Just thought I'd mention it. He's successful, single and lives 25 miles from you. And he loves children."

"Thanks for that, but no."

They'd made it out of the city and were headed into the mountains. Kate pulled out her camera and snapped a few pictures, then said, "Wendy, catch us up," Kate said. "How's your niece doing with her cancer treatment?"

"Lizzy is just over 2 years old now and doing remarkably well," Wendy said. "Better than I had thought possible. Dr. Burzynski is a miracle worker as far as I'm concerned. The tumors on her liver are gone, and there's only one left in her lungs and it's shrinking. She's going to make it."

Vivian offered another toast. "To Lizzy!"

"So how are you and Jake?" Lucy asked. "What's the latest?"

"It might be over," Wendy sighed. "He moved back to North Carolina a few months ago."

"You didn't tell us he moved," Kate said. "Did y'all break up?"

"No, we've been doing the long distance thing. He comes back to Houston at least twice a month and I went up there once, and although we've talked about me moving, it's a big commitment without a commitment."

"Don't forget Lucy's words of wisdom when she had on her beachin' bucket," Vivian reminded.

"What?" Lucy asked. "What advice did I have?"

"You said, 'Girl, don't move until there's a ring on your finger.' Those were your exact words," Wendy said.

"I said that?"

"Yes, ma'am, you did, wearing an ice bucket on your head and after several tequila shots, I might add," Vivian said. "We were shocked by your inebriated clarity."

"I do love Jake, but I can't wait forever. I'm getting old!" Wendy said.

15

"Tick tock, tick tock," Vivian said, tapping her wrist.

"Well, heck, Vivian, not everyone pops out two at a time," Kate said.

"What can I say? My ovaries are on overdrive. I would be a surrogate for any of you, by the way. But I'm not having sex with your boyfriends or husbands. They'll have to turkey baste me!"

They all agreed and clinked to that.

"So what are you going to do, Wendy?" Kate asked. "Move? Break-up?"

"I don't know. I'll figure it out on this trip."

"You gotta know when to—," Vivian said.

"Ya, ya... Hold 'em." Wendy said. "I got it."

Everyone had a good laugh at Kenny Rogers' "The Gambler."

"Look!" Kate pointed out the window to the left. "I can't believe people are still skiing."

"Loveland stays open later than most mountains," Lucy told them.

"The aspen trees are beautiful," Vivian said.

"Each grove shares a root system," Kate informed them.

"You should see them in the fall when their leaves turn bright yellow. That's one of the reasons I love living here," Lucy said as she drove past the Continental Divide in the Eisenhower Tunnel.

"So, Viv, tell us. What's the latest with Craig?" Wendy asked. "I haven't seen any screw-you-Rick-look-at-the-hot-younger-guy-I'm-dating pictures lately on your Facebook page."

"Well, lemme tell ya what happened with that. It's quite the story."

Kate rubbed her hands together in anticipation. "This sounds juicy."

"Oh, it's juicy, but not in a filet-mignon-wrapped-in-bacon kind of way."

3

As Lucy turned off I-70 onto Highway 91 toward the town of Climax, snowflakes began drifting over the SUV. Vivian felt her ears pop as she began to tell the girls about Craig.

"Y'all know I didn't date during the whole divorce, wouldn't even sleep with Jon, so I was ready to rumble after the papers were signed. My friend Monica introduced me to a coworker, Brandon, who is a perpetual bachelor but a great rebound, get-your-feet-wet kinda guy. He and I became friends, then friends with benefits. He'd fix my deck, I'd fix his—"

"Vivian!" Kate said.

"What! I'm recovering. I deserve to do whatever the hell I want. At least for a little while."

"Okay, okay."

"Anyway, he and I are friends first, and the rest is gravy. We'd text a lot, he'd come over when I didn't have the kids, etc. It was a good, no-commitment, get back on the horse kinda thing."

Snickers.

"About three months ago, I was pumpin' gas and the guy on the pump across from me struck up a conversation. Oh, and he was cute. Beautiful green eyes, dark hair, nice shoulders."

"How come I never meet a guy when I'm pumping gas?" Lucy said.

"He seemed normal enough, so we went out. It went well, and I started to see him just about any night I didn't have the kids. The sex was the best I'd had since you-know-who in college."

"Oh, I know who," Lucy said. "Mr. Ride His Bike Over, Greek Godlike Guy."

"Yep. Him."

The snow had turned to sleet, pinging off the windshield. The temperature gauge on the console read 31 degrees.

"What about Brandon?" Wendy asked.

"Oh, he rocked in the sack, too," Vivian laughed.

"No, what *happened* to him?"

"We had decided early on that we'd be supportive of one another's relationships, should we have one. No interference."

"That never works," Kate tisk-tisked.

"It did for us. He was fine with me dating Craig. He pretty much just stayed out of the picture."

"I'm surprised, but okay."

The road became slushy, and Lucy backed off the accelerator.

"Things were good for almost three months. I was even considering letting Craig meet the kids. Then two weeks ago I was sitting at work and my phone rang. It was Brandon, and he had never called at work before. He apologized but then told me that he was on Facebook and instant messaging me at that very moment."

"What do you mean?" Wendy asked.

"I mean, according to his computer he and I were having an instant message conversation, but he knew it wasn't me. He kept apologizing, saying he felt like he had to call and tell me."

"Someone had hacked into your Facebook page?" Lucy asked.

"Wow, I'm impressed Brandon could tell it wasn't you," Kate said.

"He said he knew it wasn't me because of the spelling errors, lack of capitalization, short answers, etc. I'm a very proper instant messenger. We joke about it."

"Oh no, was it Craig?" Kate asked.

"I thought it might be, so I fed Brandon a few questions. I told him to ask what I was doing that night, to which the fake me answered that I was going to a play. Which the real me was. With Craig."

Groans.

"Oh, it gets better. The fake me told Brandon that Craig and I were in love. That when you know, you know, and that I was hoping for a proposal."

"What a jackass," Wendy said.

Lucy changed lanes to skirt an 18-wheeler that had pulled over to the side of the road.

Vivian watched the trucker yank chains over a tire as she continued the story. "I fed Brandon a few more questions, then he emailed me the entire conversation, which I printed out and took home." She then recounted the entire kitchen table scene.

"What happened next?" Kate asked.

"Craig went completely berserk. He ripped my phone out of the wall, smashed a picture, threw a lamp across the room. It was very Jerry Springer, but it wasn't me being the super freak this time!"

"What'd you do?"

"Locked myself into my bedroom and used my cell to call the cops. I jumped out the window and Cooper held him back so I had time to run and hide in my neighbor's bushes."

"Yea, Cooper!" Wendy said.

"Did Craig get arrested?" Kate asked.

"No, he got away. He left before they got there."

Wendy glanced out the window, then reached for her seatbelt, which wasn't buckled. Click. "I can't believe it. You're first semi-boyfriend since Rick and he's a total whackjob."

"Yep, I know how to pick 'em. But there's more."

They rounded a corner and Lucy cut the wheel too sharply. The SUV went into a skid and fishtailed as it slid toward the guardrail.

"Ahhhhh!" they all screamed.

"I've got it. We're okay," Lucy said. "Sorry, that curve snuck up on me."

"Holy crap!" Vivian yelled. "Just concentrate on driving. I'll finish the story later."

Lucy hunched over the wheel and focused on the road. The other girls were quiet. Eventually the sleet turned back to snow and lightened up.

"Pull over, Lucy!" Kate yelled.

"What? Jesus!" she said and hit the brakes.

"We've got to take a picture with the town sign."

Vivian read the name, Climax. "Absolutely!"

"Dammit, don't scare the crap out of me like that again!"

They piled out of the car and Kate balanced her camera on the hood, set the timer and ran into place.

"Smile," she said, jumping into the shot with her arms stretched out above her head. "The Getaway Girlz have Climaxed!"

4

Coming off their Climax photo and down the mountain, Wendy picked back up on the Craig conversation. "Thank god you hadn't introduced him to the kids. How are they?"

Vivian adjusted her air vent. "The kids are doing okay. Audrey's had some counseling and seems to be opening up. The others are just too young to know what happened and why Daddy isn't home. Hell, the twins'll never know the difference."

"It might be better that they don't, Viv," Lucy said, making the turn, slowly this time, onto Highway 24 heading west.

"How has the step-monster been treating the kiddos?" Kate asked.

Wendy opened the cooler and got another beer. "I still can't believe he married her."

"I know, me, neither," Vivian said. "Y'all will never believe what his lame excuse for getting married was."

"Oh god, she's pregnant," Lucy said.

"No, but that was the first thing I thought, too."

"You should prepare yourself, because you know that'll be next."

"He had a vasectomy after I got pregnant with the twins, remember?"

"Still, just wait. It'll happen."

Kate leaned forward from the back seat. "So, if that wasn't the reason, what is it, Viv?"

"He said they were getting married because 'the kids needed a backyard.'"

"What kind of bullshit is that?" Wendy asked.

"Those are the words that came out of his mouth. Fuck him. The kids *have* a backyard. At my house. I told him, 'Tell me she's your soul mate, tell me she's the love of your life, but don't give me excuses about the kids needing a backyard.' He had no response. And now that they've bought a house you should see their backyard. I caught a glimpse of it the other day when I dropped the kids off. It's completely overgrown. The kids can't even walk back there, much less play."

"'The kids need a backyard.' Never heard that one before," Kate said.

Lucy pounded on the wheel. "He's a complete and utter asshole."

"And an idiot," Kate said.

"What a whirlwind, Viv," Wendy said. "You almost go down for murder in Mexico, get divorced, he gets married, you get a hookup, and you drop the hookup for a jackass."

"That's my life."

"Yet you're still smiling. Amazing," Kate said, patting Vivian's shoulder.

"That's just me."

It started snowing again as they passed a 6 percent grade sign and then one indicating a runaway truck ramp ahead.

"Oh-oh, maybe we'll see a ramp in use!" Lucy said.

"What are you talking about?" Kate asked.

"You'll see one in a few miles. They're only on the downhill and are for 18-wheelers that have burned up their brakes. I've always wanted to see a truck plow into one. I'll stay behind trucks when I smell their brakes burning."

"You're so weird sometimes," Vivian said. "Wanting to see a truck in trouble."

"Not in total trouble. They'd be saved! I just know the snow would fly everywhere as they barrel into it. It'd be awesome!"

Snow swirled in the wind and it was difficult to see 10 feet in front of them.

"Where are we?" Wendy asked.

"Close to Independence Pass." Lucy slowed to five miles an hour and put the SUV in four-wheel drive.

"Do I need to pull out my camera and get footage for *I Shouldn't Be Alive*?" Vivian asked nervously.

"No, I'll get us there in one piece. It just may take longer than we expected."

It was now almost a total whiteout and although Vivian couldn't see anything, she could feel the tires loose traction a time or two. *Dear Lord, I hope so. I don't want the SPS raising my children.*

"Let me tell y'all about my babies," Kate said sweetly.

"Babies!" Vivian said, happy for the diversion.

"Shaun and I adopted two standard poodles, Max and Bear." Kate pulled out her phone and showed Wendy and Vivian pictures.

"They look like cute, cuddly teddy bears," Wendy said. "I bet they're smart."

"They can do lots of tricks already. My favorite is putting a treat on their nose and making them wait to eat it."

"Torture," Vivian said, then she asked Lucy, "So how ya doing with the driving and seeing the road, because I can't see a damn thing." That wasn't entirely true. She could see the faint brake lights of a vehicle in front of them, but she couldn't tell how far in front of them.

"Ah, it's lightening up a bit. I'm okay. I promise not to go careening off the side of this mountain just yet."

"Beer me, please," Vivian said to Wendy in the back, handing her the empty.

"Maybe we should go ahead and break out the champagne," Wendy said. "If we're not going to make it, we might as well go out in style."

"No!" Lucy insisted. "We're saving that for the room."

The tension in the SUV built — Lucy concentrating, Vivian drinking, Kate praying and Wendy cursing — as they descended a thousand feet and finally made it out of the blizzard-like conditions. The snow eventually stopped altogether and Lucy took an abrupt turn onto a two lane road.

"What's with the turn?" Vivian asked, bracing herself on the console and door handle. "Another road sneak up on you?"

Lucy gave her a grin. "No, I just had an idea and we're making a detour."

"Exciting!" Wendy clapped.

Kate leaned forward in her seat. "Where are you taking us?"

"You'll see, we'll be there soon," Lucy said and clicked on her right blinker.

Soon was an understatement, as the Blue Spruce Winery came into sight. Lucy pulled in and threw the SUV in park. "Winter weather treachery equals wine-tasting debauchery!"

The log cabin tasting room nestled among the spruce trees was a great surprise to Vivian and she was ready to be out of the car. She opened her door. "I can't wait."

"It is kinda tucked away," Wendy said, shutting her door. "But it's a welcome sight after that harrowing mountain drive."

"I second that," Kate said, then had Lucy, Vivian and Wendy pose beside a wine bottle-shaped entrance sign. "Say wine and cheese!" Snap!

The crackling flames from a tall, generous fireplace greeted the four as they stepped through a pair of heavy wooden doors, trimmed in cast bronze door knobs. A middle aged woman dressed in a tweedy blazer poured wine for a couple. Delicate displays of expensive looking bottles lined the stone-clad walls, and medals adorned several magnums.

An older gentleman sporting a gray beard and burgundy ascot greeted the girls. He suggested they take a tour, personally guided by him, before tasting. He explained as he walked that the winery grew grapes on the estate, but they brought in several varietals from southwestern Colorado. He led them past the sorting area where the grapes were brought in at fall harvest, and he continued on past five stainless steel tanks where the award-winning Sauvignon Blanc aged. The air temperature dropped in conjunction with the low ceilings, and the walls closed in more and more until they stood in the middle of a damp room stacked floor to ceiling with oak barrels, aging varietals of red wine for a minimum of three years.

"This is awesome," Kate said, studying the structural integrity of the load-bearing rose-red, granite walls.

"The cave is cool, but having this as part of the winery, even better," Wendy said, clearly impressed with the operation.

"I'm ready to do some tasting," Lucy said, rubbing her hands together in anticipation.

"Me, too!" Vivian said.

Ascot escorted them to the tasting room and poured the Sauvignon Blanc first.

Wendy picked up the glass and swirled it around, took a big whiff, then sipped it while sucking in air.

"What's up with all the suckin' goin' on over there?" Vivian asked.

"I'm just appreciating the craft of wine making and the products thereof," Wendy explained.

"Do I need to suck in air?" Kate asked, swirling her wine like Wendy had.

"Yes," Wendy said. "The air opens up the bouquet, and you get a fuller taste. It will please your palette more exquisitely."

"Who are you and when did you turn into such a wine snob?" Vivian asked before taking a big gulp *sans* sucking.

"Hey, I made an A in wine appreciation in college. It was the best class. Ever."

Vivian turned to Kate. "I'm surprised you're partaking, Mrs. Might Be Prego."

"Just a sip of each," Kate said with a wink.

Ascot served four more varietals, describing them along the way. Each girl bought a bottle of her favorite. On their way out they took a short trail that led to a scenic overlook.

"Ahhhh! Help!" Vivian joked, clinging onto a large boulder that dropped to another, just a few feet down, but from the other girls' viewpoint it looked much more dangerous, as if she could fall to her death.

"Oh my gosh, that's a Kodak moment!" Lucy yelled, looking around for something stationary to set her camera on. She found a downed tree that allowed the camera angle to perfectly project the death and destruction she was shooting for.

"This is going to be so funny!" Kate giggled, fake clinging to the boulder next to Vivian.

Wendy fake-clung, too, and Lucy set the timer for 10 seconds.

"Hurry, it's blinking!" Kate yelled as Lucy ran into place.

She posed just in time for the flash, then jumped back up and checked the preview. "It's perfect. We're one-shot wonders!"

They took turns snapping a few more funny pictures and 'falling' off the cliff, then they returned to the car and piled in.

Vivian opened the door to the passenger's seat, but changed her mind. "I'm sittin' next to the bar backseat. Oops, I mean the backseat bar!"

Lucy, who had kept the tastes to a minimum, said, "Altitude ladies! You'll get drunk faster, you gotta be careful."

"Ha!" Vivian opened the cooler lid. "Little late for that."

5

The snow returned in earnest on the drive into Aspen. They slipped and slid a little but made it to The Yellow Aspen Hotel without plummeting, spiraling or bringing injury to themselves, others or the SUV.

Lucy handed over the keys to the valet who ushered them inside and then unloaded their luggage, including their backseat bar. The century-old building was boxy on the outside, but stunningly elegant inside.

Kate, being an architect, pointed out structural and design details to Vivian and Wendy while Lucy checked them in.

"You know I'll never remember what you just told me, right?" Vivian said and giggled.

Kate shrugged her shoulders. "This is a cool old place."

The bellman held the door to the elevator open for the girls before getting in with the excess of luggage.

"We're in 607," Lucy announced, pushing the 6, then she passed a keycard to each girl.

The corner room was flanked with tall, divided windows that showcased views of the mountains in two directions. The blue and white patterned bedspreads reminded Vivian of her grandmother's China. Same Blue Willow pattern almost exactly.

The bellman unloaded the luggage cart and asked if they'd like anything else. Wendy handed him a tip and said no thanks, as Vivian made a beeline for the bathroom.

When she emerged, Lucy was inspecting all of the furniture in the room. As an interior designer, she was always checking out other people's designs. She stopped at the antique desk and ran her fingers along the top then said, "Look, they even have fresh flowers in the room."

"We're high-falutin' now!" Wendy said, unpacking her suitcase.

Kate pulled one of the flowers out of the vase. "Nice touch with the tulips."

Vivian wasn't all that excited about the tulips. Unfortunately, the once favorite flower now reminded her of something she'd rather forget.

"Came with the room," Lucy said, taking the tulip from Kate and putting it in her mouth, then snapping her fingers. "Olé!"

Vivian laughed and opened the cooler and pulled out the champagne. She unwrapped the foil liner and loosened the cage. Pop! The cork flew across the room smacked into the window with a thud.

"Thank goodness that didn't break the antique glass," Kate said.

"That would have been unfortunate, but what about my eyeballs? Hello!" Lucy said. "I would have to wear an eye patch and live my life like a pirate! Arrggggh!"

"You're not a professional champagne popper like me," Wendy said.

"Yeah, but at least there wasn't a hot Mexican diving into my boobs like last time," Vivian said with a laugh, then handed the bottle to Lucy who held the glasses.

"Have you heard from Arturo at all?" Kate asked.

"Nah," Vivian answered. "I doubt I ever will. That's okay with me, honestly. I'd prefer to leave what happened in Mexico, in Mexico."

Lucy filled their rocks glasses with champagne. Vivian watched the bubbles float to the top, then pop back down, revealing the glass to be only a quarter full.

"Let's have a toast," Kate said.

They held up their glasses.

"To our second girls' getaway. Mountains, *mi amigas* and many memories."

The girls finished off their post-check-in champagne, freshened up and then decided to do a little shopping before dinner. They headed down the main drag in Aspen.

Some of the stores were closed because it was, as Lucy reminded them, "mud season." Vivian could tell by window-shopping that the stores that were open would be expensive. The first was a foofy-la-la boutique with clothing, a large glass jewelry case and wall display of sequined and bejeweled purses.

"Heyzoos Kristo," Vivian said, looking at the price tag on a purse, then dropping it promptly. "Where's the sales rack?"

Kate flitted around the store with a saleslady who placed several items into a dressing room for her. The other girls sat in the comfy chairs placed around the dressing area and waited while she changed.

Kate emerged in a flowy Maxi dress. The halter accentuated her long neck and slender shoulders. The white dress and purple flowers looked great against her skin. Vivian knew it was a keeper.

"Kate, that looks beautiful on you. You have to get it!"

"It would hide a baby bump," Wendy said and gave her a smile.

"I don't know, it's pretty expensive," Kate said.

"When has that ever stopped you?" Lucy teased.

Kate tried on a few more dresses, but none was as spectacular as the first. She bought it and added a lovely silver necklace.

Along the way to the next store, Vivian stopped to throw away a piece of gum. She pushed on the trash can lid but it didn't open. She looked at the contraption and pushed on it again.

"How the hell does this work?"

Lucy laughed at her. "It's bear-proof. You're not in Texas anymore, ladies."

Lucy pushed a secret lever and the lid opened. Vivian tossed her gum in, then tried the lever herself.

"Hmmm, okay," she said. "They really need instructions on these things."

Wendy stepped into a t-shirt shop on the corner and poked her head back out. "Y'all come in here, they have all kinds of stuff that's more in our price range."

Vivian followed Lucy and Kate into the store with its t-shirts, mugs, magnets, etc. A full-grown, taxidermied black bear stood in a corner and Vivian walked over to him. "Let's take a picture with him, he's cute!"

"He's not cute, he looks like he wants to rip your head off," Wendy said, but she walked over anyway.

Lucy and Kate joined them, too, and Vivian asked another shopper to take their picture.

Instead of saying cheese, they threw up their hands and growled, doing their best "imbearination."

"Thanks so much," Lucy said to the impromptu photographer.

Photo-op out of the way, the girls got to shopping. "Oh, look," Vivian said. "I can afford stuff in here." She picked out stuffed animals for Audrey,

Lauren, Olivia and Ben and took them to the counter. She noticed Wendy reading the label on a can of bear spray.

"Who's afraid of the big bad bear?" Vivian joked.

Wendy abruptly put the bear spray down. "I was just checkin' it out. Trash cans got me thinking."

"Uhhh huh."

"I've got to find something for Lizzie."

"Well that ain't it," Vivian smirked. "Might I recommend one of these silky smooth stuffed animals?" She opened her bag to reveal the moose, porcupine, otter and fox she had just purchased.

"Cute. I'll go check it out."

"Okay, we'll meet you next door at the art gallery."

Wendy caught up with Vivian, Kate and Lucy a few minutes later and showed off her purchase of a baby bear stuffed animal. "Found it fitting," she said.

"Check out the naked Indian," Vivian giggled as Wendy put away the bear.

"He's not naked," she replied. "He has a little bitty square covering his ding-a-ling."

"Well, I imagine there's something interesting going on under there. Who sculpted this? A man or a woman?"

Lucy read the bronze nameplate. "William Neff. I'm guessing that's a man."

"It's gotta be big then. Men tend to exaggerate."

Kate laughed. "If Shaun was sculpted, they wouldn't allow kids in."

"Oh, really," Wendy said with a butt bump. "No wonder you're almost two years in and not complaining."

Kate just smiled and turned to a painting of aspen trees.

The girls admired more of the paintings and Mr. Neff's various (semi) naked sculptures before heading back to the hotel to freshen up for dinner.

Lucy sprinted ahead and reached the hotel elevator first. She frantically pushed the button. "I gotta use *el bathroom-ola.*"

"You know, hitting the button does not make the elevator come any faster," Vivian said.

"It makes me feel better!" Lucy said, as she pushed the button three more times.

After letting Lucy into the room Vivian threw her purse onto the bed and took a deep breath. "Y'all smell that?"

"Smell what?" Kate asked. "My sinuses are stopped up. I need to use my neti pot." She then explained the saline-up-the-nose device.

"That's disgusting," Vivian said.

"It works," Kate responded. "My allergies are practically nonexistent now. And you know they used to be horrific."

"Probably from growing up in the Get-Down and being around those nasty, germy cockroaches," Lucy yelled from behind the closed door.

"First, my mom kept a very clean house. Second, I'm allergic to way more than cockroaches. However, on my skin test those came up as mega-allergic."

"You can get a brain-eating amoeba from flushing your nose out like that," Vivian said.

"Y'all are grossing me out," Wendy shivered. "Enough!"

Vivian ran her fingers up Wendy's arm in an insect-like motion. "My mom broke her toe running from a cockroach. Those suckers can fly."

Wendy swatted at her. "I like to stomp 'em and smush 'em. Pop."

"Enough insect talk, ladies," Lucy said, coming out of the restroom and throwing her hands up. "What am I supposed to be smelling?" She took a long sniff of the air. "Cuz all I smell are cleaning products, which is my favorite scent."

"It smelled like men's cologne to me when I first walked in the door, like the kind Craig wears," Vivian said. "I don't smell it anymore. I must be imagining things."

"I don't smell anything, and my sniffer works just fine," Wendy said.

"Let's get ready to go out. Layer up, ladies," Lucy said. "It'll get chilly tonight." She set out a tank top, dark purple cashmere sweater and gray wool coat.

Vivian pulled a red, short-sleeved shirt out of her suitcase. "I'm not a layer girl. I'm going to have to find something else to warm me up tonight."

"Did you see the bartender downstairs?" Wendy asked as she put on a black, turtleneck sweater.

"He looked like he could heat things up," Kate said, tugging on her Uggs.

Vivian raised her eyebrows up and down a few times. "Let's go introduce our sexy selves."

6

The hotel's Western yet refined lounge, the Tree Bark Bar, was quiet with only three patrons, an older couple drinking martinis, and a man reading the paper, sipping on a beer. The intricately carved antique woodwork caught Vivian's eye, but the main attraction was the sexy, sandy-blond bartender.

She sat down in front of the taps where he pulled a pint. Vivian took in his broad shoulders, blue eyes and white teeth and asked what his specialty was.

"Buttery Nipples," he replied with a sly smile.

"Give us a round."

"None for me," Kate said.

He got to work with the Bailey's and butterscotch schnapps and set out four shot glasses.

"What's your name?" Lucy asked.

"Eric," he said and handed Kate a glass of water, three girls a shot and then helped himself to one. Holding it up, he offered a toast, "To my favorite buttery treat."

"Yeeeee-haw!" Vivian hollered, then slammed her nipple.

"So what is there to do around here tonight?" Kate asked Eric.

"Tonight's kind of quiet since it's off-season. There's a sports bar down the street that would be okay called Bronco's. Tomorrow night is service industry night at Club Bighorn. Lots of action there, you should go."

"Will you be there?" Vivian asked, leaning toward him.

"If you're there, I wouldn't miss it."

"I'm looking forward to some Aspen action."

"Any suggestions for dinner?" Wendy asked.

"Great Italian on the corner two streets down. Tell Donatelli I sent you. In fact, their desserts are often compared to…" he leaned across the bar next to Vivian and whispered in her ear, "orgasms."

Screw the shot. That sent tingles far beyond anywhere her Buttery Nipple had reached.

Vivian recovered and ordered another round. "Eric, make us a Tree Bark Bar special."

"Comin' up!" He winked and started mixing liquors into a tin, shook it up and poured the purple, frothy liquid into three chilled martini glasses rimmed with sugar. He floated a lemon twist in the icy layer on top.

"Lovely," Wendy said, taking a sip. "And tasty."

"What is it?" Kate asked, sniffing Vivian's.

"My own little concoction."

Lucy held her glass up so that Eric couldn't see her talking behind it and whispered to Vivian, "It's his loooove potion."

Vivian giggled, took a sip, then asked Eric about himself.

He was from Montana and had come to Colorado to be a river guide. "Snow's melting and I'm about done in Aspen," he said. "In fact, you should raft the Arkansas through the Royal Gorge. There's enough snow melt to make it worthwhile."

Wendy looked apprehensive. "Snow and melt in the same sentence with rafting. I don't know."

"They have wetsuits."

"I've been down Clear Creek but never Royal Gorge," Lucy said, sipping her purple drink.

"I've been down the Guadalupe," Vivian said proudly.

"Wait, wait, wait. On a tube?" Eric asked.

"Yeah. But I almost died once. It had rained a lot and the tube rental people told me to go left at the falls but my beer cooler went right, so I went right. I flipped out of my tube but held my beer up. That's how my friends knew where I was. Thank god for Natty Lite, the homing beacon."

"This isn't the Guadalupe," Eric said. "In fact, there's no alcohol allowed. But it's a rush, nonetheless."

"Hey!" Wendy said. "I love the Guadalupe. It might not be class-five whitewater, but it serves its purpose. Lucy, I still love that picture of you wearing the giant sombrero and holding your beer up, loud and proud."

"Ugh. That was before the new me. No one can ever see that picture."

Since moving to Boulder three years ago, Lucy had transformed herself into the definition of fit and healthy.

"I keep that picture in my bribery stash," Vivian teased.

31

"You wouldn't!"

Vivian shrugged her shoulders. "No comment."

Wendy took a last sip of her purple drink and stood up. "Y'all ready for dinner?"

Vivian and Lucy polished off their drinks and said goodbye to Eric.

Picking up Vivian's glass, he brushed his fingers against hers. "Hope to see you tomorrow night."

Vivian got goose bumps on her arm and replied, "I have a feeling you will."

Vivian and the girls walked down the sidewalks in Aspen, going in and out of shops, until they reached Donatelli's a few blocks away. The hostess led them down a tight spiral staircase to the quaint basement with six tables. Claustrophobic Lucy indicated her disapproval with a not so discreet, "Ahem," so the hostess led them up a narrow staircase to the second-floor and a balcony overlooking the street.

Vivian sat down and took a look around. "Oh my god, I'm having a moment. I need some champagne."

"What?" Wendy asked.

"The mountains are so majestic, the colors of spring emerging. And the sunset is casting such glorious pink and orange rays off the clouds. I'm just having a moment. We need champagne."

"Okay, I'm in."

"I'll have a sip," Kate said.

The server walked up just in time to hear Vivian's comments. "Good evening ladies, my name is Marc. I'll be serving you tonight. May I suggest—"

Before he could answer, Lucy ordered a bottle of Veuve Clicquot.

"Wonderful choice."

While waiting on the server's return, the girls looked over the menu and decided on an appetizer of bruschetta.

"I don't eat tomatoes, but I'll eat that," Vivian said. The other girls had wanted to order "exotic" items like calamari or mussels in white wine. Vivian made gagging noises, so they decided against it.

The server arrived with an ice-filled wine bucket and two bottles.

"Did we order two?" Vivian asked. "What a bunch of lushes we are!"

The waiter smiled. "No, one bottle is compliments of the gentleman from the bar."

"How nice of Eric," Vivian said.

"Way to make friends with the bartender at the Tree Bark," Wendy said.

"Yeah, I think he's hoping to pop your cork!" Lucy laughed.

"Uh, hello! That cork was popped a looong time ago!" Kate pushed Vivian's shoulder.

"It wasn't Eric from the Tree Bark." Marc said as he presented the champagne to Lucy.

"Even better, random strangers," Lucy said and approved the champagne.

Marc laughed and poured the bubble.

Vivian held up her champagne flute. "To the majesty of the mountains."

The girls clinked glasses, then Vivian said, "So I need to finish telling y'all my crazy Craig story. He called and called for several days after the Facebook thing happened and I ignored all of them. Didn't even listen to his messages. He quit calling and a few days later, I came home and my house was trashed. I'm talking stuff broken, things thrown everywhere, the works. I called the cops and they took fingerprints, but I know it was Craig. The one thing in the house that wasn't disturbed was my bed, and there was something there that hadn't been there before. A tulip was lying on my pillow."

Wendy set her glass down. "Did he have a key? How'd he get in?"

"I don't really know how he got in. He didn't have a key and the alarm was set. I never told him the code, but I guess he knew it since the alarm didn't go off."

"Creepy," Kate said.

"Yep, it was, but it doesn't end there. A few days later an FBI agent came knocking on my door."

"The feds?" Lucy asked.

"Apparently the cops got a hit from the fingerprints they'd taken at my house, and it turns out Craig is wanted by the FBI."

"Oh my god, is he a serial killer or something?"

"No, he's wanted for credit card and wire fraud."

"Was he stealing people's identities?" Kate asked.

"Hank Tucker, the FBI agent, wouldn't go into too much detail, but evidently, Craig planted a bug into PIN pad devices in stores and skimmed people's credit card info."

"How much money did he scam?" Lucy asked.

"I have no idea and he didn't live all that flashy. He told me he was an IT consultant." Vivian sighed and shook her head. "Those poor people he robbed."

"So have you heard from him since he broke in?" Wendy asked.

"No, thank god. Agent Tucker said if Craig contacts me to let him know. Apparently, Craig moved out of his apartment right after he broke into my house and he's as elusive like that coopa, choobra..."

"A Cuba Libre?" Lucy asked.

"That's a rum and Coke with a lime, Lucy." Wendy said and laughed. "You mean a chupacabra."

"Yeah, that's it. That's what he is. But he's a cocksucker, not a bloodsucker!"

"That's really disturbing, Viv," Wendy said. "Do you think you're safe?"

"I didn't pick up on anything like that when we dated until the night I called him out. He doesn't have a history of violence, at least not in any police records."

"Tell your phone and lamp that," Lucy muttered. "What about the kids, do they know?"

"No, thank god. Rick had them for the weekend, so I had plenty of time to get things in order before they came home."

"Are you sure you're safe?" Wendy asked.

"Yes, I think it's over. I pushed him into a corner and he flipped. I think he'll leave me alone. He's got bigger things to worry about. Besides, he skipped town and I doubt he's coming back."

"I certainly hope so. In the meantime, let's toast the hot bartender who wants to share his heat with you," Kate said, clinking glasses with Vivian. "It's those darn pheromones again."

"He was flirting a little," Vivian said and took a sip.

"It's not her pheromones," Lucy said. "It's her big boobs. Let's be honest, look at those things."

Vivian looked down at her V-necked blouse and pushed her breasts together. "Whatever it is, I'm just glad I got it." She picked up her purse and pulled out two silver condom packets, then covered her eyes with them. "I'm also glad I've got these!"

7

The girls lingered over dinner, finishing both bottles, even though Kate only had one glass. Vivian savored every bite of her spaghetti carbonara and Wendy, Kate and Lucy raved over their trenette al pesto, lasagna and eggplant parmigiana. The waiter, Marc, kept dropping hints to Lucy about where he was going after his shift, to which she didn't bite.

After sharing a slice of Italian cream cake, the girls left the restaurant for the sports bar.

As they walked down the street, Vivian's phone rang. She didn't recognize the number but answered in case it had something to do with the kids.

"Hello."

"Hey Viv, how's your trip going?"

She stopped in the doorway of a bakery, covered up the mouthpiece and whispered, "Holy crap! It's Craig." She composed herself. "Uh, hi. Fine."

"Glad to hear."

Silence.

"Listen, I wanted to apologize for what I did. You were right, I should have trusted you. I don't know why I didn't. I messed up. And now I've messed us up."

She leaned against a window displaying a delicious looking carrot cake. "Uh, yeah." She let sarcasm drip off the "yeah."

Another silence.

"I'd like to see you again, Vivian. I know we can make things work. I want to see you when you're back from Colorado."

Vivian stomped her foot. "It's over Craig. There's nothing left to say. In fact, I don't ever want to talk to you again."

His voice flashed with anger. "Dammit Vivian, if you would just freaking listen—"

"No, Craig. It's over."

She hung up the phone, hands shaking and could feel the blood rushing to her face. "I've got to call Agent Tucker and tell him that I've just heard from Craig. I can't believe he called."

"I can," Wendy said, peering in the window at an éclair. "He wants to jack with you and screw up your vacation."

"We're not going to let that happen," Kate said, elbowing Lucy who was staring at the cupcakes. "No way, Jose."

"Yeah!" Lucy managed.

Vivian scrolled through her contacts and found Tucker's number.

After two rings, he answered. "Agent Tucker."

She paced in the bakery's alcove. "Hey, this is Vivian Taylor from Fort Worth. You came to my house when Craig Pearson's fingerprints came up a couple of weeks ago."

"Yes, I remember. What can I do for you, Ms. Taylor?"

"He just called me, but it wasn't from his regular number. It was one I didn't recognize."

"What did he say?"

"That he wanted to see me when I got back from my trip, and that he was sorry."

"Anything else?"

"Not really, just that he knew he messed up. He got a little mad though, when I told him it was over."

"Can you provide me the number he called from?"

She stopped pacing long enough to look at her phone and give him the number.

"Did he give any indication to his whereabouts?"

"No, sorry."

"Did he threaten you?"

"No, but he sounded mad."

"Could you hear any background noises, anything that would clue you in to where he was calling from?"

"No. I'm on a sidewalk in Aspen and couldn't hear anything but him, sorry."

"Okay, I'll run the number and see what I come up with. I appreciate your call."

"Sure. Bye."

He disconnected and Vivian dropped her phone into her purse. "It's been weeks since I've heard from him."

"I think Wendy's right," Lucy said. "He knew about this trip. He called to screw with you."

"Yeah, I guess."

They had a short walk to Bronco's.

"Let's just go inside and forget all about that jerk-wad," Wendy said and opened the door.

Vivian entered and took in the neon beer signs and what seemed like two thousand TVs. They were the only women in the place. A few men threw darts and a couple of others were playing a round of pool, but that was it. Nobody else was there. They had a seat at a table, close to the Rock-Ola jukebox, and ordered a bucket of beer and glass of water for Kate.

"Pierre says that every time he sees a bucket of beer he thinks of me, uh, I mean us," Lucy said and coughed.

"Playa del Carmen Pierre?" Vivian teased.

"You still talk to him?" Wendy asked.

"We keep in touch some," Lucy said. "It's no big deal. I'm married, we live a zillion miles apart, but he's a nice guy. Plus I feel bad for him, you know, since Jon died and I just like to check on him from time to time."

"Yeah, yeah," Kate said. "Whatever. You liked him then and you like him now."

Lucy ignored that and looked at Wendy. "Jon left him a substantial amount in his will, so he opened his own gym. Something he'd been wanting to do for several years."

"That's cool," Kate said. "You two have any plans to see each other?"

The bartender sat down the bucket and glass of water and Lucy passed them out. "No. I'm committed to making things work with Steve."

"And we support you in that," Vivian said, then held up her beer, offering a toast. "To Jon."

"To Jon," the girls repeated and joined her in remembering the best kissing (in Vivian's expert opinion), salsa dancing Canadian soap star who ever lived.

"Speaking of people from our Mexico vacation," Vivian said. "I stay in touch with Adrienne."

"She and Al were a hoot," Kate said.

"They sure disappeared from Shorty's party after the cops busted in," Wendy said. "Has she ever said anything about it?"

"Nope, and I haven't asked."

"It's got to be drugs and the mob," Lucy said, still stuck on her gangster fantasy of Al.

"Regardless, they were good to us and seem like nice people," Vivian said.

"Oh, I agree," Wendy said. "They were great."

Vivian's attention was broken by the striking man at the jukebox. His black, wavy hair brought out his ice-blue eyes. His eyelashes were so long they looked like he had taken a curler to them. He glanced over at the girls as he was making his selection.

"Any requests?" He smiled at them.

Lucy got up and went over to Rock-Ola. "Hmm…how about 'Green Eyes,' Coldplay?" She batted her green eyes at him.

After a few minutes of picking out songs, Vivian noticed that Lucy's chest was red and the color had crept up to her cheeks. *Somebody's flustered!*

A guy who had been hanging around a pool table came over to the table carrying two beers. His shirt read "I'm not Santa, but you can sit on my lap anyway." Not Santa handed a beer to the Rock-Ola guy, pulled up a chair and eased into it smoothly, draping his arm around Kate. "Who are the hotties?"

Vivian rolled her eyes and grabbed the last beer from the bucket.

Kate picked up his arm and dropped it into his lap. "I'm Kate and I'm married."

Undeterred, he said, "You ladies look like you're nice and naughty. Let's do a shot."

"Buttery Nipples?" Vivian joked.

"How about a Santa's South Pole?" Not Santa suggested, putting his arm around Vivian this time.

Ex-bartender Wendy looked skeptical. "Never heard of it."

"It's my specialty," he said and walked to the bar with Rock-Ola. They came back a few minutes later with six white shots topped with red drizzle.

"Festive," Vivian said.

Kate pushed hers away. "None for me, thanks."

They clinked and slammed, then Rock-Ola asked, "So what's on tap while you're here?"

"Spa-ing, hiking, relaxing," Lucy said, fidgeting with her naked ring finger. "No set agenda. Just fun."

Not Santa took a swig of his beer, then Kate's shot. "I think you girls should come back to the cabin with us. Get naked in the hot tub. What's more relaxing than bubbles floating around your—"

"I think we'll have to pass on that," Kate interrupted.

"You sure? We could play reindeer games." He took another swig.

Vivian finished off her beer. "I hate to burst your bubble, but as intriguing as that sounds, not tonight. I do thank you for the visit to the South Pole, though."

Not Santa made a sad face. "You're missing out on the power of the Pole."

Kate coughed, stood and picked up her purse. "I'll go take care of the tab."

"Already taken care of." Rock-Ola stood and helped Lucy scoot her chair back. "You have a nice visit. Maybe I'll see you again while you're here."

"Maybe. 'Night," she said.

Once outside, Wendy pointed to something in the distance. "What the hell is that?" She started across the street to investigate.

The girls followed her and Vivian laughed and rubbed the golden head of a male statue. He was bent over tying his shoelace and dressed in slacks, blue Oxford shirt and beige cable knit sweater.* (See appendix).

"Look, he's at just the right level!"

"You have such a one-track mind," Kate said, laughing.

Wendy got her camera out of her purse and snapped a candid. One for the scrapbook.

Vivian saw movement down the street and blinked a few times, adjusting her eyes because of the flash. The cool May wind blew and she shivered.

"I told you to layer up," Lucy chided.

She started to make a smartass remark but then saw the shadow move again. "Did y'all see that?"

"What?" Kate asked.

"I didn't see anything," Wendy said.

A couple rounded the corner in front of them, huddled together and laughing.

"Oh, nothing," Vivian said.

They walked by the windows to the Tree Bark Bar before entering the hotel. Eric was counting the cash drawer.

Vivian perked up. "Let's go in!" Before anyone could stop her, she was through the door.

Eric looked up. "Did you make it to Donatelli's?"

"We did. Excellent recommendation. You closing up for the night?"

"I am, but I'd be willing to make another round. On the house, my choice."

"They've already had a Santa's South Pole, so that's out," Kate said and giggled. "And I'm still out."

As he made his concoction, he said to Vivian, "A guy asked about you today, after you left for dinner."

"What?"

"I think he's a guest. He asked how long you'd be here."

"Who is this guy? Did he act like he knows me?"

"He didn't say your name, and I didn't tell him anything."

She pulled up a picture of Craig on her phone. "Was it this guy?"

Eric took a close look. "Nope, definitely not him." He poured four shots and topped them off with big swirls of whipped cream, then poured himself a shot of tequila.

"Here you go, ladies."

Vivian put her phone away, relieved.

Wendy picked up her shot.

"Oh no no no. No hands allowed."

"I haven't done one of these since I was in college!" Vivian said and laughed.

"What is it?" Kate asked.

Lucy, Vivian and Wendy all said in unison, "A blowjob!"

Kate made a face. "I'm not drinking, but I'm giving the toast."

They all lined up with their shots in front of them on the bar and Kate got out her camera.

"Here's to no more strange guys wanting to get us naked in a hot tub."

The girls woo-hooed, leaned over and skillfully shot their blowjobs as Kate clicked away.

"I completely disagree," Eric said, then slammed his tequila.

8

Day 2

Vivian and the girls awoke early, ready to start their first full day of vacation. Over coffee and juice around the table in their room, Lucy pitched attending a primitive wilderness school being taught just outside Aspen.

"Wilderness school?" Vivian asked.

"Primitive?" Wendy asked.

Lucy handed Vivian the brochure. "The morning class covers the basics of wilderness survival and land navigation, and the afternoon covers scouting and tracking."

"You're not taking us on some overnight hiking excursion, are you?" Wendy said. "I like the comforts of a hotel."

"Not tonight, but maybe one day we should go camping. It would be a fun girl's trip."

Vivian choked on her juice. "I don't see ever putting myself in a situation where I would need to scout or track something. I'm not much of an outdoor girl."

Kate took the brochure from Vivian and looked it over. "This sounds like fun, and after our last vacation, I wouldn't mind knowing some survivor skills."

Wendy put her feet up on the bed. "It's not like we needed to start a fire with our bare hands so we could boil water in Playa del Carmen."

"No, but we were trying to track down someone difficult to find," Lucy said in defense. "And it'd help me out living up here. My boss' sister and her husband are experienced hikers, and they recently got lost on a trail and had to be rescued by helicopter. They had some survival training, and they say it helped save their lives."

41

"Those poor people." Kate shook her head. "I think we should do it."

"Do they feed us lunch?" Wendy asked.

Lucy jumped up and down and grabbed Vivian's hand. "I bet it's a rockin' Rocky Mountain lunch. Come on, what do you say?"

Vivian thought about Lucy stuck in the mountains needing help. "If the instructor is cute, I'm in."

Kate picked up her iPhone. "Let's look him up!" She worked her phone for a minute, then showed the screen to the girls.

He looked to be in his late 30s and wore camouflage cargo pants and a tight black T-shirt, which looked pretty damned good on him.

"He is cute," Wendy said. "Okay, I'm in."

"Perhaps he'll need a volunteer to help demonstrate staying warm in the winter?" Vivian clapped her hands and then rubbed them together. "Oh, or CPR!"

"One track mind," Lucy said, shaking her head. "If we have time afterwards, I'd love to get my game on. The hotel has racquetball courts in their fitness center."

Wendy and Kate weren't interested but Vivian agreed, so Lucy called to reserve a court. After a quick breakfast at the closest thing Aspen had to a Denny's, the girls got the car out of valet and headed west of town.

The drive didn't take long, but Kate bristled when Lucy turned onto Cemetery Road.

"Relax." She gave Kate a dismissive wave. "The class meets at Sunnyside trailhead, not the cemetery. Much cheerier." Lucy pulled into a small, muddy parking lot and stopped in front of a large oak tree.

A Paul Bunyan-sized man was speaking with three other guys just past a marquee providing info and a map of the trail. It was the same guy they'd seen on the internet.

"You here for the primitive wilderness course?" he asked as the girls walked up.

Vivian felt about 3-feet tall under his hazel-eyed gaze. She imagined running her fingers through his unruly brown hair but didn't think she could reach it.

"Yes, we are," Wendy answered.

One of the other guys snickered, and Bunyan cut his gaze to him. The guy immediately stopped.

Bunyan introduced himself as Buck, and introductions were made. Vivian didn't like Chris, the snicker-er. He was about 6-foot, but looked like Tattoo from *Fantasy Island* compared to the instructor.

Buck got right to business. "The essentials in wilderness survival are shelter, fire, food and water. You need to be able to find, make and maintain shelter, fire and food, and you need to be able to find and purify water. In order to do those things, every hiker or wilderness explorer should hit the trail with their EDC, everyday carry tools."

He pulled a knife out of a sheath on his belt. "One of the most important tools out here. Whether it's cutting saplings for a tree-pit snow shelter or skinning dinner, a sharp knife is a must."

Vivian shivered. She hoped there would be no skinning demonstrations.

Buck returned the knife, then picked up his backpack. He pulled out some of the contents. "Rope, poncho and stakes for a lean-to." He threw those on the ground and reached into the bag. "First-aid kit. Should be a no-brainer, but you'd be surprised at the number of hikers who get into trouble that could have been avoided, had they had a stocked first-aid kit."

He pulled out a small brown bottle and a contraption with a pump and tubes. He shook the bottle. "Iodine tablets will kill 100 percent of the bacteria, viruses and giardia in contaminated bodies of water, but the results don't taste great." He dropped the bottle in the backpack and held up the contraption. "Water purifier, the most essential tool for the most essential element in wilderness survival. We will hike through the oaks about half a mile to a pond. Each of you will have a chance to use the pump, and I encourage you to taste for yourself." He turned and headed up the trail.

The group followed as Buck pointed out hidden dangers, identified foliage that could be eaten, animal tracks along the way, etc.

At the pond, Chris, the snicker-er, said, "No way I'm going to drink anything out of there."

A stench rose from the murky, film-covered water. Decaying plant matter along the sides left suspended particles in the muck.

"Who wants to go first?" Buck asked after demonstrating the purification process.

Vivian's stomach lurched thinking about it, but she was determined to show up the guys, so she raised her hand.

"That's what I like," Buck said. "Someone who's not afraid to take chances."

She assembled the pump as Buck had instructed, and stuck the dirty end of one tube in the pond. She put the clean end into a small plastic cup Buck provided. With a few easy decompressions on the pump handle, clear water filled the cup. She air-toasted Chris and gulped it down. It tasted a little funkified, but she forced a smile on her face.

"Who's next?" Buck asked.

One of the other guys was overeager and pumped shots for his buddies. It was the girls' turn to snicker.

Buck moved to a nearby evergreen and explained how to pick a good spot for a lean-to, then showed how to construct it using the ropes, poncho and stakes.

Lucy raised her hand. "What's the tree-pit snow shelter you mentioned earlier?"

"Let's go over here and I'll show you," Buck said, then moved off the trail into a snowy patch. "I need volunteers to dig the snow out from around this tree wide enough for two people to get in. This time of year it's not all that deep so this instruction is more for educational purposes than actual utilization, but midwinter, this knowledge could save your life. Pack the snow firm on top and inside as well."

"What do we dig with?" Wendy asked.

"Your hands, unless you brought a shovel."

"Come on, it'll be fun," Kate said and dug in. "We're learning to survive in the wilderness."

Wendy didn't look as enthusiastic.

The girls had a hole dug to Buck's specifications in no time, as the snow was more mush than powder. Vivian's hands stung from the cold and her exercise pants were muddy from kneeling.

Buck pulled out his knife and cut a few boughs off a juniper. "Place these in the bottom for insulation." They did while he cut a few more. "You would use these for cover on top."

Lucy hopped into the pit and held one of the jumper branches over her head, peeking out. "Can you see me?" she asked Vivian.

Buck laughed and reached out a hand to help Lucy up. Getting back into instructor mode, he said, "Navigating off-trail is of the utmost importance should you get lost or disoriented in the wilderness." He unzipped a pocket on his camo pants, pulled out several compasses and handed them to the group. He had them hold the compass and turn from side to side as he gave basic instructions.

He pointed out the peak to Red Mountain and went into an explanation on azimuths. Vivian tuned out the projected vector, zenith, perpendicular, blah blah. She was more interested in the rest of him.

Wrapping up the compass instruction, he handed everyone a topographical map and explained how to read it. "Now that you can read the topos, it's time to put your skills to use—"

"Tacos?" Wendy said. "I could put my skills to use eating one of those right now."

"Me, too." Vivian giggled but stopped at Buck's glance.

"Topos, as in topography," he explained.

Vivian and Wendy shared an oops moment.

Buck addressed the group. "Do you see Squirrel Lake?"

Nods all around.

"Your job is to hike there, off-trail, using nothing but the map, compass and azimuth skills I've given you. It should take you no more than 15 minutes."

"What if we get lost?" Wendy asked.

Lucy raised her map in the air. "I got this."

Buck clapped, dismissing them. "See you in 15."

9

The girls conferred over the map for a few minutes before trekking northeast toward Squirrel Lake. Mr. Snicker and his two buddies had taken off right away.

Ten minutes into their hike, Kate stopped and consulted the map. "We should have passed this stream by now." She pointed to a thin blue line about halfway from where they were to where the lake was.

"Maybe we just haven't gotten to it yet?" Vivian asked.

"I need to recheck the azimuth calculation." Kate scanned the horizon and ticked off a few points on her hand. "I think we need to head more east than north."

"Sure thing," Wendy said and they started out.

Another five minutes passed, and Kate clicked her tongue. "This isn't right. We definitely should have passed that stream by now."

"Maybe it's dried up?" Vivian said.

"Probably not, it's spring," Lucy looked at the map, then at the horizon. "By my calculations, we should head directly north. It just feels right."

Vivian leaned against an aspen. "That doesn't sound very scientific."

"You wanna figure it out?" Lucy asked.

"I wasn't paying attention! He started to sound like Charlie Brown's teacher so I checked him out instead. Fine specimen."

Kate and Lucy turned to Wendy, who threw up her hands. "Don't ask me. I hated geography in high school and used to fall asleep in class."

Kate looked at the map again. "I think we're officially lost."

Lucy looked over her shoulder. "We can't be that lost, we've only been walking a few minutes."

They studied the map together. Wendy walked the perimeter, scanning for landmarks. Vivian checked her cell phone. No service. "At least it's still early. They should find us before the creatures come out."

"I think I got it," Kate said. "If we hike a bit that way," she pointed a little to the right of north, according to Vivian's compass, "we should make it to the southern edge of the lake, instead of the east, as we had planned."

"Lead us to the promise land, sista!" Vivian said.

They started out again and hiked for 10 minutes before reaching a ravine.

"Is this the stream?" Vivian asked and sat on top of a boulder lining the edge. It started to slide and she scrambled forward, grasping for a tree.

Lucy and Wendy ran to her, grabbing her arm just in time to pull her to safety. The boulder continued to slide off the side, crunching and crushing everything in its path. The three fell in a heap.

"Oh my god!" Vivian said as she sat up. "That coulda killed me!"

Kate rushed over and helped her up. "You probably would have been impaled on something on the way down."

"We would have needed a medical chopper to rescue you," Wendy said and stood up. "That crash sounded *bad*."

Vivian dusted herself off. "Thanks for the save!"

"We get an F in primitive wilderness school," Lucy said, looking dejected. "I was sure I would ace this."

Vivian patted her back. "You did great with the tree-pit snow shelter. That's something."

"And you saved your friend's life," Buck said as he walked up behind them.

"Woo-hoo, we're saved!" Wendy said and clapped. "I am *done* with this land navigating stuff."

"How did you find us?" Lucy asked.

"At first I tracked you," Buck said and chuckled. "Then it wasn't hard to hear you, so I just followed the sound."

"Tracked us?" Kate said.

"Yes. Using the skills of Apache warriors, I can track anyone and sneak up silently."

Vivian crossed her arms in front of her chest, then raised one hand. "How Chief Buck, we come in peace. Ooohoohoohoohooo!" She popped her hand back and forth over her mouth doing her best Apache impersonation. She was one-sixteenth Cherokee so she felt semi-qualified.

"Thanks for finding us," Lucy said.

"If it's any conciliation, the guys didn't make it, either," Buck said.

47

"Is that what you're teaching us this afternoon?" Kate asked.

"The basics, yes. Let's get back to the group." He crossed the ravine and the girls followed — carefully.

Buck had the guys gather tinder, kindling and a few larger logs for his fire demonstration. He got right to it. "There are four types of campfires: cooking, warmth, lighting and signaling. Which one you build depends on your situation."

"I always thought there was a one-size-fits-all fire," Vivian whispered to Lucy.

"Me, too."

As Buck dug a fire pit, he said, "I'm not going to light the fire today, but your best bet is to carry waterproof matches with you. In the event you don't have a 21st century method for lighting fire, do it caveman style by using two sticks together in the bow-drill method or finding flint rock which can create a spark."

Kate coughed and Wendy elbowed her in the ribs. "He's not talking about *that* kind of caveman style."

"I don't even know what that would be, it just sounded funny."

"I think it would involve a lot of ughaaa wughaaa, ughaaa—"

Kate and Vivian started full-out laughing, and Lucy gave them a look.

Buck, ignoring them, threw the tinder and kindling into the pit and then used the kindling and logs to assemble the four types of fire. He concluded with the signaling fire. "Make a tripod frame over the tinder and kindling and tie the branches together with wire or evergreen branches. Light the fire and drape green leafy branches from the top of the tripod. Smoke will billow high into the sky, enabling a rescue team to find you."

"Are there smoke signals we should do?" Lucy asked.

Buck grinned. "No, the smoke is a signal itself, but if possible, light more than one of these, and make caveman sounds while you do it." Putting on a straight face, he said to the group, "Who wants to try?"

Overeager water guy was all over this, too, and stepped right up, cutting Lucy off. She went about gathering her own tinder, kindling and logs with the girls' help, and she made a bigger signaling fire than he did.

Buck gave her an approving glance, then turned his attention to the group. "Time for lunch. I brought my favorite survival snacks; hope you're hungry." He pulled a bag of dried fruit out of his backpack. "Feel free to use the water filter in the lake if you're thirsty."

48

Wendy put her hands on her hips. "He wasn't kidding when he named this course 'primitive.' "

This was not the lunch Vivian had envisioned. *Lucy's going to have to make up for this.*

She did, by whipping out the Ritz Crackers and Easy Cheese from her backpack. "Am I good or what?"

Vivian drew an A+ on a cracker and handed it to Lucy. "Way to keep me alive in the wilderness!"

A quick lunch out of the way, Buck began teaching the basics of scouting and tracking, starting with natural camouflage.

"You have to blend into your surroundings," he said as he rubbed mud all over his face, then took a bit of the tinder from the fire pit and stuck it on his cheeks. He walked to the tree line and worked a small evergreen branch into a circle and strategically placed it on his head. "Move with the landscape and observe nature." He clapped his hands, and birds flew from the trees. "What are they flying away from?"

"A predator," Overeager said.

Duh, Vivian thought.

Buck instructed the group to join him in the woods. "Observation and reconnaissance are critical." He pointed out a set of tracks and pine tree branch with the bark rubbed off. "Deer tracks, a buck. And he rubbed his antlers on this branch, leaving his scent." He walked deeper into the woods, away from the lake and any semblance of a trail. "Here's the scat."

He kept walking, the group behind him. "Keep your head up and look forward as much as possible. Look for the probable path the animal, or human, took."

"Is this how you were able to find us?" Kate asked.

Buck kept walking and said over his shoulder, "I saw some tracks from you, and where the ground was too hard I noticed decompressions in the leaves. Someone snagged her clothing on a branch and left a trace of red thread." He looked at Wendy.

She inspected her jacket. "I sure did."

"I also smelled the human scent. Vivian's perfume or lotion, I believe."

Damn, he was observant!

He crouched down and showed them smaller animal tracks. "See how these meander? Skunk. They don't have many natural predators and amble along without much concern." He stood up. "Let's see if we can sniff him out."

"Is that such a good idea?" Lucy asked.

Buck silently walked through the forest, and the group sounded like a stampede in comparison. They came to the trail leading back to the cars but Buck kept going, in pursuit of his varmint. A few feet later he slowed and then stopped.

"See that?" He pointed to a fallen, hollow tree trunk. "That's the skunk's den. The family is probably in there, as they're nocturnal animals."

Chris picked up a pebble and tossed it inside the trunk. Nothing happened, so he went to do it again. The girls backed away a few steps.

"I wouldn't do that if I were you," Buck said, also backing up.

Chris did it anyway, and a madder 'n' hell skunk emerged. It hissed and stamped its feet, raising its tail to defend its territory.

"She's protecting her young," Buck said. "Back away slowly. No sudden movements."

The girls and two of the guys complied. Chris, on the other hand, turned to run and the skunk chased after him. Chris tried to climb a tree and escape, but she turned, lifted her tail and sprayed, then casually walked back into the den.

Vivian and the girls doubled over laughing and ran back to the trail, trying to outdistance the smell.

Buck followed them. "Some people never learn."

Wiping a tear from her eye, Vivian asked, "Do you have a course in skunk spray removal?"

After everyone quit laughing, the girls said goodbye to Buck at the trail. He was staying with the guys and giving Chris pointers in how to deal with the smell. He went over directions and made sure everyone knew how to get back to the car.

"We're good," Vivian said and gave him a wave as he walked off. She watched his backside for a moment.

Lucy tugged a strand of her hair. "Come on, sex fiend. Let's go."

10

The girls were still laughing about the skunk incident as Lucy pulled out of the trailhead parking lot. "Can you believe that guy?" she said, shaking her head.

"He totally deserved it for messing with that momma," Vivian said and cracked the window. Though they didn't get sprayed, a slight hint of skunkiness clung in the air.

Wendy's laugh quieted and she made an abrupt announcement. "I've decided, when I get back, I'm breaking up with Jake. That's it. It's over."

That shut the other girls up.

A few beats later they all spoke at once. "You sure, he's a nice one?" "That's a big decision." "But I like him."

"I know. I know all of that. But I don't think he's ready to commit and I just can't move to North Carolina without a commitment. This long distance thing sucks."

Vivian turned around from the passenger's seat and looked her in the eye. "You would move to North Carolina for him? Have you ever even been there?"

"I would move if we were engaged, but I don't see that happening at this point. And yes, I've been there. I went out for Thanksgiving last year and met his family. They're all very nice and normal. They'd make great in-laws."

"Wow." Lucy looked at her in the rearview mirror. "You sure you're ready to call it quits?"

"Yes. I have to admit, I'm a little mad at him. We've talked about marriage, seemed like things were leading up to that before he moved." She fidgeted with the cup holder in the backseat. "We went to Washington, D.C., for New Year's, and no proposal. I kinda thought there would be."

"Well, who wouldn't?" Vivian insisted.

"That sucks," Lucy said.

"Yeah, tell me about it," Wendy continued. "Then Valentine's came, he flew out to see me, and again, nothing."

"Stupid Valentine's Day," Vivian remarked. "The last Valentine's Rick and I were together he gave me, and you aren't going to believe this, a JOHN DENVER CD!"

"Shut up!" Lucy said.

"John Denver?" Kate asked.

"Yep. I should have known the end was near."

Wendy shook her head. "So now, here it is, May, and we haven't talked about it since. He must not love me enough to commit, so screw it. I'm done."

"Boys are dumb-asses," Vivian said. "Stay strong, sister!"

Kate patted her knee. "I like Jake, but I hear ya. You can't wait around forever."

Lucy pulled up to the valet, and Vivian was thankful to be back in civilization. She'd had enough playing in the woods for one day. Kate went back to the room to call Shaun while Lucy, Vivian and Wendy headed for the Yellow Aspen's locker room in the fitness center. They changed out of their hiking gear, then Wendy ventured off to the steam room and Vivian and Lucy checked in for racquetball.

They were assigned the middle of three white-walled courts. The back Plexiglas wall looked onto the adjacent basketball courts and locker rooms across the hall.

Vivian reached for the flush-mounted, chrome door handle but couldn't figure out how to open it.

"What is it with you and opening things on this trip?" Lucy joked.

"It's designed weird," Vivian said. "We need Kate to figure this thing out!"

After several tries, she popped up the flush handle, rotated it and unlatched the door. Lucy started warming up and hit the ball a few times. Vivian watched it bounce around.

"You have to hit it before it bounces twice," Lucy said.

"I'm trying to!" Vivian said, but she honestly didn't realize Lucy was serious and ready to start playing.

Lucy explained the rules. "You stand in that box to serve. Then it's in play as long as it lands here." She pointed to the box in front of her. She looked at Vivian, who was giggling. "What?"

"You said box."

"OMG. Grow up! I'm not talking about your girl parts, I'm trying to exercise here!"

"I'm already sweating," Vivian whined.

"You haven't even done anything yet. We've only been in here five minutes."

They "played" for about 30 minutes before Kate walked up to the glass door carrying a large cup of coffee. Lucy hit the racquetball and it bounced off the back wall, right in front of Kate's face. Startled, she threw her arms in the air, along with her coffee. Java flew everywhere. All over the glass, her, the floor.

Kate stood still for a second, then wiped off her face with her shirt. She didn't appear to be scalded, and she frowned into the empty cup. Lucy and Vivian were doubled over, laughing hysterically. She glared at them and then walked away.

"I couldn't repeat that if I tried," Lucy said after she had semi-recovered.

"I think I'm done," Vivian said, wiping tears from her eyes.

"We still have 20 minutes on the court."

"I suck and I'm suckin' wind, especially after witnessing that."

"So what! Move your ass around and burn some calories."

Vivian wasn't pleased with the comment, but her competitive spirit insisted that she keep going. Twenty minutes later, she noticed two guys standing near the court door.

"I think they're waiting."

"We have a few minutes left," Lucy said, wiping her brow with her towel. "You're just looking for an excuse."

"Okay, I admit it. I'm ready to get the hell outta here. I've burned more calories in the past hour than I've burned in my last three rounds of sexercise."

"Don't say stuff like that around me!" Lucy smacked the ball super hard against the wall. "You know what my life's been like."

Vivian watched the ball relay around the court several times before she was able to hit it. "Speaking of that, I noticed you fidgeting with your nonexistent wedding ring last night while you were flirting heavily with Rock-Ola."

"I wasn't flirting heavily." Lucy slammed the ball again.

"Okay, you were flirting lightly, but you were flirting," Vivian said and hit the ball after two bounces. "Your cheeks were rosy pink, as were the tops of your breastabules."

"He was cute." Smack. "I was titillated." The ball bounced directly back to her. Smack. "I used that word just for you, by the way."

"Yeah, I figured." Vivian swung and missed.

"Time's up." Lucy snatched the ball as it passed near her.

Vivian didn't argue, and they gathered their things. She noticed someone pass behind the two guys who were waiting. That someone looked like Craig, her ex.

Lucy tossed the ball in the air. "You know, if you'd practice, you could be pretty good. You have good hand-eye coordination."

Vivian dropped her racquet. "Uh, yeah."

Lucy it picked up, and one of the waiting guys opened the door. Vivian looked around the basketball court but didn't see anyone resembling Craig.

Where did he go? Then she saw the exit door close and walked toward it.

"Viv, where are you going?"

"I thought I saw…"

Lucy looked around. "What?"

"Oh, nothing. I think I'm too hot. I'm seeing things."

"There's a water cooler. I recommend you use it."

Kate walked up with a fresh cup of coffee and a clean shirt. Wendy came down the hall glowing pink.

"I recommend the steam sauna," Wendy said, looking relaxed. "Twenty minutes in there and a cool shower, and the toxins are gone. I feel invigorated!"

"I prefer to detox without feeling like I'm in Pasadena in July," Vivian said.

Lucy checked her watch. "My appetite has been invigorated and I'm ready for dinner."

Vivian's stomach rumbled on cue. "There's my vote for food. Let's go get ready."

They walked into the hotel and Vivian saw Eric behind the bar. She fluffed her sweaty curls and told the girls she'd meet them in the room.

"But you stink," Lucy said.

"I won't get too close, and I won't be long."

She went to the far end of the bar and called, "Hey, cowboy." Exaggerated Texas accent. "How are things in these here parts?"

"Hey, there, little lassie," Eric said, pretending to tip an invisible cowboy hat in her direction. "I'm doin' mighty fine. Looks like you are, too. Have a good day?"

"Sure did. Now it's time for dinner."

He looked her up and down. "Hope you're planning on meeting me for SIN later." His tone got serious. "I know a great spot for dessert."

Vivian winked at him, turned and walked out of the bar.

11

Vivian got into the elevator, her cheeks blushing. She fanned herself. *Damn, Eric is hot!*

A man in his mid-40s stuck his arm in the doors just as they were closing; they opened and he got on.

"That was a close one," he said.

"You can say that again," Vivian said, pushing the 6. "What floor?"

"Same, thanks."

"So what's going on in Aspen tonight?" he asked.

"Night out with the girls for me," she said. "We tend to make trouble wherever we go."

The doors opened and she stepped off.

"Be careful out there," he called, walking the opposite way.

She let herself into the room where the girls were in full swing getting ready. Lucy was in the middle of opening a bottle of wine, Kate slaved away over an ironing board and Wendy was wrapped in a towel heading to the shower. She stopped.

"Did Mr. Buttery Nipple butter you all up?" she joked.

"That stick of butter is still in its package, thank you very much," Vivian replied, placing her purse on the entry table. "But he reminded me about SIN night. We are *so* going!"

At that moment Lucy's wine cork pulled free. "I'm in!" she said with a laugh. "Who wants a glass?"

Two "me's" chimed in unison.

Lucy poured three, small plastic cups with pinot noir and handed them out. Wendy took hers, held it up and said cheers, then shut the bathroom door.

Vivian turned her head and sniffed the air. "I smell it again."

Kate stopped ironing for a second. "Smell what?"

"I swear it smells like cologne. Craig's cologne."

Lucy swirled the wine glass. "The only thing I smell is this fine bouquet emitting from my glass."

Vivian walked around the room. "Remember when we came in earlier, I thought it smelled like cologne then, too?"

"I only smell the heat from the iron," Kate said. "But I didn't really notice anything before."

Lucy ran the straightening iron through her hair. "What's wrong, Viv? You missin' a man's scent already?"

"Hardly! I don't need no stinkin' or sexy smellin' man! They're just nice to have around occasionally for—"

"Yeah, yeah, we know," Lucy huffed.

They continued to get ready, primping, straightening, perfuming. Vivian put her final touches of lipstick on and looked at her ears. *Earrings.* She picked through her jewelry satchel for the silver and turquoise dangle earrings Kate had bought her in Playa Del Carmen. They went perfectly with her black and turquoise, tight, v-neck wrap shirt and blue jean mini-skirt, but they didn't go so well with her bumblebee pendant. Craig had given her the necklace for their three month anniversary and in honor of Audrey starting school next year as a Libby B. Staten Bumblebee. Though she didn't care for costume jewelry, or really any jewelry other than earrings, she had taken to wearing the piece often.

"Y'all about ready?" Lucy asked. "I'm hungry." She buckled her red, sling-back FMPs that provided the perfect accent to her clingy black, scoop-neck dress.

Wendy and Kate were both wearing jeans. Kate had ironed a crisp white cotton blouse, and Wendy sported a sleeveless black silk blouse with hints of deep purple and teal.

Vivian heard sirens and walked toward the window overlooking the main street. Two police cars, a fire truck and ambulance screeched to a stop in front of the hotel about the same time.

"What the hell's going on?" Lucy asked, joining Vivian at the window.

Wendy and Kate walked over too.

"Dunno. Fire alarm isn't going off. Probably some medical emergency."

They gathered their purses, Wendy grabbed a wrap, and off they went.

The hotel's front entrance was blocked off, so they walked to the concierge.

"What the heck's going on?" Kate asked.

"There's been an accident out front. You'll need to exit through the rear, I can show you if you like."

As they walked, Lucy asked for dinner recommendations. He suggested Moose Crossing, modern American cuisine with Colorado flair, within walking distance and happy hour for the next 45 minutes. Sold!

They passed Club Bighorn on the way, and Kate pointed out the flyer in the window announcing service industry night. "This is where Viv'll be committing SIN later tonight. I can't wait to watch this!"

This got a round of woo-hoos.

A black cat darted across the street in front of them. Vivian hoped Kate wouldn't notice.

She did.

"We have to turn around and go the other way around the block."

"What? Why?"

"The black cat crossing is bad luck. We can't continue on our current path."

"Doesn't that rule only apply if you're in a car?" Lucy asked.

"Don't encourage her," Wendy said.

"This goes back to way before cars were invented," Kate defended. "Remember what happened after you broke that mirror in Mexico?"

"Fine, we can work up even more of an appetite," Vivian said. "Let's do it, make her happy."

They took the long route around the block, window shopping along the way.

When Lucy pulled the door open to Moose Crossing, the girls entered a timber wonderland of wooden chairs, tables, walls, lamps. The only things not made of wood were the taxidermy animals perched here and there, looking ready to attack.

The girls were seated next to the large stone fireplace complete with mounted moose head.

"I hear y'all have happy hour," Lucy said to the waitress.

"We do. Moosehead Lager pints are on special. It's from Canada. I like it because it's not too heavy."

"I dunno, I'm a Dos Equis girl," Vivian said.

"Let's just get a bottle of wine," Wendy said.

The waitress gave her a wine list, and she chose a Sequoia Grove cabernet. "One of my favorites."

"They serve weird animals here," Vivian said, looking over the menu. "Elk, venison, buffalo, rabbit. Poor little Thumper and Bambi."

"It's not weird, Viv, it's exotic," Kate said. "Branch out."

"I'm having a salad."

"Let's get a few different things and share. Viv, you have to at least try it. Expand your taste buds."

The waitress appeared with the wine and poured Wendy a taste. She approved so the waitress poured each of them a glass, except Kate who had water.

Lucy ordered the Rocky Mountain elk loin, Wendy the rabbit-rattlesnake sausage (Vivian made a gagging sound), Kate the wild boar ribs and Vivian a Caesar salad.

As the waitress left to turn in the order, Kate offered a toast. "To our second girls' trip and expanding our taste in food and wine."

"And men," Vivian threw in.

"Cheers!"

Clink.

"So how are you handling single mom-dom?" Kate asked.

Vivian picked up her glass and took a long drink. "It's not been easy. I've tried to make everything as seamless as possible for the kids, but it's so hard. Working full time, keeping Audrey and Lauren in dance classes, and my god, the laundry. It's never-ending. And now…" Her voice broke.

They all were quiet. Wendy got out a packet of tissues and gave Vivian one.

"With them married, she shows up to everything. It feels so forced. She never looks like she's having a good time. Or even cares about the kids. It's like it's all for show."

"I just don't see why he decided to marry her," Lucy said. "Do you think it was to save face? Like, to say to the world, 'Yes, I left my wife and four kids, but look, I married the other woman so I did it for a good reason?' "

Vivian took another tissue. "I don't know. He keeps making bad decision after bad decision. Every time I talk to him he sounds about ready to jump off a bridge."

"Let's hope if he does he makes it look like an accident so you can collect the insurance," Wendy said, half joking.

Kate reached for the bottle and refilled Vivian's glass, emptying the wine bottle. "He is officially the world's biggest cow turd."

"First-class douche bag," Wendy added.

"A dipshit of mega magnitude," Lucy said.

"Y'all are making me feel better," Vivian said, cracking a smile.

Wendy ordered a second bottle of wine that arrived with their dinner. Kate made Vivian a plate that had mostly salad but also some of everything.

"Expand your horizons, Viv."

Vivian did and, once finished, offered an opinion. "Not bad. The elk loin is pretty good, but the wild boar ribs don't taste like any pig I've ever had. The rabbit-rattlesnake sausage just tastes like sausage. That I can handle."

"You're crackin' me up," Lucy said. "You and your critique."

"I'm forced to watch Food Network while I get my pedicure."

The waitress cleared the table and came back with a dessert tray. "Can I interest you in a dessert tonight?" She went through her spiel, and the girls decided on the molten lava cake with drunken berries and a banana pudding.

Lucy poured the remainder of the wine into each of their glasses.

"Oh my god, is that George Clooney over there?" Kate asked.

"No…is it?" Vivian craned her neck.

"It does kinda look like him from the side," Wendy said.

Lucy picked up both of the wine bottles and stuck the openings to her eyes.* "Where? Where's George? I don't see him."

"Oh god, she's doin' the wine goggles," Vivian said. "What's next?"

"If you could meet any celebrity, who would it be?" Lucy asked, setting down the bottles. "Mine would be Beyoncé." She did the "Single Ladies" hand wave.

"You're not single," Vivian pointed out.

Lucy shrugged and resumed seeing the world through her wine goggles.

"It's a good song and good choice," Kate said. "But I'd love to meet Ron Paul. He's the only one playing for a different team."

Vivian slapped the table. "Matthew McConaughey. He's sexy."

"Yes, but he's married now," Kate pointed out.

"The question was meet, not marry."

"I love the way Matthew talks, he has the best drawl." Wendy took a sip of wine before continuing. "I'd love to meet Ellen DeGeneres. I watch her show every day and she cracks me up."

"She does a lot of good for a lot of people," Vivian said. "I like that about her and I'd like to meet her, too."

The waitress placed the lava cake and banana pudding in the center of the table, then added four forks and spoons next to them.

Lucy tilted her wine goggles up to the waitress. "Is that George Clooney over there?"

The waitress laughed and said, "No, but it does look a lot like him."

"Damn, he's hot. I was ready to get looney for Clooney."

The girls laughed at her and with her, then dug in on dessert.

Wendy took a bite of the cake, scooping up a raspberry. "I think Lucy's as drunk as this berry."

"I'm on vaca and I'm not drivin'," Lucy said.

They clinked wine glasses to that, then slowly finished off the desserts.

"About time to head over to Club Bighorn," Kate said, scooting her chair and rubbing her tummy. "Can someone carry me?"

"I'll carry you now if you carry me later," Vivian said.

"I think Eric's gonna carry you later," Wendy smirked.

"You gonna find out if he hazza big horn tonight?" Lucy slurred.

Vivian tilted her wine glass up and finished off the last bit. "Big horns do make me happy."

12

The girls paid their tab and made their way out of the restaurant. Lucy secretly posed behind "George" while Vivian snapped her picture. George was none the wiser, and the girls cracked up about on their way to SIN.

Club Bighorn wasn't what Vivian expected. She figured another dead animal type of place, but instead it was trendy modern. Across the lounge spanned a cantilevered polished concrete bar and oversized chairs and couches with ottomans shaped like marshmallows. In the club, a large disco ball veiled in a chandelier glittered above the dance floor, and the ceiling was punched with a thousand pinpoint LED lights that randomly changed colors in a mesmerizing rhythm. Occasional laser lights shot around the dance floor and a DJ played tunes from a booth in a corner.

"Anyone see Eric?" Kate asked.

Vivian looked around the 20 or so people in the club. "Not yet. He's probably wrapping things up at Tree Bark. He'll be here."

"Time for shots!" Lucy said, heading to the bar in the lounge.

"Hey, there, y'all got any specials?" Wendy asked the bartender.

He smiled, showing off the dimple in his left cheek. "Bighorn bombers, my specialty."

"Let's have 'em!"

He flipped bottles, shook up the concoction in a tin, and poured out five shots. He handed them to the girls and held one up himself. "Bombs away!"

"Bombs away!" they cheered.

Lucy plopped down across an ottoman and hung her head off the edge. "Take my picture!"

"Look at you, being sexy showing off your cleavage," Kate said as she snapped the camera. "You need to send this to Steve. He'll like that."

"One would think," Lucy replied.

"Let's go dance," Wendy said. "I gotta burn off some of that lava cake."

"Don't Stop 'Til You Get Enough" by Michael Jackson played, and Lucy moonwalked her way to the middle of the dance floor. She spun around, doing her best MJ impersonation. Wendy did the knee, foot-shake thing, and Kate went "Wooo," rising onto her toes, and grabbed her crotch. Vivian laughed and pulled out the snap move.

The DJ played great song after great song. "When Doves Cry," "Groove is in the Heart," "Can't Touch This." The girls danced and danced until Eric came up behind Vivian and put his hands around her waist.

She turned around and smiled at him. "Hey, you."

"Mmm, you look good," he said and moved his hands lower down her back, just above her ass. "I like the way you dance, too."

Vivian shook her hips with a little more enthusiasm. "I used to take belly dancing."

"Damn, that's sexy. Did you wear one of those veil things?"

"Nah, but I do have a sexy little bangled scarf that makes fun noises. But I only break it out for special occasions, and since I wasn't anticipating any special occasion, I didn't bring it."

"That's unfortunate. Tonight will be classified as a special occasion."

Vivian giggled. *Yeah, baby!*

They danced to the end of the song, then Eric asked if anyone wanted anything to drink. Time for more cocktails. The group ambled to the bar, and Eric shook hands with the bartender. "Hey, Lorenzo. How 'bout a round of bombers?"

The bartender got right to it, tossing the bottles with flair.

"And how about a round of waters, too?" Wendy, the walking pharmacy, ordered.

Shots were served, and Eric offered a toast. "To special girls and special occasions." He flashed a sexy smile at Vivian and drank his shot.

Vivian hummed with anticipation and smiled her sexiest smile back. Flirting was definitely coming easier these days.

A couple of guys with long-sleeved white shirts and black slacks walked in. One of them clapped Eric on the back. "Hey, bro, how's it going? What the hell happened at The Aspen tonight?"

"Man, some guy did a header off the 6th floor. It was crazy. Police everywhere."

"Alcohol's a depressant, dude. You gotta quit over-serving your guests."

"Yeah, yeah. Here, let me introduce you to some lovely ladies." He made the introductions, saying the guys worked at the tapas bar a few blocks over. They talked shop until three girls walked in wearing similar uniforms. The bar started to fill up and Eric said hello to almost everyone, never taking his hand off Vivian's waist and occasionally brushing it across her butt.

Wendy, Kate and Lucy headed back to the dance floor, which was now packed. Eric and Vivian joined them for a song, then headed back to the bar and had another shot. As they were served, Vivian ran her hand down Eric's chest. "When does the special occasion of this evening begin?"

Eric leaned down and kissed her. Tongue was involved.

"That was just a sneak peak."

Damn skippy! Vivian thought but said, "Looking forward to the full feature."

They moved to a cocktail table near the dance floor, and the other girls joined them just as "Pour Some Sugar on Me" blared through the club.

"Who sings this song?" Vivian asked.

"Def Leppard," Lucy yelled. "You know, with the one-armed drummer." She took a sip of her vodka cranberry and glanced to her right. A one-armed guy had just walked onto the dance floor and stared right at her. Lucy spewed her drink, laser lights shining through the spittle particles floating in the air around them.

Eric, Vivian, Kate and Wendy couldn't hold back laughter as Lucy tried to recover.

Vivian turned to Eric. "Might be time to go."

Eric looked pleased. "Let me tab out."

Though tipsy themselves, Wendy and Kate gathered up Lucy and headed to the door. Eric and Vivian met them outside, and he walked them back to the hotel. The heel taps on Wendy's boots had fallen off from all her dancing, and the walk back was clanky and loud.

At the door to the hotel, the girls started to go in but Eric said, "Sorry, ladies, I can't. Once I'm off for the night, it's not allowed."

Vivian looked disappointed.

He pulled her toward him. "But you're welcome to go back to my place."

Vivian blushed and felt giddy. She glanced at the girls. "I'll be in later. I have my key."

"But what about the buddy system?" Kate asked.

"Buddy system?" Eric asked, raising his eyebrows. "That sounds intriguing."

"Not that kind of buddy system!" Vivian laughed and gave him a push. She turned toward the girls. "It's fine. We're not in Mexico anymore and we know where he works."

She linked arms with Eric and said over her shoulder, "Don't wait up."

13

Eric opened the door to his apartment and moved aside so Vivian could enter. The efficiency was dark, except for the Christmas lights that ran around a wall-length mirror on the other side of the room. They lit up the bed.

This is gonna be awesome, she thought.

He closed the door behind her. "Let me get a light on," he said and scooted past, grazing her gently as he did. It sent tingles down her spine, slowing in all the right places.

Her eyes had begun to adjust to the darkness when he clicked on a small desk lamp across the room.

"Mind if I borrow your bathroom?" she asked.

"Of course not," he said, then leaned down and kissed her passionately, moving his hands in a massaging motion along her waist. After a moment he pulled back. "Right through there." He pointed down a short hallway. "You want something to drink?"

"Maybe just some water. Thanks."

She walked through the small kitchen and saw the sink filled with dishes. *Ick.* Only a few steps beyond was the bathroom. She flipped on the light and heard him in the kitchen, getting her a glass of water. She smiled.

At first glance, the bathroom wasn't too bad. A blue towel served as a rug and another hung over the plaid shower curtain, which was pulled to. Vivian was tempted to look into the tub, but after the kitchen sink, she decided against it.

She freshened up a bit, including taking a dab of toothpaste and rubbing it over her teeth. She flipped upside down, fluffing her hair and shaking it out. It was still sweaty from dancing, and the curls closest to her neck had kinked up. She leaned in close to the medicine cabinet mirror. She noticed mascara smudged underneath her eyes and looked around the cluttered sink for cotton balls, then laughed. *Who am I kidding?* She tore off some toilet paper and wiped it away.

Her phone buzzed with a text message from Lucy.

Hey trashy! Wendy said to wrap that rascal you naughty girl!

She couldn't help but smirk. She dug in her purse and pulled out one of the condoms she had made rubber eyes with last night at dinner, and checked the expiration date. It was good for another year, good to go. She clicked her purse closed, keeping the condom packet in hand, glanced at herself one last time and opened the door.

She hadn't had a one-night stand in more than 10 years, and even then she'd only had a couple. She was A-okay with it, and had one expectation: sexceptionally fun sex. No holds barred, get crazy, grab this bull by the horns! Her previous sexcapades had all been just that, and she hoped this night would be no different. He lived in Colorado, she in Texas. They both knew what this was.

Eric had turned on soft music and changed into jersey knit shorts. Nothing else. It was still dark in the room, but Vivian could see the shadow of his lean, muscular frame. Images raced through her mind. She laid her purse on the back of the couch but kept the condom.

"Hope you don't mind. I had to get out of those clothes."

"Uhh, no, I don't mind." She traced her fingernails up his arm and took a deep breath. He smelled good. A mix of cologne and manliness.

He ran his fingers down the front of her blouse, grazing her breast. "Maybe you should do the same." He ran his finger back up her breast and placed his fingers under her chin, kissing her gently. His other hand slipped up the back of her shirt. He pulled her close and swayed a little to the music. His shorts didn't leave much to the imagination, and she could feel his excitement. *Not bad.*

It was just dark enough that Vivian felt fairly confident in her body. She'd been going to the gym and working hard to get her pre-twins figure back. She still had a way to go, but the darkness provided enough cover that she kicked off her shoes, threw off her clothes except for her bra and panties, and jumped on the Christmas-light bed.

Eric followed, smoothly slipping next to her. "Aren't you a spunky little thing?" he murmured, his lips already to her neck, wrapping his arms around her.

"That I am."

***

Vivian quietly closed the door to the apartment and slipped her shoes on. *Freakin' walk of shame,* she thought as she looked around. She adjusted her clothes, then dug into her purse, pulling out an ink pen. She twisted her curly hair around and then stuck the pen so that it stayed up off her neck. She clicked her purse closed and cursed to herself. She hadn't found her new, hot-pink bra in the darkness and didn't want to make a big deal out of it, but that sucker cost $40.

She walked to the road and turned north, toward the hotel. Eric had offered to accompany her but she had insisted, no, it wasn't necessary. It was only a few blocks.

She hugged her arms close to her body. The temperature had dropped several degrees and she was chilled. She heard a noise to her left and looked that way. All she saw was a trash can.

Shit. Bears. Do bears eat at night? Probably. Oh my god, I probably smell good to a bear.

Pheromones. Sweat. Sex.

Holy crap, I'm going to be a sauced-up, sex-sauced, tasty bear snack!

She picked up the pace, looking around. It was close to 4 a.m., and the streets were desolate. *One block down, one to go.*

Vivian's purse popped open and her phone dropped to the ground. She stopped to pick it up, and again she heard something. Her breath was loud in her ears, her heart pounding. She heard a shuffling to her left and then a weird click.

Fuck it.

She wrapped one arm around her boobs and ran.

14

Day 3

Ughhhhhhhhhhh."

Vivian stirred on the couch. Then she heard it again.

"Ughhhhhhhhhhhhhhhhhhhhhhh."

She opened her eyes and looked toward the groan. It was Lucy.

"Are you okay?"

Lucy just "ughed" again.

Vivian got up, went to the bathroom and brought Lucy a glass of water.

"There's ibuprofen in my purse," Wendy said quietly. "Give her some. Dammit. Give me some, too."

"Why did y'all let me drink so much wine?" Lucy whimpered.

Kate kicked her covers off. "It wasn't the wine, it was the bombers. I'm dying, too."

Vivian handed Kate three ibuprofen as well.

"You don't seem like you're hurting too much, Viv," Wendy said. "Did Eric sober you up?"

Vivian shook her head. "Not hardly."

Kate tisked. "Well, that's what you get for being semi-slu—"

Vivian cut her off, pointing at her. "I am not slutty, I'm opportunistic. There's a difference. But oh my god, it was…awful. Horrific. Terrible. And I had such high hopes."

"He was so cute," Wendy said. "Was it his equipment?"

"No, the equipment was fine. He got all 'sweet' on me."

"Sweet?" Kate asked.

"Yep. And cuddly. He wanted to spoon."

"Before or after you did the nasty?" Wendy asked.

69

"Both."

"Ughhhhhhhhhhhhh." Lucy groaned again.

"Such a waste of what I thought was going to be fantastic. He had the ultimate bachelor pad. Mirror on the wall, twinkly lights casting a naughty glow on the bed. I thought it was going to be amazing. But nope. He became all 'sweet.' Disgustingly so."

"Bummer." Wendy got up and started brewing some coffee. "And your first one-nighter since the divorce. Crappy start."

Lucy jumped up and ran to the bathroom.

"She thinks so, too," Kate said.

Retching sounds emanated from behind the closed door.

"Poor thing," Wendy said. She knocked on the door and let herself in, taking her bag of remedies with her.

A few minutes later they emerged and Lucy lay down.

"I'm going to hop in the shower," Vivian said, reaching for a change of clothes. "Oh crap, I forgot."

"What?" Wendy asked.

"I couldn't find my bra last night when I fled from Eric's apartment. I've got to go back and get it. It's brand new and cost me forty smackers."

"I want to see his apartment," Kate said.

"I'll go, too," Wendy said. "Let's get cleaned up, grab some breakfast and then we'll go. Do you remember where he lives?"

"I think I can find it."

They took turns getting ready. Lucy went last, somewhat recovered after napping for 45 minutes. They grabbed a quick breakfast at a coffee shop a few doors from the hotel and made their way to Eric's.

The bad replica of an alpine chalet complex was vintage 60s and was laid out like a motor lodge, with the doors opening right onto the parking lot. Upstairs, a balcony ran end to end with a thin metal railing supported by oversized faux beams.

Vivian headed up the stairs, the girls marching behind her. "I hope I can remember which apartment is his." She stopped in front of 4B and knocked. She glanced down and saw a flowerpot and said, "No, not it."

She looked in the window to 5B. "This is it. There's the mirror and Christmas lights."

"I've got to see this," Kate said and pulled out her camera.

Vivian rapped lightly on the door. "I kinda hope he's not here."

Lucy giggled. "An awkward morning is better than a boring night."

"Yeah, but it turned out to be a boring night, so if I see him now, it's going to be both." Vivian tapped on the door again.

Eric wasn't home. "Thank god! But how am I gonna get my bra?"

"Try the door," Wendy said. "Maybe he left it unlocked."

"Is that breaking and entering?"

"Technically, but we're not breaking."

Vivian turned the knob and looked at Wendy. "It's unlocked."

"Great, but we need lookouts. Lucy, let's go downstairs and watch for him. Vivian, if we see him, we'll use code word 'ice cream.' It saved us in Playa del Carmen, it can save us again."

Vivian waited for Wendy and Lucy to walk downstairs and get into position. Kate snapped a picture of Vivian opening the door.

She walked in and immediately noticed the dishes still piled in the sink.

"Definitely the right place."

Kate took a picture.

Vivian kicked around a pile of clothes that were by the bed but didn't see her bra.

"Did you leave it in the bathroom?" Kate asked, taking a picture of the bed, mirror and lights.

"No, I only went once and left there with my clothes still on."

"Check the bed."

Vivian grabbed the navy and white striped comforter and threw it back.

Perfectly placed in the middle bed was her hot pink bra. Kate took a picture. Vivian picked it up and Kate snapped another.

"Hooray!" Kate cheered.

"Let's get the hell outta here."

They left the apartment, closing the door behind them, and heard Wendy and Lucy faintly talking about ice cream.

"Oh no! He's coming! Let's go down the other side and sneak around the back."

The metal stairs threatened to give away their presence and they moved along the back of the building, passing a laundry room that would have given Lucy the shudders. Kate stuck her head around the corner and saw Wendy and Lucy talking to Eric, whose back was to her. She waved her arms, and

Wendy glanced in her direction and gave a slight nod. Kate saw them give him a hug, then he turned and went up the stairs toward his apartment.

Wendy and Lucy started down the street, meeting up with Vivian and Kate, and they all hustled back toward the hotel.

"It was about right here that I thought I was going to be bear food," Vivian announced as she passed a bear-proof trash can.

"What are you talking about?" Wendy asked.

"Seriously. I heard a noise over by the trash can and got to thinking about bears eating at night and that I probably smelled yummy to them. After-sex smell, ya know?"

"Viv, bear sex probably smells a lot different from human sex, so bears wouldn't have been after you because of that," Lucy said. "They'd just eat you because you were readily available, walking down the street in the middle of the night."

"That makes me feel so much better!"

"Speaking of death, to stall Eric, we asked him about the accident at the hotel yesterday," Wendy said. "Turns out, they think that guy might have been murdered. Eric said the room had been trashed and looked like there had been a struggle."

"How creepy. And it was on our floor," Kate said.

They went through the front entrance of the hotel and Vivian couldn't help but look toward where the guy had fallen.

Getting on the elevator, Lucy asked, "Did you find your bra at least?"

Vivian whipped it out of her purse and waved it in the air. "Ta-da!"

This brought a barrage of laughter.

Back in the room, Vivian said, "I don't know about y'all, but I'm ready to get out of Aspen. I've had my fill of this town for now."

"I'm ready to get to Vail!" Kate said.

"Me, too!" Wendy said. "Let's pack it up and move it out."

The girls packed, then called the bellman to get their luggage. Vivian checked them out of the hotel while the girls waited out front.

The reception clerk handed her an envelope with a Yellow Aspen Hotel emblem on it. "This was left for Vivian Taylor."

Vivian glanced at it. *Great, probably Eric leaving me a sweet note and his number. Blah.* She shoved it into her purse.

She met the girls out front with the car, which was already loaded up with the bellman's help, and they zoomed out of Aspen.

15

On the drive to Vail, Lucy noticed a big section of dead trees and explained the cause. "Pine beetle. It's devastating groves and groves of pine trees. It's horrible. Researchers are working to figure out how to get it under control, but right now there's not a lot that can be done."

They rounded a bend on the downhill stretch. The brake pedal didn't feel quite right under Lucy's foot. The road flattened out and she dismissed it.

"I hope they figure out how to save the trees," Kate said.

"Yeah, apparently it takes something like six straight days of below-freezing temperatures to kill the beetles. We get cold weather, but we don't stay below freezing for that long."

The road started descending again, and Lucy tapped the brakes going around a bend. "My brakes feel funny," she said. The road straightened out, and she kept her foot off the gas.

"What do you mean, funny?" Wendy asked.

"There's less resistance on the pedal." Lucy tried again. "My foot is practically to the floor."

"That's not good," Wendy said.

"They felt fine on the way here."

"Pull over!" Kate said.

"Can't until we get down the pass." The speedometer crept over 60, even though Lucy kept her foot on the brake pedal.

"Try pumping them," Wendy said, leaning over the seat. "Build up pressure."

They passed a 6 percent downhill grade sign. Lucy rapidly pumped the brakes, but no response.

"Oh my god, we have no brakes!"

As the road quickly descended, the speedometer zoomed past 80. Lucy swerved into the left lane to avoid an RV that crept along in the right. The old man gave them a dirty look as they flew past.

"I'm too young to die!" Kate wailed. "And I might be pregnant!"

"Let's not panic," Wendy said, sounding a little panicked. "Pump them again."

Pump, pump pumppumppumppump.

"Nothing," Lucy said but kept the pedal to the floor anyway.

"We're going way too fast!" Vivian said.

They soared past a couple of cars and an 18-wheeler and were rapidly approaching a blue and silver pickup ahead.

"He's gotta move," Wendy said. "Honk!"

Lucy laid on the horn and flashed her lights. The truck swerved out of the way with inches to spare.

"Ahhh! That was too close!" Vivian said, gripping the oh-shit handle.

Reading the sign in front of her, Lucy swerved into the right lane and clicked on the hazard lights. "Buckle up!"

"Oh god, are we…?" Kate said, as Lucy drove straight ahead rather than taking the bend in the road.

Lucy gripped the steering wheel, gaze intense, barreling toward a runaway truck ramp. "Hang on, ladies!"

They all screamed as the tires spewed gravel as the SUV ran up the incline. Snow and slush flew everywhere, covering the windshield as they careened halfway up the ramp. Lucy mashed the emergency brake pedal and they jerked to a stop. "*Aye carumba!*"

Vivian slapped her hands on the dashboard as the momentum carried her forward, then slammed her back into her seat. She blinked and stared through the windshield covered in dirty snow, and up at the mountain looming before her.

"Holy fuckbuckets, Lucy. Good thinking."

"Thank god. We're alive!" Kate yelled.

"Jesus," Wendy said and let out a sigh. "Way to go, Danica Patrick."

"I can't believe it," Lucy said, releasing the wheel. "I finally got to experience a runaway truck ramp, not just see it. They really work!"

"Amen to that!" Wendy said.

The snow surrounded the vehicle so the girls had to shove on the doors to get them open. Vivian slipped on the ice a little, before catching herself on Kate's passenger door. "Whoa! Looks like we're going to need some help getting out of here."

"Do *you* need some help getting out of here?" Kate asked.

Though Vivian's knees were a little weak, she wasn't about to admit it. "Nope, I'm fine, but Big Bertha here isn't." She slapped the roof. "And good grief this thing is filthy now."

Big Bertha was now covered in muddy grime.

"Let's just hope some 18-wheeler doesn't fly down the mountain and need this ramp right now." Lucy blew out a sigh and kicked at the bank of snow. "I guess we need a tow truck."

They walked down the ramp while Lucy called a wrecker service. She gave their location and was told it'd be at least 45 minutes.

"I need a drink," Vivian said. "I'm gonna hit the back seat bar. Anybody want anything?"

Everyone nodded, even Kate.

"I'll come help you," Wendy said.

A few minutes later, Vivian and Wendy walked back down the ramp with four margaritas. "I mixed 'em up good, ladies," Wendy said. "Enjoy."

They found a few boulders and sat down, drinking their margaritas while they waited. It ended up being a two-margarita wait. Kate took pictures to document the moment and her near-death experience. She also called Shaun and told him how much she loved him and the dogs.

Lucy posted a picture to Facebook with the caption, "It's not just for trucks anymore!" which received numerous comments and "likes." She also received a very worried call from her mother.

"That's why I ignored my mother's Facebook request," Wendy said.

"I can relate," Vivian said. "I tried, but she called and said I was the only one who had not accepted her friend request. I claimed ignorance, but that only got me so far."

"Y'all are awful," Lucy said. "Your mothers are so sweet."

"I didn't let my mom know what crazy things I was up to in high school or college, Lucy; I'm not sure I want her to know what craziness I'm up to now," Wendy said. "I'm not ready to admit 'The Boat.' "

"The Jack Daniel's incident?" Vivian asked.

"Yep."

A toothless tow truck driver arrived and hooked up the SUV. All four girls piled into his wrecker and he towed them down the mountain. He dropped them off in El Jebel at the closest garage.

The girls waited in a coffee shop across the street while the mechanic worked on Lucy's SUV.

Vivian went to pay for her snack and saw that Yellow Aspen Hotel envelope in her purse. "I forgot all about this."

"About what?" Kate asked.

"The front-desk guy said this was left for me. I'm sure it's from Eric, his phone number or something."

"Ooooh, let's read it," Kate said. "See what your sweetie-pie said."

The bell above the door chimed, and the mechanic walked in and approached their table.

"Yer all set. The brake valves over both front tires was loose, fluid sprayed damn near everywhere. The reservoir didn't have no fluid left, which is why yer brakes didn't work."

"That's weird," Lucy said. "Why would the valves be loose?"

"Did ya have 'em serviced lately? Cuz a bad mechanic coulda forgotten to tighten 'em."

"No. I just had the oil changed, but they didn't mess with the brakes, only checked the fluid."

He scratched his chin. "It's kinda squirrely that both of 'em was loose."

"Could they have worked themselves loose from general wear and tear?" Wendy asked.

"You do go off-roading a lot," Vivian said.

The mechanic shrugged and handed her a bill. "It'd take some doing." He left them to their thoughts.

Vivian still held the hotel envelope. She opened it. "What the hell is this?" She threw a picture of herself down on the table for the girls to see.

"That's what you wore last night," Lucy said.

"Yeah, but I'm by myself and, if you notice, I'm not wearing a bra," Vivian said. "That means it was taken after I left Eric's."

"Holy shit, Viv," Wendy said. "That's messed up. Do you think he followed you?"

"He offered to walk me back but I said I'd be fine. He was snoring by the time I walked out the door."

Kate pointed to the picture. "Then who could have taken this?"

Vivian put it down. "The same person that messed with the brakes."

Only one name came to mind.

16

It has to be Craig," Vivian said, looking at the picture of herself on her walk/run of shame. "I was so excited when we booked this trip, and it was before he freaked out on me, so I told him where we were staying. Even showed him the website."

Kate pointed to the picture. "So you think he was there in Aspen and followed you back from Eric's?"

Wendy stirred her coffee. "It takes some skills to tamper with the brakes enough that they don't go out until we're out of town and going down the mountain. Is he capable of that?"

"I'm beginning to realize that I have no idea what he is capable of, but who else could it have been?"

"Have you seen him in the last two days?" Kate asked.

Vivian started to answer "no," but then thought about it. "Yesterday morning, playing racquetball. As I opened the door to leave the court, I thought I saw him. But it was just the back of him, and the guy disappeared through a door, so I dismissed it. Figured surely, no way it was him."

"He's spying on you," Lucy said.

"Fuck," was all Vivian could say to that. Then something else clicked in her brain. "The cologne."

"We didn't smell it, though," Kate said.

Vivian shook her head. "I could have sworn I did, but only for a second."

"Why would he try to kill you, though, Viv?" Kate asked. "For breaking-up with him?"

"He must be super pissed-off you slept with Eric," Wendy said.

"Is his ego that sensitive or is he a control freak?" Lucy asked.

"He's obviously not the person I thought he was. Stealing people's credit card info and spying. I found out the hard way that he has a temper when he tore up my house. The FBI agent told me that he has something like 20 aliases."

"Is Craig even his real name?" Wendy asked.

"I don't know."

Kate shivered. "This feels like my grasshopper dream."

"What?" Vivian asked.

"Last night, I dreamt I was walking on a familiar path in the middle of a field. A few giant grasshoppers started springing up out of the tall grass on either side of me so I walked a little faster. More grasshoppers sprang out of the grass, some jumping across the path in front of me. I ran, trying to get away from them, but the faster I ran, the more there were and the less control I had over my legs. I finally had no control at all and they crowded me, their creepy little legs crawling all over me."

"That is so weird," Wendy said as she brushed away imaginary grasshoppers from her arms.

"Did you get away from them?" Lucy asked.

"One minute they surrounded me, and the next I was at a serene, beautiful lake holding a fishing rod. I reached onto my shoulder and grabbed a big grasshopper. I looked into his eyes before I stabbed the fishing hook through his exoskeleton. I can still hear the crunch."

"Ewww," Vivian said.

"Was that the end?" Wendy asked.

"I cast out the line and there was a sharp tug. That's when I woke up."

"What do you think it means?" Vivian asked.

"It means stay the hell away from grasshoppers!" Lucy said.

Kate thought for a moment. "I don't know. I usually have family visit me in my dreams, not insects. I think Craig's not done with you."

"That being said, I think we should *not* stay at the hotel in Vail," Vivian said. "Craig knew what hotel I was going to. I think we cancel and find something off the beaten path."

"Done," Wendy said, pulling out her phone. "I'll call them and cancel the reservation."

"Where should we go?" Kate asked. "I think somewhere *not* near a lake."

"I'll call my friend Blair," Vivian said. "She just took her second honeymoon near Vail."

"Second?" Lucy asked.

"Yeah, her first husband died about two years ago."

"That sucks. Was he old?"

"In his mid-50s. Not old by any means. She's totally loaded now."

Vivian called Blair, who suggested The Ridge in Bachelor Gulch. She raved about the impeccable service and the luxurious spa at the isolated mountaintop resort 15 minutes outside Vail.

Kate called the hotel and made a reservation.

"Vivian, you need to call the FBI," Kate said when she got off the phone. "This is serious."

"Yeah," Lucy said in a huff. "Craig tried to kill us. *All* of us!"

Vivian rifled through her wallet. "I have his card right here, I'll step outside and call him now."

"Not alone," Wendy said. "The buddy system is officially back in effect."

"We'll go get the car," Lucy said, motioning to Kate. "Then we'll pick y'all up."

Wendy and Vivian went outside. Her hands shook as she dialed the number.

As soon as he answered the phone Vivian said, "Hi Agent Tucker, this is Vivian Taylor again and I think Craig may have tried to kill me." Her voice caught and tears rolled down her cheeks.

"Are you safe? Are you okay?"

"I feel like I'm safe for now and I wasn't hurt."

"What happened?"

"I'm on vacation in Colorado with my friends and our brakes went out. We almost flew off the side of a mountain, literally. We had the car towed and the mechanic told us the brakes valves were loosened."

"What makes you think Craig played a role in this?"

"Someone left an envelope for me at the front desk of my hotel, and it had a picture of me from late last night."

She hesitated. *Should I tell him the whole story?*

"I was, uhhmmm."

God this is embarrassing.

"I was leaving a guy's apartment."

"Go on."

"I also think he may have broken into our room. I thought I smelled his cologne on two different occasions."

"Was anything in the room tampered with? Was there a note with the envelope?"

"The room seemed fine, and there wasn't a note in the envelope. It just had my name on the front and my room number."

"Don't handle the envelope or picture anymore. If you have a bag or something you can seal them in, that'd be best."

"I'll find something."

"Where are you now?"

"We're still in the town where the tow truck driver brought us, El Jebel. We're about to leave, though, for The Ridge Hotel in Bachelor Gulch. We canceled our original reservations at the hotel in Vail and just booked this one."

"That's good. I'll send agents from our Denver field office to meet you this afternoon. Have you contacted the local authorities?"

"No. Were you able to find out anything about the phone number Craig called me from yesterday?"

"It was a disposable cell and he's probably ditched it by now. I was able to trace it to a retailer in Denver but he paid cash. He is obviously escalating. Get in the car and go to The Ridge. Don't make any additional stops. Be aware of anyone who could be following you."

"Okay."

"Is the number you're calling from the number I have on record as your cell?"

Vivian needed to sit down. She felt lightheaded and reached out to Wendy for support. "Yes, it's my cell," she said, and they disconnected.

Vivian pulled the phone away from her ear, still dazed.

"What'd he say?" Wendy asked.

Before she could answer, Lucy and Kate pulled up and they got in.

"Tell us, what'd Agent Tucker say?" Wendy asked.

"He said that Craig's behavior is escalating and we need to be careful and watch out for him in case he's following us." She used the side-view mirror to look behind them. "And to go straight to the hotel."

"You got it," Lucy said and pulled onto the highway.

"Did he say anything else?" Kate asked.

"He told me to not touch the envelope or picture anymore and to put it in a bag. I guess they'll try to get prints off of it. Lucy, do you have something I can put it in?"

"There's a grocery bag in the back seat pocket."

Wendy held open a bag and Vivian dropped in the envelope before continuing. "The only other thing was that he'd call the office in Denver and have agents meet us at the hotel."

"At least he's taking it seriously," Lucy said, "because I was ready to send a strongly worded letter to the oil change place. If I find out it was Craig who did this, I may go ballistic on his ass."

"Let's have them check for bugs in the car," Wendy said. "I realize we're not in Mexico, but we're not taking any chances."

"And tracking devices," Kate said.

"We should stop now and look for tracking devices," Wendy said. "Al showed us the one he found, maybe we'd be able to recognize another."

Lucy pulled onto the shoulder and the girls got out.

Holy crap, Vivian thought. *Here we go again.*

17

The search for listening or tracking devices on Lucy's SUV turned up nothing, so the girls got back on the road. It took an hour to reach Avon, where Lucy turned off to ascend the mountain to Bachelor Gulch. About a quarter of the way, she rolled into a security checkpoint. The guard called the hotel and confirmed they were guests prior to allowing access.

"That makes me feel better," Vivian said as the gate arm lifted.

The road wound up the mountain a few miles. Just past the tennis courts, Kate gasped.

Lucy slammed on the brakes, which were now working quite nicely. "What? What is it?"

Kate pointed out the window to the left. "Bighorn sheep!"

"Jesus, you scared the crap out of me. I'm on edge here!"

"Sorry, but I've never seen one."

"Me, neither, but it's just a sheep. It's not Bigfoot!"

"Aren't bighorn sheep just about as elusive?" Vivian asked. "I've stopped at that stupid scenic overlook in Georgetown several times and have *never* seen one. Ever."

"Well, I've seen 'em, and now so have you," Lucy said. "I have a constant fear when I'm driving in the mountains that one is going to fall off a cliff and land on my windshield."

"It is weird how they can balance like they do," Vivian said. "Lucy, if only you were that sure-footed."

"Yeah, yeah, I'm a klutz. I know it." She followed the signs to the hotel and pulled under the portico.

Two valets opened their doors and helped them out. One asked Lucy if they needed assistance with their luggage.

"Wow," was all she could manage as she took in The Ridge.

Wendy spoke up as she opened the back hatch. "We need help with all of this." The cargo area was completely full, as in up-to-the-ceiling, can't-see-out-the-rearview full.

Kate and Vivian were oblivious to the luggage conversation and had moved toward the double front doors that the valets held open.

"Gorgeous," Kate chimed, in awe of the stately stone and timber-beamed lodge with its two guest wings angled out like massive rock shoulders toward the entry court.

"When do we move in?" Vivian asked. She liked the seclusion and the security and was glad she called Blair.

The girls were drawn into the cozy lobby where four armchairs and a table sat in front of a wood-burning fireplace. Before they could sit, a host appeared and introduced himself as Matt. He welcomed them and offered a complimentary glass of champagne.

"That sounds lovely," Lucy said, looking over at the girls with amazement.

Kate stopped him. "Thank you, but can I have a glass of sparkling water instead?"

"It would be my pleasure," the host said and walked off to fulfill their requests.

The girls giggled and golf clapped at his response. They turned to the left and walked past a swanky restaurant on their way to the front desk. A large basket of fruit graced the polished mahogany counter. Bananas, apples, oranges, you name it. A beverage station held two 3-gallon glass servers, one containing lemon slices, the other strawberries.

A man whose name badge read Trey checked them in.

Vivian leaned against the check-in desk and asked, "Did you used to have a masseur here named Rodney?"

Trey looked up from his computer and grinned. "We sure did. Rodney is a good friend of mine."

The girls laughed and Vivian clapped. "He was my masseur on the beach in Playa del Carmen. He was so much fun."

"He knows how to have a good time, that's for sure," Trey said. "We miss him around here."

"If you talk to him, tell him we said hi!" Lucy requested.

"You got it." He got back to checking them in and due to construction on the fourth floor, he upgraded them to a mountain-view room with a fireplace. "Your room is on the eighth floor. You are on three, which is the main floor, so the construction shouldn't be a problem, but we like to let all our guests know to avoid four. You shouldn't be disturbed by the noise, but if you have any problems, don't hesitate to call the front desk. We want your stay to be as pleasant as possible."

"Why, thank you," Vivian said. "We want our stay to be as pleasant as possible, too."

"Yeah, especially after the drive up," Wendy said. "How secure is this place, by the way? We've had some security issues recently."

Trey's demeanor turned serious. "Our guests' safety is of utmost importance. We've had numerous political figures, sports celebrities and movie stars on our property and have never had an incident. Do you have any special needs?"

"No, no. Everything's fine," Vivian said.

Wendy leaned over the counter. "We'll let you know."

Trey gave a smile, then said, "Would you ladies like a tour of our *very* safe and spectacular facilities?"

Wendy looked pleased and Lucy answered, using her line from earlier, "That would be lovely." She held up her glass and clinked with the girls.

Trey looked past them and snapped above his head. Matt, the host, appeared by their side and led them a few steps away into the great room. Vivian tuned out whatever he was saying and focused on the view out the windows, which perfectly framed the snow-covered mountains. The snow had melted off in places, but it was a beautiful sight for this Texas gal all the same.

"Cocktails, blah blah…Timberline…blah blah…wireless." She didn't hear much. The majestic view overpowered her senses, and she felt herself start to relax.

The girls looked out the floor-to-ceiling windows in awe. "I need my camera," Kate said, digging in her purse.

Matt held the door open leading to the back of the property and continued the tour. "We have a large patio for you to enjoy, including the fire pit. We light this every evening and have s'more kits available for purchase in the Timberline Restaurant."

The view was even more amazing outside, and the girls posed in front of the ski lift for a picture. Matt snapped a few, then escorted them past the fire pit to a patio filled with tables and chairs. "This is the outdoor dining for Felix, our signature restaurant." He swept his arm out in a grand gesture to the left. "As you can see, here is our heated, Olympic-sized swimming pool.

Nestled in the aspens just beyond are two hot tubs." He spun to the right and gestured again. "And here is a third, larger hot tub." He walked up a few steps and through a door, back into the hotel and the fitness center. "Towels are available here," he said, pointing to a large wooden shelf filled with fluffy, bright-white towels.

"We have state-of-the-art exercise equipment and a workout room with free weights, yoga mats, exercise balls, jump ropes and a number of other items to ensure a perfect workout."

Lucy nudged Vivian. "We'll be spending some time in here. Circuit training, here we come!"

Vivian rolled her eyes and took a sip of her champagne.

They walked down a short hallway. "This elevator will take us down to the spa where we have steam rooms and a dry sauna, plunge pool, showers, the grotto, a lounge and numerous services available such as facials, massages and more for your relaxation pleasure."

"Now we're talking," Vivian said as they entered the elevator. Matt pushed the B button.

As the doors opened Vivian knew she was in heaven. The aroma de spa, hidden lighting, soft music and muted colors exemplified tranquility and instantly melted the knot in her chest.

"I love the feel in here," she said. "Blair rocks!"

A beautiful young woman introduced herself as Suri and guided them through the spa. They passed a desk with robes, then entered a locker room complete with a long vanity supplied with brushes, combs, deodorant, lotions, razors, cotton balls, blow driers and an array of hair products.

"Look, y'all," Kate said. "There's enough stuff here for us to do up some big-ass Texas hair."

"I may be inclined to tease it up for a special occasion while we're here," Vivian said.

"Hell, just being here is a special occasion in my book!" Wendy said.

"Yeeeeeeehaw!" Lucy yelled.

A pair of women in robes, their hair wrapped in towels, walked into the locker room and stared at them. Vivian waved.

Suri led them down a dark hallway and turned to the door on her right. "Here you will find the ladies-only grotto, dry sauna and steam room. The small pool at the end of the room is the cold plunge, which I highly recommend you dip into after detoxifying in any of the three amenities here."

"I see myself needing to detoxify," Wendy said. "Can't wait to try the steam room."

"Dry sauna for me," Kate said. "My sinuses will thank me."

Suri led them out of the room and to the right, through a door with a sign stating, "Shhh. Treatments in progress." The ladies lounge was a few steps down the hall, and they went inside.

"This is where your massage therapist or aesthetician will pick you up, should you schedule any treatments. However, you are free to use the lounge at any time."

The sharp scent of burning wood drew Vivian's attention to a crackling fireplace on the far wall. She imagined herself in an overstuffed chaise, pampered skin wrapped in a cushy robe and snuggled under one of the cozy blankets that adorned each ottoman. She didn't feel like leaving, but Suri opened the door, leading them farther down the hall.

Lucy pointed toward an exit door. "Does this lead up to the fitness area?"

"No, it leads out to the west side of the hotel," Suri said, pushing open a large, wooden door with an iron scroll handle.

Warmth and humidity enveloped them within seconds.

The cavernous, underground grotto was the most impressive part of the spa. A waterfall cascaded from the rock wall, splashing into a hot tub large enough for 50 people. Candlelight flickered from wall sconces. Four lounge chairs beckoned at water's edge, behind which a table offered a tray of rolled washcloths covered in ice, topped with sliced cucumbers. A beverage station filled with ice water sweated in the humidity.

Lucy flicked a melting ice cube off a cucumber slice and stuck it into her mouth.

"Those are for the bags under your eyes, Lucy!" Vivian said, "not for your stomach!"

"I'm hungry and need a snack," Lucy replied. "I've had a stressful day, what with the flying-down-the-mountain, near-death, brakes-failing, we-almost-died-two-hours-ago drama."

Suri looked at Lucy with wide eyes. "Is there anything I can get you?"

"Yes," Wendy answered for her. "Back to the bar."

"It would be my pleasure."

Everyone's new favorite words.

18

The girls golf clapped after the elevator doors closed in the spa.

"It would be her pleasure," Kate said. "I love that!"

"I know," Vivian said. "It's so much better than just plain ol' 'thank you.' "

"I vote we just head back up to the room, hit the cooler and get Wonkita a snack," Wendy said. "After all this, I'm ready to see our room."

Lucy's nickname, Wonkita, started in high school, compliments of the otherwise all-male drum line.

Vivian smacked the 8 button, where they got off.

Kate slid the card into the reader and pushed the door open.

"Damn, it smells good in here," Vivian said. "What is that?"

"Lavender and juniper, maybe?" Wendy said, tossing her purse on the nightstand.

"It is caressing my nasal passages," Kate said, sniffing the air.

"Are we in a Danielle Steele novel?" Lucy asked. "Caressing your nasal passages? Really?"

Vivian inhaled deeply. "Whatever it is, it is definitely caressing my nasal passages." She walked past the two queen beds and built-in armoire hiding the TV and pushed back the curtains at the sliding glass door. "Holy fuckbuckets. Would you look at this view?"

"Kodak moment," Lucy yelled, scrambling for her camera.

Kate slid the door open. "I see myself enjoying coffee out here every morning."

"And we should definitely call for room service," Wendy said. "It would be their pleasure!"

"The sky is so blue!" Kate said, stepping outside. "It's not this blue at home."

"That's because you live in the big city," Lucy said. "Pollution."

Vivian sat down and took a deep breath. The few clouds cast fleeting shadows on the mountain, which was still patchy with snow. The muddy ski runs zig-zagged through the trees with their early bits of color. She heard a giggle from below and saw a couple frolicking in the pool. The image of Rick and the SPS popped into her head. She looked away and took a sip of her wine. *Get a room!*

Lucy came back inside and heaved Vivian's large orange suitcase onto the bed. She balanced her camera on top, set the timer and ran into place. "Suck it in, girls!" Click!

They set to unpacking. This was the kind of place where you wanted to empty the luggage and never leave.

"We'll have to go find the bellman downstairs and tip him," Kate said, unzipping her bag. He had delivered their luggage and backseat bar to the room while they were on their tour.

By the time they were finished, the drawers bulged and the armoire cabinets barely shut, but all their shit fit.

Wendy set up the bar on the built-in chest of drawers and cracked open a bottle of wine. She poured a bit for everyone but Kate, who stuck with sparkling water, and they toasted to "the majesty of the mountains."

Lucy's snack run in Boulder a couple of days ago was coming in handy now as she got out the grapes, Parmigiano-Reggiano, asiago and Colby jack cheeses and cracked pepper water crackers. The girls took their munchies and wine out on the balcony.

Vivian snubbed all that and brought out her insisted-upon Easy Cheese and Ritz Crackers, which Wonkita was extremely embarrassed to purchase.

"I still can't believe you made me buy that," Lucy said, indicating the can of cheese.

"Don't knock it," Vivian answered. "Look at the cute things I can make on my crackers." She held up a squirty cheese smiley face.

"Gross," Wendy said. "Do you even know what's in that stuff?"

Vivian shoved the entire smiley cracker in her mouth and shrugged. "Roo rares."

The cracker gone, Vivian said, "Now this is the life. I need to wake up to this view every morning. My oak trees aren't bad, but the neighbor's fence is."

"I hear ya," Wendy said. "The refineries aren't exactly a scenic overlook, either. Smokestacks spewing fire and god knows what else."

"You can see a refinery from your house?" Lucy asked.

"I can see *two.* Both from my front windows."

"Take a deep breath and revel in this while you can," Kate said.

She did.

They enjoyed their snackage, the wine and the view. The couple they dubbed the newlyweds had moved and were mackin' down in one of the hot tubs nestled between the aspens.

"FIFTY PERCENT CHANCE!" Vivian screamed out, but there was no stopping those two.

"Vivian!" Kate said.

"It's true. Look at the statistics."

In the hot tub next door, four women in their 30s woo-hooed the couple.

"Look, they're here on a girls' trip like us," Lucy said.

"Mmm mmm mmm, what do we have here?" Vivian asked, standing up and looking over toward the fire pit. "Check out that fine specimen."

The girls followed her gaze and saw a trim man wearing sunglasses, white oxford shirt and dark slacks.

"Cute," Wendy said, pouring a little more wine.

"I guess he's getting a tour, too," Kate said.

He was with Matt, the host, who pointed at chalets on either side of The Ridge.

"Is he taking notes?" Wendy asked, peering over the railing. "Oh my god, I think he is."

"I'm all about details, but that's going a little far," Lucy said.

"Maybe he's gay and getting Matt's number," Vivian said.

"Shut up, Matt isn't gay!" Lucy said.

"How do you know?"

"I know."

Lucy reached for a cracker, missed and instead knocked the entire packet off the railing. It landed directly in front of Slacks and Matt.

Slacks looked up to their balcony as the girls hastily retreated into their room.

"Did he see us?" Kate squealed.

Vivian stepped back out on the balcony and peeked over the railing. Slacks had moved on and the crackers were gone. "Now that's service! Let's drop something else!"

"No!" yelled Kate and Lucy at the same time.

"What's he doing now?" Wendy asked.

Vivian peeked again. "He's getting something out of his pants."

"This is getting good!" Lucy said.

"Wait, wait. It's just his phone."

Vivian's ringtone, which she had dubbed "wannabe porno music," went off.

"What a coincidence," Lucy said. "He's calling someone and your phone is ringing."

Vivian looked at her phone but didn't recognize the number. She hit receive.

"Hello?"

"Is this Vivian Taylor?" a deep voice asked.

"Yes, that's me."

"Ms. Taylor, this is Agent Wade Nelson with the Denver FBI field office."

19

I'm here at the hotel and need you to meet me in the lobby as soon as possible. I was told you have some evidence. Please bring that with you."

"I'll be right down," Vivian said and hung up the phone.

She turned to the girls. "That was the FBI guy. He wants to meet me in the lobby and to bring the envelope and picture."

Wendy grabbed her purse. "Let's go!"

"This is so exciting. An FBI agent! And he's cute!" Lucy said.

"If he's anything like Agent Tucker, it'll be all business. They know their stuff."

"Still…," Kate said.

"In the books I read they're always tall, dark and handsome," Wendy said. "Unfortunately, often they turn out to be the bad guys."

"Let's not keep him waiting," Lucy said, heading to the door. "Maybe he's only a bad boy in a good way."

They joked about "bad" qualities down the hall and into the elevator. Vivian started singing "Bad" by Michael Jackson. The girls chimed in and were really getting going when the elevator doors opened.

There stood the gorgeous guy they'd been spying on from their balcony. He was 6 feet tall, athletic build, mid- to late 30s with some serious, dark green eyes. Standing next to him was a tall woman in her mid-40s, dark brown hair, fit, wearing trim black slacks and a cotton-candy-pink blouse.

Vivian stepped out of the elevator first. He glanced at the necklace before looking her in the eye. He stuck out his hand.

"Ms. Taylor, I'm Agent Wade Nelson, and this is Agent Gloria Cervantes."

Vivian shook both their hands. "Hi, thanks for coming. These are my friends, Wendy Schreiber, Kate Troutman and Lucy McGuire."

Kate couldn't help but correct. "Actually, I got married last year, and I just changed my last name to Jameson."

"Nice to meet you all. Let's have a seat," Nelson said, and glanced at the bumblebee pendant again before gesturing toward the great room. Vivian, self-conscious, touched it.

He sat down in an oversized chair, with Cervantes opposite. The girls lined up on an adjacent couch.

"Agent Tucker gave us some background," Cervantes said, "but let's get the facts straight. Please start from the beginning, how you met Craig to now."

Vivian gave the lowdown in detail, from meeting at a gas station up to the picture and brake incident. "I thought he cared about me, but if so, why did he try to kill me? Kill us? He's obviously not the person I thought he was."

"People often aren't," Nelson replied. "May I see the picture?"

Vivian reached into her purse and pulled out the plastic grocery bag containing the envelope from the Yellow Aspen Hotel. "Here you go."

Nelson snapped on a pair of latex gloves before handling the envelope. He studied the picture. "And you're sure this was taken last night in Aspen?" He handed the picture to Cervantes, who had put on reading glasses as well as gloves.

"Yes, absolutely. The only time I was by myself last night was late on my walk of shhh… uh, my walk back to the hotel. After..."

Nelson raised his eyebrows. Cervantes coughed.

"Do I have to explain?"

"I get the gist," Cervantes said, "but we need to know who, when and where."

Vivian sighed. It was a part of the night she'd rather not remember. She divulged all. Well, almost all. The FBI didn't need every gory detail.

"Did you see anyone at all on your walk back to the hotel?" Cervantes asked.

"No. I heard a noise near a trash can and thought I was about to be bear food, so I hauled ass outta there. I didn't stop to look around."

"Do you think Eric could have followed you?" Nelson asked.

"I doubt it. He was snoring by the time I walked out the door." Vivian was starting to get irritated. She knew who took the damned photo, and she wanted him caught.

Nelson put his hands up in defense. "Just covering all the bases, Ms. Taylor. We'll run this for prints and see what turns up."

"Thank you. Are y'all going to check out the car? Because you may find evidence that indicates Craig was involved."

"We did a quick search for listening and tracking devices and didn't see anything," Wendy said. "But we're not the experts so we certainly could have missed something."

"I've already requested the car be pulled from the valet," Cervantes said. "We'll look for devices, check out the brakes and look for fingerprints, but I doubt we'll find any useful prints because of the repair. We will also conduct a thorough inspection of the hotel and grounds before returning to Denver tonight."

Nelson pointed to the bumblebee on Vivian's chest. "Where did you get that?"

Vivian touched the pendant. "Craig gave it to me for our three-month anniversary. It's the mascot of the school Audrey will attend next year. I keep waiting for it to turn my neck green and some of the rhinestones to fall out."

"Call me if Craig contacts you again or if you see anything suspicious." Nelson stood and handed each of the girls his card but paused when he got to Wendy. She had to tug twice to get the card from his grip.

"Do you have any questions?" Cervantes asked.

Nelson fidgeted with the buttons on his shirt cuffs. "I've provided security a picture of Craig that they are distributing to all staff."

"Thank you both so much," Vivian said, getting up. "I really appreciate y'all coming up here from Denver."

Vivian shook their hands, then the agents turned and walked out of the great room. The girls remained.

"My first experience with the FBI and I'm tellin' ya, my heart is going ninety to nothin'," Wendy said. "And I don't think it's because of the case."

"He is officially hot." Kate fanned herself. "Do you think they're more than FBI partners?"

A man wearing a starched white shirt, jeans and a crisp brown apron appeared. "Ladies, can I get you anything?"

"Do y'all serve pitchers of margaritas?" Vivian asked as she sat down in the chair Nelson vacated.

"I'm sorry, we don't. However, we do serve individual margaritas."

"Oh my god!" Lucy yelled.

"*What?*" the girls asked in unison.

"It's *Cinco de Mayo!*"

"Holy shit," Wendy said. "You scared me. I thought you saw Craig or something."

Vivian shook her head and told the perplexed waiter, "Give us four, please." After he walked off, she said, "I'll buy this round since it's my ex-dumbass-boyfriend who's causing all this mess. I'm really sorry, y'all. We seriously could have been killed."

"It's not your fault, Viv," Lucy said, putting her feet up on the large wooden table in front of them. "You couldn't have known he was going to turn into a stalker-gone-wild."

"I know, but still. I wonder if I missed any signs."

"Quit thinking that way," Wendy said.

"Yeah, it's not going to do any good," Kate added.

The server arrived with the margaritas. "Anything else right now?" he asked.

"You wouldn't happen to have a twelve-gauge, would ya?" Wendy asked.

"Excuse me?"

"Just kiddin'," she said with a grin.

She leaned forward and held up her margarita in toast. "We're smart. We're resourceful. Who the hell needs a gun?"

Clink!

20

After a few sips, Kate pushed her margarita away. "I can't drink this. I feel sick."

Vivian put hers down, too, and looked at Kate. "Are you pregnant? Oh my god, you're pregnant, aren't you?"

Kate hesitated. "Maybe. I am for sure not feeling right."

"We've got to get you a pregnancy test," Vivian said. "Instant gratification!"

Lucy and Wendy hopped off the couch, margaritas in hand, and headed toward the gift shop to see if The Ridge supplied pregnancy tests.

The waiter reappeared and looked at Kate's practically untouched drink. "Is something wrong with your margarita?"

"No, I'm just not feeling very well. Can I get some sparking water instead, please?"

"Of course." He reached down to take away her margarita, but Vivian stopped him.

"Hold your horses there. I'm sure that will be consumed, no problem."

He smiled and walked away.

Lucy and Wendy reappeared. "Negative on the pregnancy test," Wendy said. "However, we stopped by the front desk and Trey said he could get one, but it would be a few hours."

"The front-desk guy is getting me a pregnancy test?" Kate asked.

"Yep! It's his pleasure!" Lucy said.

The waiter brought Kate's water and Vivian paid the tab.

"Hey, preggers, you feel like you can handle goin' to the grotto?" Vivian asked.

"I might not be," Kate said and took a sip of water, "but yes, I can lounge around and throw a cold washcloth over my face. Sounds perfect."

Trey wasn't at the front desk as they walked by, but Kate blushed anyway. Once in the room, they got ready for their initial grotto experience.

"Those margaritas were great," Wendy said, covering up her hot pink bikini with a plush, white Ridge robe. "Let's get another round in the grotto."

"Uh, not no, but *hell* no," Vivian said, inspecting the contents of the cooler. "That round of margaritas cost me 75 smackers."

"Holy crap," Wendy said. "You didn't say anything."

"I said I'd pay, but I thought y'all should know. I was going to load up the cooler but let's just take a bottle of wine."

All wearing robes and cotton Ridge slippers, the girls stepped on the elevator. Lucy carried the ice bucket with a bottle of sauvignon blanc sticking out of it.

"We're so classy," Wendy said, holding up three plastic cups.

Kate hit the B button. "You can take the girl out of the Get Down, but…"

"Yeah, yeah," Vivian said and looked down at her slippers. "These may accidentally end up in my suitcase."

Lucy bent over a bit to look at hers. Her rear stuck out, hitting the emergency call button. The girls jumped as a shrill bell sounded.

A voice sounded over the PA system.

"What's your emergency?"

No one could speak. They were laughing too hard.

"What's your emergency, please?"

"Lucy has a bubble butt!" Vivian yelled.

"Hey!"

Wendy composed herself. "Sorry, sir. Lucy bent over and hit the button with her very muscular gluteus maximus. Everything is fine."

"Not a problem, Enjoy your stay."

"I can't believe you told him I have a big butt!" Lucy butt-bumped Vivian.

"I didn't say big, I called it bubble-licious."

The doors opened and Kate said, "We better take it down a notch or they aren't gonna let us in."

Suri greeted them and asked if they'd like to book a service during their stay. All services were 35 percent off due to mud season.

"Score," Vivian said, "What are my options?"

Suri handed them a list — massages, facials, seaweed wraps, manicures, pedicures, mud baths.

"I'd like to have a 60-minute massage tomorrow, please," Vivian said.

"Wonderful. I have 10 a.m. available with Mindy or Stefan. Do you have a preference?"

"Oh, I'll take Stefan. I like strong hands."

"Great. Please be here 20 minutes prior to the appointment, and Stefan will meet you in the ladies lounge."

"Yay!"

Kate and Lucy also booked massages and Wendy a facial for around the same time.

"Thank you, ladies," Suri said. "Enjoy your time in the spa today."

"Thank you," they chimed as Lucy pulled open the door to happiness.

The girls had the coed grotto to themselves, so each claimed a lounger by tossing her robe on it and kicking her slippers underneath.

"Ahhh," Vivian said, dipping down to her shoulders. The green hue of the water brought out the green sparkles in Vivian's black, low-cut one-piece.

"You're going to have to drag me out of here," Kate said, sitting on the edge, legs dangling in the warm water, light from the sconces shimmering off her blue iridescent bikini top. "This feels fantastic."

Air filled Lucy's black and silver tankini as she floated over to Kate and the wine bucket. She popped the cork and poured three plastic cups. Wendy got Kate a glass of orange-infused water from the beverage station before stepping in.

"*Gracias*," Kate said.

"*De nada* and happy *Cinco de Mayo*!" Wendy said.

"You mean happy *Drinko de Mayo*," Vivian laughed.

"*Aye ya yai ya yai*!" the girls cheered.

"We should go out for Mexican food tonight," Wendy suggested. "I could use a giant, big-as-yo'-face burrito."

"Oh yeah, definitely," Vivian said.

"Okay, but I'm warning you," Lucy said, shaking her head. "It's not going to be the Tex-Mex y'all are used to. There's no Chuy's here."

"That's all right, it'll be fine," Kate said.

"Maybe they'll have good drink specials," Wendy said. "Better than the $75 margaritas at The Ridge."

They clinked their plastic cups together again.

Lucy took a sip of wine and eyed the beverage station. She got out of the water and came back with cucumber slices for everyone.

"We can finally relax now and I think we need a picture of us doing it. Kate, get your camera ready and girls, prepare to relax!"

Lucy, Wendy and Vivian got into place, cucumbers over their eyes while Kate hopped out of the hot tub and got the camera situated just right on one of the loungers. She set the timer, then splashed into the pool and swam up next to Lucy just in time for the flash.*

The girls then grabbed their cups of wine and had another toast. "To relaxing at The Ridge!" Vivian said and had a sip of wine, then set her cup on the ledge.

She floated over to the waterfall that cascaded from the rock wall and stood underneath. She tilted her head back, letting the water splash over her.

"You know, with the right lack of attire that'd make a naughty picture," Kate smirked. "Should I get out my camera?"

"Use 'em to reel in the next Mr. Right," Lucy said.

"Or Mr. Right Now," Vivian said. "I'm in!"

21

ou are not going to take topless photos in here, are you?" Wendy asked.

"Sure," Vivian said. "Why not?"

Kate fished the camera out of her bag. "Lucy, why don't you stand by the men's entrance and kinda block their view if the door opens?"

"I'm on it, but I want mine taken, too. I haven't told y'all, but I went to a plastic surgeon a few weeks ago and I'm getting a reduction."

"I want one," Vivian said, "or at least a lift. Two for one. Two for one!"

They laughed.

"I need before-and-after shots. We'll have to come back to take the afters."

"You got it," Kate said.

Lucy stood guard at the men's door and Wendy at the ladies' while Vivian untied the neck of her swimsuit and lowered it to her waist. She posed under the waterfall. Kate snapped away. The camera flash was blinding in the dim light, but exhilarating.

"Why do I get the feeling this isn't the first time you've done this?" Wendy joked.

Vivian grinned and switched poses.

"Yes, give us a dramatic Playboy look," Kate said, laughing and clicking away.

She switched again.

"Damn, girl, you're a natural!" Kate shifted the camera and moved to one knee. Click. She stood back up and stepped into the water to her knees. "This one's pretty close. Work it, sister!"

Vivian was cracking up, as were they all. Their cackles echoed off the walls.

Vivian tried to quiet them. "Shhhhh, someone's going to come in."

They couldn't stop.

A few shots later, Vivian retied her top. "This is probably the trashiest thing I've ever done."

"Umm, hello," Wendy said. "What do you consider last night?"

"I don't want to ever think about that. In fact, if we never talk about it again, I'll be very, very happy. Now get your boobs in here."

"Unh uh. No way. Not gonna happen," Wendy said, shaking her head.

"Come on, Wendy, I promise they will only be seen by you," Kate said. "Well, and us."

"Jake might like it," Lucy teased.

"Any man would like it," Wendy said, "but I don't know. It is pretty trashy."

"Live a little," Vivian urged.

"Don't be a wuss," Lucy teased.

Wendy hung her head a little and sighed. "Okay, fine. But only a few, and before I expose myself, you both have to look down the halls and make sure no one is coming."

"Okay," Vivian said. "Now get naked!"

Wendy grabbed her wine and gulped it down. "Liquid courage," she said and stepped back into the hot tub.

Vivian and Lucy each peeked down the halls and gave the all clear.

Wendy dipped down below the water and unhooked her bikini top.

"Check again, just in case," she said before removing it.

They did.

"CLEAR," Vivian yelled and took a sip of wine.

"Clear," Lucy said, giving a thumbs up.

Wendy flung her top toward Kate. "Make it snappy!"

"Give me sexy," Kate said and started clicking.

Wendy kept her arms over her chest and managed a tentative smile.

"Run your hands through your hair," Kate said. "Head back, close your eyes, arch your back. That's it! Just pretend you're taking a shower."

"I don't do this in the shower," Wendy said but did as Kate instructed. "Especially in front of three people."

"Make love to the camera," Vivian squealed.

"Work it, baby," Lucy said.

Wendy turned to the side and gazed over her right shoulder, giving a sexy look. In that instant the men's locker room door flung open, shoving Lucy aside, and Agent Nelson barged in.

Wendy gasped and stood frozen.

Nelson locked eyes with Wendy and stared. After a few too many seconds, he turned and went back through the door.

The girls really started to laugh, except for Wendy, who looked horrified.

"Oh my god, you were supposed to be on guard, Lucy," Wendy said, lunging for her top floating in the water. "He just saw my boobs!"

"I'm sorry, I was mesmerized by the sex you were exuding! I'm impressed, by the way. I didn't know you had that in you!"

"I should have known better. Vivian called it and someone did come in."

"Technically, he just saw the side of your boobs," Vivian said.

"That doesn't make me feel any better."

Kate turned to Lucy. "Do you still want your before? But we gotta make this quick. I have a feeling we're about to get busted. No pun intended."

"And we need to find out what Agent Nelson wanted," Vivian said.

"Oh yeah, it's my turn!" Lucy walked toward the hot tub. "And then I'm ready for some Mexican."

Lucy got in place and promptly showed the ladies her ladies. Kate snapped away as Wendy and Vivian kept laughing and poured themselves another glass of wine.

Vivian held up her glass. "Shake 'em, hooker!"

"My, what large breasts you have," Wendy said.

"Not for long," Lucy said and smiled into the camera. Click click!

Kate wrapped it up and Lucy put the girls back in place right before Suri walked in with fresh towels. "You girls sound like you're having a good time."

"That we are," Vivian said and got back into the hot tub.

"Can I get you anything? A menu perhaps?"

"No, thank you," Kate said. "We're going out for Mexican food tonight."

Suri smiled, tidied up the beverage station and left.

"I think it's officially time to get ready for dinner," Wendy said. "Kate's hungry."

"Maybe she's feeding two," Vivian said and gave Kate an inquisitive glance.

"We'll know soon enough, compliments of Trey!" Lucy said.

Vivian's phone chimed and she got out to check it. "I have a voicemail. I didn't even hear it ring."

"We're in the basement, so I doubt you get service down here," Kate said.

"It was probably Agent Nelson. Let's go up and get ready for dinner," Vivian said.

They went up the elevator, without incident this time, to their room. Vivian checked her voicemail.

"It was him. He said to call him back."

Wendy looked at her, worried and wide eyed. "Oh shit."

22

Vivian called Agent Nelson back, taking care to hit the right buttons, which wasn't the easiest after the margaritas and wine.

He answered on the first ring. "Nelson."

"Hey, it's Vivian. I got your message."

"We've completed the inspection on Mrs. McGuire's car." He paused for a moment. "I'm afraid we did not obtain any evidence. There were no fingerprints or any other forensic evidence we could find."

Vivian wanted to scream but contained herself. "Well, thanks for checking." She started to lower the phone.

"Ms. Taylor, what are your plans for the evening? Are you leaving the premises?"

"We were talking about getting some Mexican food to celebrate *Cinco de Mayo.*"

Nelson cleared his throat. "Where are you going and when?"

"Don't know exactly, but probably in about an hour. You and Agent Cervantes heading back?"

"Soon, but let me know where you go. You can text me."

Click.

Vivian threw the phone on the bed.

"What'd he say?" Wendy asked.

"They didn't find anything on the car that tied to Craig."

"Not a big shocker there," Lucy said.

The girls took turns getting ready, then headed down to the concierge for a Mexican food recommendation. He suggested El Sombrero, in the town of Avon.

The valet brought Lucy's SUV around, they piled in and Lucy drove down the mountain, through the security post, past the colorful row of flags and the roundabout and to the other side of I-70.

Vivian texted Nelson.

El Sombrero for dinner. On our way.

Lucy came to a stop in front of a tacky, pink and teal stucco restaurant. "Are y'all sure you want to do this?"

Kate opened her door. "Absolutely."

"This is gonna be bad," Wendy said, sniffing the air. "No hint of greasy chip aroma. Not good. I hope the salsa doesn't suck. That's always the telltale sign."

The girls walked in and were greeted by a guy wearing an enormous sombrero. Vivian elbowed Lucy in the ribs. "Bring back any memories?"

Lucy narrowed her eyes at Vivian and shook her head. "Zip it."

They were seated at a table by the front windows, overlooking the parking lot. The host put down their menus and whipped maracas out of his back pocket. He shook them as he sang the specials to the tune of happy birthday.

"Hot tamales for you. And a chimichanga, too. Chili con queso, fried ice cream, shrimp fajitas for two. Ole!"

The girls clapped at the performance.

"That was fun!" Vivian said after he walked away, still shaking his maracas.

A server approached carrying chips and salsa.

"Do y'all have any *Cinco de Mayo* drink specials?" Wendy asked.

"*Cinco de* what?" he asked.

She sighed. "Never mind, we'll have a pitcher of margaritas."

He ran off to get the goods, delivered them and the girls toasted to "*Cinco de Drinko.*"

Kate dug into the chips and salsa. "Oh, this is good."

Vivian took a bite and made a face.

Wendy looked at her. "*No bueno?*"

"Too tomato-y."

Wendy dipped a chip and tasted, then shook her head. "No spice. I need about half a bottle of Cholula to make this edible."

"I feel like I'm eating ketchup," Vivian said.

"I told you," Lucy said. "This is *not* Tex-Mex."

Wendy tried another bite. "I could use some of Casa Ole's green sauce right about now, and some of the Don'Key's red sauce."

"Mmmm, that would be good," Kate said, munching on chip number seven or eight.

"Let's just roll with it," Vivian said. "It's *Cinco de Mayo*, for god's sake, and as Texans, what other options do we have?"

"Not any good ones," Lucy said.

The waiter arrived and they ordered a variety of food, none too complex. They stuck with Mexican basics, hoping for the best.

The food arrived two pitchers in, which helped to mask the blandness.

"I need some fresh jalapeño," Wendy said, peeking inside a triangle of quesadilla. "That's the only thing that's going to save this meal."

"Holy crap, you're going to fry your taste buds," Kate said.

"I can take it."

Mid-burrito, Vivian looked up and saw Agent Nelson at the bar. "Look who's here."

"Who?" Kate asked, finishing off her chimichanga special.

Vivian indicated to the bar with her fork. "Him."

Wendy, who was mid-sip, spewed margarita across the table and coughed.

Nelson looked over at them and nodded.

"Jesus, when is he going back to Denver?" Wendy asked. "I can't handle seeing him after my indecent exposure."

"Flasher," Lucy teased.

"You were supposed to be my lookout!"

Lucy picked at her plate. "I failed. If it's any consolation, the door did knock me out of the way."

"No consolation."

Lucy shrugged and pushed her half-eaten tacos away.

The girls finished their half-ass Co-Mex dinner and pitcher and paid the tab.

On the way out, Vivian stopped in the bar to talk to Nelson. Wendy steered off to the front door.

"What are you doing here?" she asked.

"Grabbing dinner while Cervantes wraps up at the hotel."

Vivian glanced at his to go order sitting in front of him — three Styrofoam containers and a bag of chips. "So we're keeping you informed, we need to stop at a liquor or grocery store before heading back to The Ridge."

Lucy stood next to Vivian. "We can't afford the drinks at The Ridge."

The bartender overheard the conversation and offered, "There's a liquor store a couple of blocks down on the left."

"Thanks," Vivian replied, then said to Nelson, "We'll hit that before going back."

Nelson pushed his barstool back. "You have my number if you need it."

Nelson looked past them at Wendy and adjusted his shirt collar.

Vivian smiled. *He's got a crush. How cute.*

"Bye," Kate said and walked toward the door to meet Wendy.

They piled into the car and Lucy pulled onto the street. "Women on a mission. We need refreshments."

A few blocks later, Wendy, in the back seat, leaned forward and pointed across Lucy. "There's Beaver Liquors."

"With a name like that, we gotta stop," Vivian said and laughed.

Lucy flipped that bitch around the roundabout and pulled into the parking lot, screeching to a stop.

Kate grabbed her camera. "We've got to document." She instructed the girls into place under the green neon sign, put the camera on the back of a sedan parked beside them and set the automatic timer. She ran into place just in time.

The girls took several more goofy shots and were still laughing as Lucy held the door open.

A young guy sat behind the counter. "I was beginning to wonder if you were going to make it inside."

"We had a few pictures to take first," Kate said. "Are you even old enough to drink?"

"We get that a lot, and I am."

The kid seriously looked maybe 18. Mohawk, nose ring, eyeliner but a big, friendly smile and he knew his way around the goods. After helping them select a couple of bottles of wine, Baileys and butterscotch schnapps, he insisted on taking their picture with the Beaver Liquor mascot, Woodchuck. Judging by his yellowed front teeth, brittle eyes and a thick

106

layer of dust, he looked to be an old, *old* taxidermied beaver. Backwards baseball cap and Mardi Gras beads completed his ensemble.*

"Hands down, that is the ugliest thing I have ever seen," Wendy said. "And it kinda freaks me out a little."

Lucy took a step back. "Ugh, he's nasty. Good grief."

"Poor little beaver snatch," Vivian said, taking a step forward and leaning in close to his beady eyes. "Bless his poor little dead, removed heart."

"Did you just call him a beaver snatch?" Kate asked just as Young'un said, "Say Woody" and snapped the picture.

They were all caught with different expressions of beaver admiration, which made the picture an instant classic.

They paid, then Young'un pointed them to the Beaver Liquor souvenir shop with its T-shirts, hats, koozies, bottle openers, magnets, stickers, flip-flops, sweatshirts, boxer shorts, edible panties and everyone's favorite, Beaver Balm.

"It says 'for soft and supple beaver lips,' " Lucy read off the label.

"We all need that," Kate said and then grabbed a handful of Beaver Balm and a pair of boxer shorts for Shaun that said "I'm a beaver liquor."

Everyone else loaded up on stickers, magnets and "I ♥ beaver liquors" T-shirts and a few more Beaver Balms.

Young'un helped them out to the car with their plethora of beaver goods.

I hope he makes a commission off all the beaver crap we bought, Vivian thought.

They gave him a high-five and got their beaverness in the car.

"That was a beaver-lickin' good time," Lucy said and expertly steered them onto the road, headed back to The Ridge.

23

The valets opened the hotel doors for the girls at the same time, making for a grand entrance. Vivian giggled to herself. *I could get used to this!*

They stopped by the front desk, and Trey handed Kate a discreet paper sack. "For you, Madame. It was my pleasure."

Vivian was the most excited. "I just *know* it's going to be positive!"

"It could be the altitude," Lucy said. "It does weird things to people."

Once in the elevator, Lucy made an announcement. "I have a surprise!"

"You hired a stripper?" Vivian asked.

Lucy gave her a "no, smart-ass," look.

"Somethin' sweet?" Wendy asked.

"Maaaaaaaaybe…," Lucy said.

"It's chocolate, isn't it?" Kate said. "Something chocolate? I could use some chocolate."

"As a matter of fact, it is partly chocolate. I have stuff for s'mores!"

Woo-hoos all around.

"First things first," Vivian said. "Kate's got a plastic stick to pee on."

They hustled into the room, and Kate went directly to do the pregnancy test. Wendy opened one of the bottles of wine and quickly poured three glasses and got a bottle of water ready for Kate, in case congratulations were in order.

"How's it going in there?" Vivian called through the door, excitement building.

"Hurry up!" Lucy said.

Kate emerged a few minutes later, a smile on her face.

"Well?" Wendy asked, handing her the bottle of water.

Kate reached for Wendy's glass of wine instead. "Negative!"

"You sound happy about that," Vivian said with a twinge of disappointment.

"Although we've been trying, the idea still freaks me out a little. And besides, I want to be with Shaun when we get the news."

"Yeah, yeah," Lucy said. "We get it."

"It's all good," Wendy said. "If you're happy, we're happy."

"Yes, but I think you should start poppin' 'em out soon," Vivian said. "As y'all reminded me several times on my 30th birthday, we're not spring chickens anymore!"

"Let's take the wine and go down to the great room for now," Kate said. "I'm suddenly feeling much better and ready to sit on those comfy couches and enjoy this glass."

Lucy packed up the s'mores supplies and another bottle of wine, and they left the room.

Vivian walked into the great room and came to an abrupt stop. Wendy ran into the back of her and muttered, "No."

Agent Nelson sat in a high-backed, leather chair, his back to the windows, watching people come and go.

Recovered from her surprise, Vivian said, "Didn't expect to see you here."

He stood as they approached. "I'll be staying overnight. Right across the hall from you."

Kate wrung her hands. "Why? Did something happen?"

"Those were the orders I received. No need to be worried." He looked around at the surroundings, then at Wendy. "The hotel is so nice I didn't want to argue."

Right, Vivian thought but said, "Where's Cervantes?"

"She took the evidence back to Denver." He changed the subject and asked, "Any problems getting back to the hotel?"

"Negative, ghost rider, but we did have a Beaver Lickin' good time!" Lucy said, holding up her wine, which spilled a little on the carpet. "Whoopsie!"

The girls snickered and Wendy looked uncomfortable. "Let's go outside to the fire pit," she suggested.

"Why don't we sit here with Agent Nelson and enjoy a glass of wine first," Vivian said, sitting on a couch. "Would you like some?" she asked him.

"I'm set." He held up his rocks glass with some kind of clear, carbonated beverage. "Please, call me Wade." He sat back down.

Wendy pulled at the neck of her sweater as she sat in the chair opposite and the farthest away from Nelson.

They cheered to working brakes and a lack of stalkers.

"So how long have you been in the FBI?" Vivian asked.

"Almost two years."

"Ever busted anyone in the mob?" Lucy asked.

"Oh no, here we go again," Kate said and laughed. "You'll have to excuse her."

Nelson laughed and said, "I could tell you, but then I'd have to whack you."

Kate glanced at his left hand. "Are you married?"

"No."

"Girlfriend?"

"What is this, an interrogation?"

"It's just gettin' to know you questions," Vivian said. "This is hardly an interrogation. We've been there, done that, and this ain't that."

Nelson raised his eyebrows and cocked his head.

Vivian raised her glass. "Here's to Mexican police work!"

"Screw that," Wendy said, refusing to toast. "We solved that crime. Otherwise, you were goin' down!"

"And not in a good way," Lucy added.

Nelson just shook his head. "Care to elaborate?"

"No, that was our last vacation," Vivian said. "You can read all about it in *Escándalos.*"

"You're not married and no girlfriend," Kate pressed. "Is there a, uh, boyfriend?"

Wendy choked on her drink for the second time that night, and Nelson answered quickly, "No. I just don't have a lot of time for a significant other."

"That's a bummer, but sometimes significant others cheat, lie and steal your Facebook password," Vivian said.

Kate waved off Vivian's comments. "Wendy, you look like a Ralph Lauren model, sitting there in that chair wearing your preppy turtleneck, your hair shining and spilling over your shoulder, your brown eyes sparkling."

"Hot momma." Kate flipped more of Wendy's hair over her shoulder.

"Boom, chicka-baobao," Lucy sang.

"I need more wine," Wendy said, getting up and reaching for Lucy's bag o' goodies. She dug around for a minute. "We forgot the wine opener. I'll run up and get it." She walked toward the elevators.

"Buddy system!" Vivian called, then looked at Nelson. "Maybe you should make sure she gets there safely."

He took the hint, downed his drink and followed.

24

Wendy stepped into the elevator, and as she turned she saw Nelson walking toward her. She frantically pushed the door close button. *Come on, come on, close!*

Just when she thought she was in the clear, an arm flew into the doors, causing them to retract. Nelson stepped in.

"Oh, sorry, I didn't see you," Wendy said, hitting 8, then taking a step back.

"Your friends said something about the buddy system?"

"Yeah, we had to implement that down in Mexico. She's got four young kids."

"I read her file. She was blessed with attractive children."

Wendy thought of one of her favorite musicians, Josh Weathers, and his song "I'm Blessed." She loved that song. *Blessed to walk, blessed to talk, blessed to breathe, blessed to open my eyes... and see. Blessed to be alive and well. By the way I'm livin' now, you probably couldn't tell. I am blessed!*

The doors opened to the floor and she stepped out first as Nelson protectively ensured the doors were not going to close.

She let them into the room and started searching for the bottle opener. He went out to the balcony as she scrounged around the table.

"It's a gorgeous night out," he called, looking up at the stars.

"You should see it during the day." She found the wine opener and pushed the curtain back. "I found it. You ready, Agent Nelson?"

"The stars are amazing," he said. "And like I said earlier, call me Wade."

She reluctantly joined him on the balcony, and her insides did a flip. *What am I doing? What am I doing?*

"So what about you, are you married?"

"Nope, not me."

"Is that the big dipper?" He pointed to the sky, then let his arm drop down behind her and grazed the small of her back.

"Uh, no, Wade. I think that's the little dipper, actually."

He turned and looked her in the eye. "It's the big one."

She looked back at him, unsure of what to say. After a few seconds she started laughing and turned to bail, but Wade grabbed her hand.

"I'm sorry for this afternoon. I should have looked away immediately. I don't know why I didn't. I should have, and I apologize."

"Let's just pretend like it never happened."

"Deal," he said, squeezing gently. "I'll leave that out of my official report."

She drew her hand back and laughed. "That's probably a good idea."

A gust of wind kicked up and blew Wendy's long, brown hair across her face. Wade pushed it back, tucking it behind her ear. Her skin tingled where he'd touched her face and sent shock waves through her body. She wanted to kiss him.

Her body said "yes," and her mind said "no" and "why not" at the same time. He was hot, of that there was no doubt, but she loved Jake, didn't she? Did he love her? Why did Wade's touch feel so good? *Dammit.*

She pushed away the urge. "So what do you think about Craig? How dangerous do you think he is?"

"I'm not sure yet. Craig is a wanted criminal and I plan to apprehend him, but at this point it looks like Vivian screwed around with a bartender who probably snapped that picture just to mess with her for leaving. It was sent in an envelope from where the guy worked."

"Hmm, I don't know."

"Guy had a bruised ego."

"What about the brakes?"

"I couldn't find anything that had been tampered with, and she'd had an oil change the week before. Those types of places mess things up all the time."

Wendy wasn't ready to buy what he was selling, even though it was possible. She was quiet for a moment. "So you don't think it was Craig? It's all just coincidence?"

"We'll know more if Agent Cervantes pulls any prints off the picture." He put his hand on hers. "But I don't think there's any real danger."

She held up the corkscrew end of the wine opener. "They're probably ready for more wine by now." She turned and went inside.

He sighed, then followed and slid the door closed and locked it.

She grabbed the bottle of Baileys and butterscotch schnapps on her way out. "I'll make us all Buttery Nipples out by the fire."

"Sounds tasty." He gave her a sly smile.

Damn, why did I say that? She made a beeline for the elevator, hitting the down button four times before the doors opened.

They both reached for the lobby button, their hands grazing. Wendy didn't step back this time, allowing him to stand close to her. Much closer than was necessary. The doors opened and he excused himself.

Wendy met the girls back in the great room. "Ready for the fire pit?"

"Y'all were gone for a while," Vivian said. "We figured you were heatin' things up in the room and wouldn't need the fire pit."

"There were some sparks but no full-fledged fire."

"Oooouuuu," the girls said.

"Do tell," Kate said.

"Ouu, nothing. He apologized for staring at my boobs. No biggie."

"Nothing? No kiss, no flirting?" Lucy asked.

"There might have been some minimal flirting. Can we please go outside now? He'll be back any sec, and I don't want him to know we're talking about him. The whole situation is still a little uncomfortable."

The girls went outside and grabbed the last four chairs by the fire. A couple to their left were holding hands and giving googly eyes to one another. A group of girls, all 25-30, sat to their right. One of them sat along the ledge rimming the fire pit, her butt crack exposed.

"There's no way she doesn't feel her ass hangin' out, as cold as it is out here," Wendy whispered.

"She knows. She just doesn't care," Lucy said, then got to work on the s'mores, commandeering two skewers and sticking marshmallows on them. She thrust them into the flames. "I'm stickin' 'em in, ladies."

"That's what he said!" Vivian said, opening the package of graham crackers. "I like mine flamin' hot, by the way."

"Are we still talking about marshmallows?" Lucy asked.

"I like mine hard and gooey, all at the same time," Kate said, then ripped open the Hershey's package with her teeth.

"Y'all and your sexual innuendos," Wendy said.

"Let's move on to something else that cracks us up," Vivian said and indicated to the butt-crack girl with her glass of wine. "In case I haven't told y'all, you should *always* say no to crack."

"Does that window have a crack in it?" Kate said, pointing to a nonexistent window.

Nelson came out carrying some firewood. He stood on the brick ledge and threw it on the fire.

"I'm not a crack whore," Lucy said and pointed to butt-crack girl with a skewer.

Nelson's line of sight followed the skewer and he almost fell off the ledge.

"Is it me, or is there a full moon out tonight?" Kate asked.

"Oh, it's definitely a moons-over-my-hammy type of night," Vivian concurred.

"A blue moon type of night, definitely," Wendy said. "But since we don't have any, let's do a Buttery Nipple!" The two liquor bottles were already cold from sitting outside behind her chair, so she poured them out in little plastic cups she'd grabbed from the water station.

Wendy passed out the shots and Vivian held hers up proudly. "To an *ass*tonishingly good friendship that is blooming from the *moon*ing we are *crack*ing up at, *butt* does anyone know a good plumber? *Ass* we are in need of one, right now right this very minute."

"Bluuuuuue moooooooooooooooooooooon," Lucy started singing.

Nelson, getting into the ass groove, said, "Can you please pass me a graham *crack*er?"

With that, it was on.* The girls, Nelson and the couple next to them cracked joke after joke. Ass-girl never indicated she heard or cared that they were making fun of her mostly bare butt cheeks.

Wrapping up the ass jokes, Vivian said, "I think I hear wolves howling at the moon," which instigated howls at the moon from the girls, the couple, even Wade.

"Aooooouuuuuuhhhhh," they bellowed.

They enjoyed the fire for a while longer, then the girls decided to pack it up, and Nelson escorted them upstairs.

As Lucy closed the door to their room, she yelled, "That was fantabulASSSSSSS!"

25

Day 4

Vivian awoke to the sound of the sliding door closing and water running in the bathroom. The warm, cozy bed enveloped her, and she snuggled deeper under the comforter, pulling it over her head.

Lucy's perky voice chimed, "Rise and shine, sleepyheads."

Wendy groaned, flipped over and plumped her pillow.

Guess she's not ready to get up, either, Vivian thought.

"Kate's already up and at 'em," Lucy said as she pulled back the room-darkening curtains. "It's a beautiful day outside, and look at this view."

Vivian didn't move.

"I said," Lucy said, yanking the covers off Vivian's head, "look at that view!"

Vivian peeked with one eye, then promptly shut it. "It's too bright."

Lucy smacked Wendy on the butt, then yanked her covers off, too. "Up!"

"I thought we were here to relax," a sleepy Wendy said. "That's exactly what I'm doing."

Lucy jumped from one bed to the other. "We've got big plans today. We work out, then we spa, then we bike ride in Vail, then we fire pit. Come on! Get up up up!"

"Bike ride?" Wendy moaned, still in bed.

"Yes! Vail Village reminds me of Switzerland, so picturesque. I've already reserved bikes for us today at 5, and I know the perfect place to watch the sunset. I even bought special snackage for the occasion. Then we'll ride back into town and go to dinner at Hail-Yeah, the only 'casual' place in Vail."

"When did you go to Switzerland?" Vivian threw a pillow at Lucy.

"I haven't, but I've seen pictures."

116

"Whatever," Wendy said and rolled out of bed.

Vivian thought about the day's activities, and that spa idea was enough to get her moving. "I'm in for your itinerary," she said to Lucy, then grabbed her comforter and a box of white powdered donuts and joined Kate on the balcony.

"Mornin'," Kate said and took a sip of her coffee. "Breakfast of champions, I see."

Vivian popped a whole donut into her mouth. "Roo row rit." She coughed, and a cloud of powdered sugar floated in the sun's rays.

Wendy had poured herself a bowl of cereal and stepped out just in time for the sugar cloud. "You should balance that with a banana at least."

Vivian shook her head and licked her fingers. "I think I'll just balance with another one of these."

Lucy and Kate grabbed granola bars for breakfast, then the girls changed into their workout gear.

Vivian knocked on Nelson's door and let him know about their workout and spa plans.

Lucy marched down the hall. "The workout starts now. Forget the elevator, we're takin' the stairs down."

Kate slumped her shoulders. "That's eight floors."

"Nine, actually. We're going down to the lowest level. You can do it." Lucy pushed open the door to the stairwell.

The girl's steps echoed as they marched down the nine floors. Their soles squeaked on the turns as Lucy periodically cheered them on.

Overall, not too bad, but she can forget it if she expects me to go up this way! Vivian thought.

"Ladies, ladies, ladies!" Lucy chanted as they walked into the gym. She took in all of the equipment and was happy to find everything they needed. "Have I got something fantastic in mind for us today! I've been working with a new trainer and I have written up some of my workouts for us to try. It's a circuit that we will do three times – you may feel like you are going to die, but I assure you, you won't!"

Vivian kicked a machine. "I have high blood pressure, remember. Don't kill me."

"You'll be fine." Lucy went around the gym setting up the various stations and providing a demonstration on each one. Vivian, Wendy and Kate made faces and sounds at each of the activities. Without missing a beat, Lucy got everyone in position and yelled, "On your mark, get set, go!"

Moaning and groaning, her reluctant subjects began the workout. Lucy, with her unwavering enthusiasm, refused to allow even the slightest amount of slacking off and ignored the "drill sergeant" and "Trainer McGuire" comments coming out of the girls' mouths.

As round one neared completion, Lucy was just getting warmed up. The other girls sounded as if they were injured, or perhaps, dying.

"So much whining!" she yelled, then tossed them each a towel. Lucy took a quick sip of strawberry-infused water. "If y'all are this worn out after one round, this should be your wake-up call – this is exactly what you should be doing several times a week so you *don't* die."

Wendy, who was actually the least whiny during round one, got off of her machine and draped her towel around her neck. "I'd like to be able to walk tomorrow, so I'm done."

"Come on, Wendy, you can do it. Keep going," Lucy encouraged.

"Nope, stick a fork in me. I'll be in pain as it is, but no need to add insult to injury."

Lucy was disappointed, but knew better than to mess with Wendy when she'd made up her mind. She focused her attention to Vivian and Kate, who, after seeing Wendy's retreat also said they were done.

"Oh no, no, no," Lucy said, showing no mercy. "It gets easier. Keep at it."

Round two was surprisingly quiet. Lucy assumed that they either needed all of their breath for the workout, or simply didn't have enough oxygen to make a sound. Either way, she was happy they had cooperated and remained encouraging of their efforts.

"Last round!" Lucy yelled.

Vivian and Kate responded in unison. "Thank God!"

Lucy rolled her eyes and continued to push them through exercises. Vivian and Kate's form rapidly deteriorated and they did a few less reps despite Lucy's vigilance, but they managed to complete the workout. At the end of the last set, Vivian and Kate threw themselves on the floor, gasping.

"I can't believe you do that almost ever day, Lucy." Vivian sucked in some air. "I think my lungs are collapsing. Call a medic."

"You did great for never working out. If you keep at it, you, too, could have my fine form." She did a Vanna White sweep up and down her side.

Kate bent her knees, but otherwise made no move to get up. "I don't have time to do this on a regular basis."

"You have to make time." She glanced at the floor, then back to the girls. "There's no telling how many germs you're rollin around in down there. Y'all should get up."

Vivian and Kate stayed put and continued their death rattling.

Lucy offered them each a hand and helped them up. "Might want to hit the hand sanitizer on the way out." She pointed to a dispenser, turned and headed toward the door. "You've been detoxified of all, well, some of the alcohol you've consumed, and this workout is going to make you appreciate your massages all the more."

"But I wanted to feel good in my massage," Kate said. "I hope the pain searing through my body doesn't interfere."

"That's exactly why I stopped," Wendy said. "I was thinkin' ahead."

Lucy harrumphed at that.

"As long as my masseur is cute and has strong hands," Vivian said as the door to the gym closed behind her, "I'm going to forget about pain and stress and everything else. My relaxation begins now!"

26

The torture of Wonkita's workout behind them, the girls headed to the locker room to shower before their massages.

Once clean and comfy, they each claimed a lounger in the ladies lounge.

Vivian looked over at Lucy. "I notice you avoided the Gravitron during our workout today."

Lucy gave her the stink eye.

"What? I'm just sayin'."

"Say nothing."

Kate looked at Vivian. "What's a Gravitron?"

Vivian glanced at Lucy. "It's an amazing piece of exercise equipment that, unfortunately, isn't for the short in stature."

Lucy huffed, then walked to the beverage station. "I don't need to hear this story. Living it was bad enough."

Wendy put down her magazine. "This sounds good."

"Oh, it is," Vivian smirked. "We were in college and Gabrielle had free visitors passes to her gym, so the three of us went.

"Lucy wasn't the gym connoisseur she is today, and neither of us knew how to work most of the machines. I stuck to the usual equipment, you know, stuff like the rower and the treadmill, but Lucy wanted to try out the Gravitron. It was smack dab in the middle of the gym. It must have been their newest toy, and they were showing that bad boy off.

"She decided to give it a whirl and stepped on the platform. She was then automatically boosted up to a bar about eight feet in the air."

"Boosted her up?" Wendy interrupted.

"It had some kind of hydraulic motor or something. I dunno, but it kinda just popped her up there. It was really cool."

"Huh."

120

"So Lucy grabbed the bar and pulled herself up to where her chin was just over it. Well, the little booster step then went down, leaving her hanging there."

"Oh no."

"Oh yes. She hung on for a few seconds, her feet dangling, and started searching frantically for a step, any step. Of course, the platform was long gone and she didn't know how to make it come back up."

"Did you help her?" Kate had a blanket pulled up to her nose and was giggling behind it.

"I didn't know what to do, so down she came with a loud thud!" Vivian smacked her hands together. "She was sprawled out, flat on her ass." She laughed again at the memory.

"Is this where you helped her?" Kate asked.

Lucy turned from the beverage station, dunking her tea bag. "No, she *never* helped me."

"It was funny. I did my usual point and laugh, then pretended to not know her. I am ashamed to admit, but then I walked away."

"You did not." Wendy threw her magazine at Vivian, which missed.

"I did."

"It really is amazing she's still your friend," Wendy said.

Lucy grabbed a dried banana chip and threw it at Vivian. "That thing almost killed me!"

"Oh, you were fine, and it was damn funny!"

The door to the ladies lounge opened and a tall, thin, middle-aged man wearing a tight black T-shirt and black slacks entered.

"I'm looking for Vivian," he said.

Vivian picked up the dried banana from her lounger, popped it into her mouth and waved. "That's me!"

"I'm Stefan. I'll be providing your massage today."

"Excellent," Vivian said, as he turned back toward the door. She turned to the girls and gave a thumbs up. "See y'all later in the grotto!"

Stefan led her down the hall to the Snowflake room.

"Please disrobe to your comfort level, remove any jewelry and lay face down here," he said as he pulled back the sheet. "Do you have any areas that require special attention?"

"My lower back sucks since I had the twins, but other than that, the usual. I don't want any of that deep tissue, stick-your-elbow-in-my-back business, either. I just want to feel good. You know, relax."

"I understand completely." He folded the sheet on the massage table back, smoothing it gently. "The table is warmed and ready. I'll be back in a few moments to begin." He stepped out and closed the door behind him.

Vivian didn't have on any jewelry or a stitch of clothing, so she placed her robe on the hook on the back of the door and slipped under the sheet. She stuck her face into the oval cutout and wiggled around to get comfortable.

I bet this will be the best massage ever.

She closed her eyes and took a deep breath. *It smells wonderful in here. I wonder what that is. Juniper? Not piney enough. Juniper mixed with something?* She took another deep breath. *Lavender? Honey? Heck, I don't know.*

She turned her attention to the music. *Are these chanting monks?* The next song began and sounded like wind blowing through trees, caressing a chime from time to time. While she enjoyed it, she'd enjoy it more if her masseur was already at work. *What's takin' him so long? My time better not have started yet.*

After another couple of minutes, the door opened and shut with a thud.

The masseur stood over her and cleared his throat loudly, then cracked his knuckles, one by one. Apparently ready, he slid the sheet down to her waist, then poured warmed oil onto her back. He rubbed his hands back and forth across her back, though not with much finesse. He moved from her upper back, to shoulders to neck, then abruptly to her lower back, almost on her butt. Vivian squirmed a little, and he moved back up to the middle of her back.

As he worked she could feel him close to her. His breath was steady as he glided his hands along her back, running them along her side and occasionally touching the side of her breasts.

After a few minutes he pulled the sheet up to her shoulders, then flipped it off of her feet and legs. He pushed it high, all the way up to the top of her thighs.

Don't they usually do one leg at a time?

He squirted oil onto her right leg, then began kneading her calf, working his way up.

I hope he comes back to my feet. That's one of my favorite parts.

He went up over her knee, both hands around her thigh, his fingers getting a little closer than professional boundaries dictated.

This is gettin' weird. I didn't take this for a happy ending kind of place.

She was about to say something when he started on her other calf.

He has the roughest hands I've ever felt for a masseur.

As he began to work his way up past her knee, she knew she was going to have to say something. His touch had become even more sensual.

An "mmmmmmmmm" escaped his lips as his hand moved up her thigh, moving the sheet and exposing her ass.

That's it!

She sat up and flipped over, grasping at the sheet to cover herself.

What the…

27

Holy *shit* what are you doing here?" Vivian yelled.

He put his hands up in defense. "Take it easy, take it easy."
Vivian jumped off the massage table and tugged the sheet around
her. "Craig, get the hell out of here."

"Vivian, I need to talk to you. Don't you know how much I love you?"

"You are a maniac. Get *out* of here!" She made a break for the door.

He stepped in front of her and grabbed her arms. "Run away with me.
We can be in another country in a matter of hours." His eyes pleaded, wild
and intense. "Grab your things and let's go."

"You are crazy! My kids! I'd never leave them!"

"We'll start our own family. Vivian, I love you." He shook her a little.
"We're meant to be together!"

"Oh my god! HELP! HELP ME!" she screamed, trying to loosen his
grasp.

Craig shoved her against the wall, covering her mouth with his hand.
"Shhh, I have money, Vivian. I can afford anything you want. We can live on
a beach somewhere. It'll be perfect. Just us."

Vivian continued to struggle, turned her head away from his hand and
screamed again. "HEELLLLLLLLLP!" Her sheet had fallen to the floor, but
she didn't care. All she wanted was to get away.

The door burst open. "Hands up!" Agent Nelson rushed into the room
followed by a security officer. They ran around the table on either side.
Nelson reached Craig first and grabbed his left arm, trying to wrap it around
his back. Craig twisted and punched him in the face. Nelson hammered Craig
with a fist to the nose and another to the gut.

Craig answered with a double jab to Nelson's right kidney, who recoiled,
dazed.

"Craig, stop it!" Vivian yelled.

Craig spun and gave the security officer a right hook that knocked him
back into the wall. He slumped to the floor.

Vivian screamed again. Craig grabbed her arm and ran for the door, dragging her with him.

Nelson jumped over the table onto Craig's back, causing the connection between Craig and Vivian to break. Nelson wrapped his arm around Craig's neck, choking him. Craig twisted and threw an elbow back into Nelson's face. Crack! Nelson staggered. Craig ran out of the room. Nelson recovered, then got up and charged after him.

Vivian scooped up the sheet, shielding herself, and ran into the hall. The security officer had recovered and ran out behind her, yelling into his walkie-talkie. "Confirmed assailant, Craig Pearson, Caucasian male, wearing black T-shirt, black pants. Running in spa corridor. Request police backup. Need medical assistance."

At the end of the corridor, a masseuse stepped out of a therapy room, right in Craig's path. He shoved her out of the way. She yelped in pain as she slammed against the wall. Craig flung the exit door open and hauled ass up the stairs into daylight.

Wendy ran out to see about the ruckus and Nelson smacked right into her, both of them falling to the ground.

"You okay?" he asked, jumping off of her.

"I think so," a startled Wendy answered.

Nelson took off, back in pursuit.

Lucy and Kate rushed out of their therapy rooms to Wendy and helped her up.

Vivian reached them. "Oh my god! Are you okay?"

"Holy shit! What's going on? Was that Craig?" Wendy pointed in the direction the men had run. Her face was covered in bright orange goop.

"Yes," Vivian said. "Are you bleeding?" She pointed to a red smear on Wendy's neck.

Wendy touched the spot and looked at her blood-smeared fingers. "It's not mine. I think Wade was bleeding."

"Where are the police?" Lucy asked the security officer.

He held up a finger as he listened to the information being relayed. "Subject just ran out west spa stairwell exit. I repeat, subject exited west spa stairwell. Request police backup and medical assistance."

Lucy and Kate's masseurs checked on Wendy's aesthetician, who was holding her shoulder, whimpering.

The security officer lowered the walkie-talkie and instructed everyone to go into the ladies lounge. "Stay there. I'll be back in a few minutes." He hustled down the hall, toward where Craig had disappeared.

Wendy fanned her face. "I gotta wash this shit off. It's starting to burn."

Her aesthetician got back into Ridge mode. "Oh yes, I'm so sorry. Let's get that off you." Still holding her shoulder, she turned to Kate's lady. "Please go into my room, get a hot towel and remove her peel. Afterwards, please apply the papaya-infused whipped moisturizer. Liberally."

Kate's masseuse took care of Wendy while the rest of the group went into the lounge and had a seat.

A bloody-nosed and beat-up Stefan sat in a chair, ice pack to his forehead.

Vivian sat down on his ottoman. "Oh my god, Stefan, I'm so sorry you got caught up in this. Are you okay?"

Stefan lowered the ice pack and squeezed Vivian's shoulder. "I'll be okay. I'm just glad to see that you are, too."

"What happened?" Kate asked, gently. "Where did Craig come from?"

"I don't know," Vivian said. "All I know is that he pretended to be Stefan. I was about to tear into him for getting too handsy, then I turned over and saw it was Craig."

"I would never get too handsy," Stefan said. "I was about to knock on the door to the treatment room when I was ambushed. Craig, you called him, grabbed me and forced me into the electrical closet on the connecting hallway. He covered my mouth in duct tape and hit me in the face a few times until I passed out."

"Oh, Stefan, how horrible!" Lucy had sat down next to him and now leaned over, hanging on all the details.

Wendy came into the room rubbing cream on her face and sat in the other chair next to Stefan. They got her caught up on the events, and she said, "Stefan, how did you manage to get help?"

"Thankfully he didn't knock me into next week, but I'm not sure how long I was out. It was hard to move, but I knew I had to get help, so I crawled out of the closet and managed to stumble to the spa's front desk."

Vivian's hands shook as reality set it. Tears spilled from the corner of her eyes. She sniffled and Lucy handed her a tissue. It wasn't until Kate hugged her that she started to really lose it.

"I can't believe that just happened. He wanted me to run away with him! To leave my kids!"

"Oh, Viv," Kate said, giving her a squeeze. "He's obviously crazy if he thought you'd do that."

"Yeah, you'd never leave them. Ever," Lucy said and grabbed more tissues out of the box beside her.

Stefan patted Vivian's back. "They'll catch him."

"Thank goodness Wade busted in when he did," Wendy said.

"Yeah, Viv. God knows what he could have done to you in there," Lucy said.

Two medics arrived, each carrying portable medical kits. "We had a call that someone needed medical attention," the first one said.

"Over there." Wendy pointed to the aesthetician.

The security officer came through the door. "Is everyone okay?"

They all nodded, and he walked over to the medics. After a few moments he turned to Vivian. "Are you hurt?"

"No, I'm okay. Did y'all catch Craig?"

The security officer looked down, then said, "As of right now the suspect is still at large. However, the Avon police have arrived and are searching the hotel and the grounds. I expect Agent Nelson will be back soon and will want to talk to you."

"At large?" Vivian asked.

28

Wendy smacked her hand on the end table beside her. "Dammit, that is so not good."

Vivian threw her tissue into the trash. "I can't believe Craig got away."

The security officer glanced at Vivian, still wrapped in a sheet. "Perhaps you would be more comfortable if you met with Agent Nelson upstairs?"

Vivian glanced down. "Yeah, I'll go get dressed."

"I'll be waiting at the spa check-in to escort you."

With that, the girls said goodbye to Stefan and made their way to the locker room, changed and then met the security officer. He shuffled them into the elevator and led them to a private boardroom on the main floor. He disappeared when Nelson walked in a few moments later.

Nelson had a scrape on his cheek and a fat lip. He motioned for them to sit down. "Craig got away."

"What happened?" Vivian asked.

"He had a motorcycle hidden in the trees, just on the other side of the road. He was able to evade the Avon police. We don't know his whereabouts."

"Damn." Wendy summed up the situation.

"So what do we do now?" Vivian asked. "We thought changing hotels would keep him from finding me, but clearly that didn't work."

"I suggest you pack your bags and head back to Denver International. Catch the next flight home."

"What makes you think he won't come after me there?"

"Yeah, and what about the kids?" Kate asked. "She can't risk putting them in danger."

Nelson didn't answer right away.

"I will *not* put my children at risk."

128

"Stay here in the hotel for the rest of your vacation. The staff and security officers are all aware of the situation."

"Would you give your sister the same advice?" Wendy asked.

Nelson considered the question for a moment before answering. "I can stay another night."

Vivian looked at Nelson. "I'm not going home with Craig out there and risk anything happening to my kids."

"Understood. I have to consult with Agent Cervantes, but the first thing right now is to keep you safe. Since I'm staying, and with your permission, I will arrange for us to have adjoining rooms. You girls need to stick together, and I need to know where you are at all times." He glanced at Wendy, then quickly away.

"Permission granted," Vivian said.

"How did Craig know where we were?" Kate asked.

"I'm going to figure that out. I will need access to all of your belongings." He stood. "I'll be right back." He went just outside the door, leaving it cracked behind him.

"It's Mexico all over again, but with our consent this time." Lucy shivered with the heebie-jeebies.

"I don't think he's got cooties," Wendy said quietly, winking at Lucy. "But if it makes you feel better, we'll get you some Lysol."

Trey walked up and conferred with Nelson for a moment, but Vivian couldn't hear what was said. Nelson took a call, and the girls sat silently until he opened the door for Trey a few minutes later. He handed everyone a new room key. "Ladies, you are now in the two-bedroom Presidential Suite, with an adjoining room for Agent Nelson. We've arranged for your belongings to be moved once you've packed. We're horrified at what occurred and want to do everything in our power to ensure the remainder of your stay is pleasant. We're taking care of the room upgrade, and obviously there's no charge for today's spa services. Plus, we've arranged for you to have lunch at the Timberline, if you'd like."

"Thank you so much," Vivian said, standing up. "I appreciate y'all looking out for us, and the generosity."

"It's our pleasure and the least we can do after what happened."

Nelson approached with an Avon police officer. "Vivian, this officer is here to take your statement and help you file a restraining order."

The officer stuck out his hand. "I'm Lieutenant Martin." He led her to the far end of the table, away from the girls. In addition to some documents, he pulled out a small notepad and pen. "Tell me what happened."

Vivian described the events from the moment her masseur picked her up in the ladies lounge to sitting in the boardroom.

The lieutenant tapped his pen on the table. "Do you have any idea how Craig could have known you were here?"

"No, we changed our hotel reservation at the last minute. We were supposed to be in a hotel in Vail."

"I want to be clear. You jumped off the table, he held you against your will, grabbed your arms and slammed you against the wall?"

"Pretty much, yeah."

"We'll be filing assault and battery charges against him. Would you like to file a restraining order?"

"Yes. Absolutely."

He pushed the paperwork to her. "Fill this out and sign at the bottom."

She did.

Martin handed her a business card, his cell number written on the back, then took statements from Lucy, Wendy and Kate. He spoke to Nelson briefly, they shook hands and he walked out of the boardroom.

"Are we done?" Lucy asked. "I've had about all the cops and robbers I can handle."

"Yes, for now. I need to follow up with Agent Cervantes on some things and we need to get your luggage packed so it can be moved. I'll go through your belongings carefully in the new accommodations."

"I need a beer," Vivian said. "Or five."

"Let's go to the Timberline," Wendy suggested.

Kate linked arms with Vivian. "Let's go getcha five. We're not going anywhere today."

They left the boardroom and followed Nelson to their room, where they threw their clothes into suitcases and repacked the bar. Two bellmen arrived and loaded up two carts. "We'll ensure these arrive at your new room."

Wendy handed them a tip. "Thanks."

"It's our pleasure."

Nelson went with the bellmen to the new room. The girls headed to the Timberline and took a table by the window.

A waiter delivered menus and asked if they knew what they'd like to drink.

"Dos Equis, extra lime for me," Vivian said without hesitation.

Lucy said she wanted to celebrate being alive and ordered a split of champagne. Kate and Wendy both ordered a glass of cabernet.

Vivian glanced over the menu and stopped at the list of fancy margaritas. The waiter delivered their drinks and she pointed out, "Did you know y'all forgot the decimal here?"

He didn't even look down. "No, ma'am, there's no mistake. That's a $500 margarita."

"Holy guacamole!" Lucy yelled.

Vivian fanned herself with the menu and asked, "Does that come with a little sumthin' sumthin' extra? Like an orgasm?"

"What the hell do they put in that thing?" Wendy asked.

"Only the best ingredients, including Barrique de Ponciano Porfidio tequila."

"Bet y'all don't sell too many of those, do you?" Kate asked.

"You'd be surprised." The waiter smiled and tucked the serving tray under his arm. "We also have a $1,000 margarita."

"Heyzoos Kristo, does that come with two?" Vivian snickered.

"Let's order a round and see if Trey will cover it!" Wendy said and clapped.

"That's typically not a complimentary cocktail," the waiter informed them.

Vivian squeezed lime into her beer. "After the day I've had, I think I deserve it and all its pleasures."

29

The girls finished their delicious, free (yay!), and for Vivian, mostly liquid lunch in the Timberline, then headed upstairs to check out the accommodations in the Presidential Suite.

Vivian stepped into the foyer, mouth agape, and started giggling. "My gosh, I'm downright giddy!"

"Like a picture out of a magazine," Kate said. "It's perfect."

"It's a helluva lot better than our regular-ass room," Lucy laughed. "Not that it was bad, but come on!"

The girls entered the living room, marveling at their surroundings. Lucy called them into the kitchen, where she was opening the drawers and cabinets.

"They have all the top-of-the-line gadgets," she said and pushed buttons on a Vitamix blender. "Wolfgang Puck would approve."

Nelson got up from the dining table and pointed to their purses. "May I?"

The girls said yes.

He began rifling through their purses. "Those are your rooms," he said, pointing to the bedrooms to the right of the kitchen, "and that door," indicating a door on the far side of the living room, "goes to my hotel room and needs to stay unlocked at all times. I can't help you if I can't get in here."

"Got it," Vivian said.

The balcony ran the length of the suite, and the views from the top floor were even more majestic than on the eighth. "I will so be having breakfast out here," Kate said, draping herself against the railing. "Crepes. Not Vivian's powdered donut death of a baked good."

"You know you like them," Vivian said.

Lucy yelled from the master bath, "Come check this out!"

Vivian hustled in to see what the fuss was about and found Lucy spread eagle in the ginormous jetted tub. Her hands and feet didn't even touch the side.

Vivian jumped in as Lucy scooted over. "I bet we could fit 10 people in here, maybe more." She looked up to see Agent Nelson's face in the doorway, turning red. "Maybe we'll try that later."

"This makes me wanna go get in one of the real hot tubs," Kate said.

"Yeah, I don't want to be cooped up in the room," Vivian said.

"Let's swimsuit up," Lucy said, hopping out of the tub. "Wait a second, we're supposed to be at the bike rental place in two hours."

Nelson shook his head. "You'd better cancel."

"Why?" Wendy asked.

Nelson cut his eyes to her. "You're safer here on the property."

"Could some of your guys pose as other bikers or skateboarders or something?" Kate asked.

Nelson shook his head. "We couldn't cover Vivian completely, or the rest of you. It's best to cancel the bike ride."

"You're probably right." Lucy looked disappointed. "No sunset soirée for us, I'm afraid."

Aw, she went all out making plans for today. Vivian flashed with anger. *Stupid-ass Craig.*

They unpacked again, set up their new, improved and larger bar, got changed, including their Ridge slippers and giant, plush robes.

Lucy looked at Vivian as they stepped into the living room. "You going to wear that necklace? I thought you were worried it would turn green on ya? The hot tub'll do it."

Vivian unclasped it and set it down on the kitchen counter. "Thanks for reminding me."

Kate set her watch on the counter, too and told Nelson they were ready to roll.

"I've got to make a few calls," he said. "I'll keep an eye out from up here. The Avon police are on the grounds."

"Okey doke," Vivian said, grabbing her room key, then said to the girls, "Grab your trashy, truck-stop hats."

Lucy put on her hat. "Check."

Wendy pulled two bottles of wine off the bar, an opener and four cups. "I've got all we need right here!"

They chose one of the hot tubs tucked in an aspen grove, in clear view of the four Avon police officers standing guard on the patio. The girls threw their robes on a lounger but kept on their hats. Kate turned on the timer and bubble spewed out of the jets.

"What happened to your leg?" Lucy asked Wendy.

Wendy looked down at the baseball-sized bruise on her thigh. "Kate kicked the crap out of me in her sleep last night. I screamed, but you lushes didn't even stir."

"I'm really, really sorry," Kate said as she stepped into the hot tub. "I was karate chopping a bear."

"Is Shaun battered and bruised?" Lucy asked.

She shook her head. "No. Usually my dreams don't involve martial arts, but a bear was attacking me. I had to defend myself."

"Well, you've got one hell of a karate chop!" Wendy rubbed her leg gingerly.

"I had a lesson from my cousin, Thai, before the bear charged me."

"At least it was your cousin and not one of your dead relatives," Vivian said.

Kate looked down at the water. "Oh no, he's dead."

"What?" Wendy asked.

"He was killed by a drunk driver seven years ago."

"Oh my god, I'm sorry," Vivian said. "I assumed because he was your cousin he'd be young…and alive. Sorry."

"It's okay, you didn't know. He visits me in my dreams." Kate reached for a cup of wine that Lucy had poured. "I always feel empowered after he visits, like I'm ready to take on the world."

"To Thai and feeling empowered," Lucy said, holding up her cup.

The girls cheersed, and the two closest Avon officers stepped a little closer, evidently curious about the noise.

Vivian put down her wine and floated in the bubbles. She poked her toes out of the water, checking on her pedicure and thinking about what Kate had said. "You know, this conversation has done a little something to empower me." She put her feet down and stood up. "I'm thinkin' we need to get our asses on those bikes and do what we came here to do. We will not be prisoners in our hotel, fabulous though it is. We are on vacation! To hell with Craig, and if we can catch him, all the better."

"Now that's what I'm talking about!" Lucy slammed her cup down, spilling wine onto the ledge of the hot tub. "I forgot to cancel that reservation anyway, so they're still expecting us."

"Let's go tell Wade," Wendy said. "He's not gonna be happy."

"After the lesson I had last night, I can take Craig down in one chop!" Kate chopped the water. "Let's go!"

"I can vouch for that!" Wendy splashed Kate with her own karate chop.

They sang "Everybody was Kung Fu Fighting" and had a slow-motion kung fu fight among the aspens.

Vivian's cup soon filled with more water than wine and she tossed it out. "I'm boiling. I'm gotta go cool down." She dried off, wrapped her robe around her and went just outside the fence surrounding the two hot tubs. She took off her slippers and stood barefoot in the snow. *"Aye yai yai*, that's cold!"

One of the police officers spoke into his walkie-talkie, and two of the other guys moved up the mountain a bit on either side.

Lucy joined her, not even bothering to put on slippers. She scooped up a handful of grassy snow, packed it and beaned Vivian. "Of course it's cold, it's snow!"

Vivian dug up a handful of the slushy, muddy stuff and chunked it at Lucy, smacking her right in the boob.

"Dammit, the ta-tas are off limits!"

"Sorry!" Vivian said, throwing another snowball at her. "My aim sucks." She got Lucy in the other one.

"Oh, it's on now!"

Kate and Wendy couldn't resist, not bothering with robes or their slippers, and the four lobbed grassy, globby snowballs at each other, everyone getting properly covered in cold muck. They then took pictures lying in the snow and a shot of their Ridge-slippered feet in a snow circle.

Agent Nelson cleared his throat. He held Vivian's phone.

"Oh, hey," Vivian said. "Didn't see you come outside."

"I need to ask you a few questions."

"Okay."

Vivian and Nelson walked to the fire pit and sat down.

"Were you aware that your phone has an application installed that details your location?"

"Is that something from the manufacturer to help find it if I lose it? Like GPS?"

Nelson shook his head. "No, this was purposefully installed on your phone."

"I don't remember putting anything like that on it."

"Where did you buy it?"

"From the service provider. I've been with them for years."

"Is there anyone else, other than Craig, who could have access to your phone and installed this?" He showed her the app.

"I don't think so. It's rarely far from me."

Nelson went to push a button on the screen. "I'm going to uninstall the app."

"Wait." Vivian put her hand on his. "We've decided we *are* going on that bike ride. Screw Craig."

30

Nelson did his best to talk the girls out of the bike ride, to no avail. Vivian was emphatic. "I'm not going to let him make me feel like a victim. We're going, and I hope to hell he shows up."

"I think it's a bad idea." Nelson turned and went inside.

The girls grabbed their stuff and went upstairs to get ready.

Nelson met them in the room and sat them down. "Since I can't stop you from going, I'll be tracking your whereabouts." He handed Vivian a black pager-sized device. "Keep this on you at all times."

"Sure," Vivian said and slipped it in her pocket.

"I planned for us to toodle around Vail Village, have a picnic in the Betty Ford Alpine Gardens and then ride along Gore Creek on the Vail Pass Trail," Lucy said. "You okay with that plan?"

Nelson sighed. "This bike ride needs to wrap up before the sun goes down. I don't want you out after dark on the bikes. You need to go straight to the Gardens for the picnic. And before you ask, no alcohol."

"Dammit," Wendy said.

"After the picnic, head down to Vail Pass Trail and continue west along Gore Creek until you get to Lionshead Place. You'll take that directly back to the bike shop." Nelson paused and looked each girl in the eye. "Understand?"

Vivian, Kate and Wendy said "yes" and nodded.

Lucy added, "We might do dinner at Hail-Yeah in Vail."

"Call me after the ride and let me know if you do. But for now, pack up and get going. It will be dark in a few hours and I'd like you to be back here."

Lucy and Kate packed crackers and sliced cheese into a small cooler and Vivian grabbed her can of Easy Cheese. They said goodbye to Nelson and scooted out the door.

Lucy drove down the mountain and into Vail Village. The girls walked into the bike shop and were greeted by a guy with jet-black, long hair, his arms covered in tattoos. Vivian smelled a hint of patchouli. He handed each of them a pen and paper. "You'll need to fill this out and sign the waiver."

Vivian read through the disclosures. Ruff Riders Bike Shop was held harmless for injury, death, dismemberment, accidents resulting from stupid people doing stupid things, pedal impalements, rabid dogs, bear attacks, you name it.

"I feel like I'm reading the mumbo-jumbo of mortgage papers," Wendy said, holding the pen above the signature line. "I get enough of this at work." Wendy was a loan officer at a mortgage company, and while she liked her job, the underwriting blah blah got old.

The clerk gathered the signed papers and passed out helmets as Lucy put on her backpack. He led the girls outside and got the bikes adjusted to each individual height. "Be careful and have fun," he said as they pedaled away.

Vivian fumbled a little, then got her balance and rode ahead a few paces.

Lucy quickly caught up. "No getting ahead of us, Viv."

"I'm just getting back into the swing of things, here. Trying to figure out gears and stuff."

Kate whirred up next to Vivian. "This town is so cute!"

They cruised past a hotel that looked like a chalet, then a ski shop, a confectionary and a couple of artsy boutiques.

They approached Vail Valley Drive and Lucy squeezed the brake, leaned to the right and made the turn with ease.

Vivian wobbled as she tried to coordinate the brake and turn.

Wendy zoomed past. "Problems?"

"It's been awhile. The only bikes I own right now have three wheels and sit two inches off the ground."

The girls pedaled, four across, down the street . It wasn't long before Lucy led them off the main road and onto a trail. They followed it a mile or so, then came to their stop — the Betty Ford Alpine Gardens.

Vivian's phone rang as she put down the kick-stand. It was Nelson.

"Everything all right so far?" he asked.

"Yep," she answered, "except my bike skills are rusty." She clicked off.

The girls parked their bikes and walked past the pavilion, through the gate and meandered along the path. They stop to admire plants and flowers along the way. Vivian tried to look like she didn't have a care in the world as she shuffled around some downed needles of a lodgepole pine.

"I sure hope Craig has kept tabs of your location, Vivian, and shows," Kate said and took a picture of tulipas maximowiczii. "I'm ready for him to go down." Another click.

"Me, too," Lucy said. "We need to get back to our regularly scheduled vacation."

"I'm a little nervous about what will happen if Craig shows," Wendy said. "How fast can the Vail PD get here? What if he tries to kidnap you?"

Vivian shook her head. "With y'all here, no way. You're as bad as Lucy and her mob fixation. If it makes you feel better, Wendy, you can be in charge of calling the police." Most of her believed that.

The girls decided the meditation spot was the best place to picnic. All was quiet except for the rhythmic splash of the waterfall and occasional bird cries. Vivian sat on one of the benches overlooking the pond and looked around. "Too bad I don't meditate."

Wendy gave a nervous laugh. "Who can calm their mind enough to meditate? Mine won't shut off."

Kate sat down on the bench next to Vivian. "With everything that has happened, meditating has helped me put it all into perspective. The brakes, the spa."

"When did you meditate?" Vivian asked.

"This morning, before you got up."

Lucy sat her backpack on a boulder. "Meditating is overrated, but if you were going to do it, this is a magnificent spot. We need a picture."

Kate perked up. "Go over by the waterfall and I'll get one of y'all."

Vivian, Lucy and Wendy hiked up a trail encircling the pond. Halfway to the waterfall, Vivian heard something, stopped, and turned to pose.

"I can't get the waterfall from there, keep going!" Kate yelled and waved them on.

The waterfall was loud, but Vivian heard something else. She didn't see anything and kept going around a curve, toward to a big boulder. The sound intensified. She looked by the path, next to the boulder, and her heart skipped a beat.

"RUN!"

31

Vivian took off back down the path, grabbing Lucy's shirt and pulling her along. "Run!" She yelled at Wendy as she passed her. Vivian screamed at the top of her lungs the rest of the way down the trail.

"What? What's wrong?" Lucy asked, for once scrambling to keep up with Vivian.

Wendy hurdled over a rock and landed next to Vivian at the base of the trail. "Is it Craig?"

"SNAKE!" she screamed and jumped up onto the meditation bench next to Kate. She danced around, unable to stop moving her feet, still in fight or flight mode. "Holy shit. Holy moly. Jumpin' Jack Flash," Vivian rasped and bent over, hands on knees, breathing hard.

Lucy and Wendy jumped onto the other bench and Kate stood up next to her.

"What kind of snake?" Lucy asked, not winded.

Even though he hadn't touched her, she could feel him sliding up her leg. "Oh my god, a rattlesnake." She took a few huffs, then continued, "It almost got me. It was all curled in a ball and its head was stickin' up, ready to strike. I almost died! *Again*!"

An older gentleman in khakis, white long-sleeve shirt and wide-brim hat approached. "Everything okay?"

She let out a big sigh. "Heyzoos Kristo, there's was one pissed off snake back there!" She pointed toward the waterfall.

Lucy jumped down from the bench and put her hand to her chest. "I thought you were being attacked by that maniac or something!"

"At this point I'm not sure which would be worse," Vivian said and sat down, being sure to put her feet up on the bench. "That was one ticked-off reptile!"

Wide-brim hat guy said, "Good news is since it's springtime the snake most likely cannot move very fast. It was out sunning, or warming, its core body temperature."

Vivian narrowed her eyes and looked at him. "Who are you?"

"I'm an employee here. Joseph Phillips, ma'am. We post warnings about snakes and other potential dangers near the entrance."

She pointed into his chest. "Well, that slimy, little guy seemed quite able-bodied to me."

He nodded his head, hesitated, then said, "In reality, snakes are not actually slimy. Their skin appears—"

Vivian outwardly cringed and Wendy butted in. "Thank you, but I think we've had enough reptile facts for the time being."

"Enjoy the rest of your visit," he said and ambled off.

"Let's go have our picnic snackage over there," Lucy said, pointing to a sunny spot near the pond but further from the waterfall.

Vivian didn't feel like eating anything, but remembered the squirty cheese awaiting. Cheese always made things better. "Excellent idea." She hopped of the bench determined to get over the willies from the snake.

The girls sat down in the grass and Lucy dispersed the goodies.

Kate took a bite of asiago and cracker and said with a full mouth, "You know what would make this much better?" She swallowed, then continued, "The Moose Crossing's rattlesnake sausage!"

Wendy laughed and choked on a cheesy cracker. Crumbs flew out of her mouth.

"I know where we can get some fresh!" Lucy said, then popped a grape in her mouth.

"That's my first time to hear a rattlesnake!" Vivian said. "Thank god they come with a built-in alarm system."

They finished up, loaded the remaining items back into Lucy's backpack and walked back to their bikes. Joseph, the employee, nodded as they took off for Vail Pass Trail. It wasn't far to the trail and Lucy made a sharp right turn onto it.

A three foot iron fence separated them from the creek. The mountain cliff went straight up on the other side and trees sprouted out from between the rocks along the banks.

They went along for a mile or so, Lucy and Kate out in front, then Vivian and Wendy brought up the rear. There were no additional snake or nature incidents and no sign of Craig. They came upon the wooden plank bridge crossing Gore Creek and Vivian came to a stop quickly. Wendy had to swerve to keep from slamming into the back of her.

"Is something wrong?" she asked hopping off her bike, looking around.

"My calves are on fire," Vivian said, kicking her legs and flexing her feet. "They burn like an inferno in hell."

Wendy propped her leg up on the rail, touching her nose to her knee. "Hell is an inferno, Viv."

"Exactly!" Vivian watched her stretch. "Geez, you're so bendy!"

"I may not be the most fit, but I'm flexible!" Wendy threw her other leg up, touching her fingers to her toes.

Lucy and Kate reappeared from around the bend.

"What the heck?" Kate said, skidding to a stop beside them.

"I needed a break, my legs are burnin'," Vivian said, looking at her feet and considering bending over to relieve the burn in her calves. "It's official, I'm outta shape."

"Have some water," Lucy said and handed Vivian the line to the CamelBak.

Vivian had a sip of water and looked around, but didn't see anything odd. Like she'd know what odd was for the trail, but she didn't think Craig was lurking close-by. "Let's get a quick picture." She pointed to Wendy and Kate, still on their bikes. "Y'all get together. Let me take a picture of you on the bridge." Snap!

"Now take one of me and Lucy real quick."

Vivian and Lucy posed playfully on the bridge with their bikes as Wendy took the picture. "I *really love* those neon yellow shorts you're wearing," Wendy said to Lucy. "They really pop against the evergreen background."

"Hey! These are my favorite biking shorts," Lucy defended.

"Yeah, you just like that extra padding on your tush," Vivian said, smacking her ass.

She heard a splash and looked over Wendy's shoulder. "What was that?" A few baseball-sized rocks splashed into the creek. Her gaze traveled from the creek up the mountain. "I see something moving up there." *Oh shit, maybe Craig is closer than I thought!*

Lucy pointed to a guy hustling through the trees. "Is that Craig?"

Not taking any chances, Wendy pulled out her phone.

Vivian squinted. "He's too far, I can't tell."

The man was approximately 50 yards away and hauling ass up the cliff.

Kate started pushing Vivian. "Abort! Abort! Let's get out of here!"

32

Vivian and the girls hopped back on their bikes and pedaled as fast as they could away from Gore Creek. In town, Vivian saw a cop getting on his bike in front of a restaurant.

"Help!" She called, squeezing the brake handle. She wobbled as she approached.

"What's the matter?" The officer caught her bike and helped her stop.

Vivian steadied herself with one foot on the ground. "I think the guy that might being trying to kill me is across the creek running on the mountain. You have to help me, please!"

"Slow down and give me some details," the officer requested.

As calm but quickly as she could, Vivian gave him the CliffsNotes version of the Craig situation.

"You can verify all of this with Agent Wade Nelson with the FBI," Wendy said when Vivian was done.

The officer turned around and barked commands into his walkie-talkie. "Go directly to the bike shop and stay there until an officer meets you."

Vivian heard shouting coming from across the creek as they made their way back to the bike shop. The black-haired guy greeted them like he didn't have a care in the world and asked about their ride. Vivian briefly wished she could have a little of whatever he looked like he was on.

Wendy called Nelson and told him what had happened. He promised to be there within 15 minutes. After what felt like much longer, a grim-faced Nelson joined them.

"Did they catch him?" Wendy asked, letting down her ponytail and shaking out her long, brown hair.

"Was it Craig?" Kate asked.

"Vail PD chased the suspect a good way across the mountain and was able to apprehend him."

"And?" Vivian asked.

"It was a local man training for an Ironman, not Craig."

Vivian shook her head in disgust. "Dammit. I was hoping this was over."

Nelson looked at her. "I was hoping so, too. But good job on being vigilant and getting help from the police immediately."

"Thanks."

Bike riding adventure over, Nelson led the girls back to the car.

Kate sat in the passenger seat, legs dangling out of the car. "Son of a biscuit eater, that was freakin' stressful." She let out a big sigh. "I need to relax."

"Amen!" Wendy said. "Where are we going?"

"I'm not going anywhere with Lucy wearing that." She smacked Lucy's banana-yellow ass. "And I think I've had enough excitement for one day."

"Let's just order a pizza and take it back to The Ridge," Lucy said. "There's a Pop's Pizza a few blocks down. It's good stuff."

"That sounds like a good idea," Agent Nelson said, opening the back car door for Wendy. "I'll be right behind you the whole time."

Lucy called Pop's as she drove and ordered two large pizzas, a veggie and a pepperoni. She and Wendy ran inside to pick up the goods.

"Sorry all this crap is ruining our vacation," Vivian said to Kate as they sat in the SUV. "I know it's not turning out like we planned."

"It's okay," Kate said. "It's not your fault. We still got in a nice, scenic bike ride and an unexpected encounter with nature! It just ended with a little more excitement than I was expecting, but I should be used to that with you by now!"

Vivian smiled at her. "I'm not generally a chaos creator. Troublemaker, yes. But not usually chaos."

A few minutes later, Wendy opened the car door and sat down with the two pizzas in her lap.

"I can't wait to get back to The Ridge before I have a piece." Kate turned around from the front seat and flipped open the lid. "It smells fantastic!"

"Mmmm." Vivian reached for a slice.

They munched on pizza while Lucy drove back to the hotel. They dropped the car off with the valet and took their pizza to the fire pit where a middle-aged couple lounged with glasses of wine. Vivian noticed a couple of bottles poking out of a bag.

Nelson had followed them back to the hotel and walked with them out to the fire pit. He sat at a table on Felix's patio and got busy on his phone.

The woman had stylish, cropped black hair. She looked over at Wendy, who carried the pizza. "Gosh, that smells good."

"We'll share if you do." Wendy gestured toward the bag. "We have more than we can eat."

The man wore a sweatshirt depicting a stick figure falling out of raft that read, "I survived the Royal Gorge." He pulled out one of the bottles of wine and sat it on the ledge of the fire pit. "I'll run inside and get a few more glasses."

"Woo-hoo!" Lucy said and then introduced herself and the other girls.

"Nice to meet you," the lady responded. "I'm Anne. My husband's name is Loren."

"Veggie or pepperoni?" Wendy asked.

"Veggie, thanks!" Anne said. "So where are you guys from?"

"We're all from Texas, but Lucy lives in Boulder now. What about y'all?"

"We're visiting from Minnesota. We're on our honeymoon!"

Loren arrived with four glasses, pulled the cork and poured.

"Would you like a slice?" Wendy asked him.

"Sure, thanks," he said and picked out a meaty wedge.

Vivian held up her glass. "Happy honeymoon!"

They clinked and sipped.

"So has it been magical?" Kate asked.

"Yes, absolutely," Anne answered, squeezing Loren's hand. "We went rafting this morning. It was gorgeous and so much fun. Loren went for a swim, though!" She giggled behind her wine glass.

"Yeah, yeah," he laughed. "We hit a rough patch and I got pitched."

Vivian shivered. "Bet that was cold."

"We were all wearing wetsuits, but yes, it was still cold."

Anne finished her slice, then asked, "What about you girls? How's your trip been?"

All four looked at each other, none answering right away, then Vivian spoke up.

"It's not exactly been what we were hoping for. We've hit our own rough patches."

"What do you mean?" Loren asked.

"Vivian's ex-boyfriend is stalking her," Lucy blurted. "He's wanted by the FBI and everything!"

"Oh my gosh, you are *those* ladies," Anne said. "We heard about a guy attacking a woman in the spa this morning."

Vivian waved. "Yep, that's us."

"What happened? Are you okay?" Loren sounded concerned.

Vivian gave a recap and noticed Agent Nelson listening in. She figured she better not give all the details, but then Lucy said, "He escaped through the emergency exit and hasn't been seen since. The cops can't find him. We thought he was spying on us during our bike ride today, but it turned out to be some other poor shmuck in the wrong place at the wrong time."

Nelson walked over and sat down across the fire pit and gave Lucy a stern look.

Loren asked, "What does the guy look like? Should we be concerned?"

Vivian figured the more people who knew what Craig looked like, the better. "I've got his picture right here." She saw Nelson give a slight nod and then handed Anne her phone.

Anne leaned in close and looked at the image. "I think I've seen him," she said and paused a moment before snapping her fingers. "Yes, I'm sure we saw him last night on our way back to our room from dinner. He was dressed in a white jumpsuit, the kind a painter would wear. He got off on the fourth floor, and I remember thinking it was odd that anyone would be working so late." She looked at Loren. "Remember, honey?"

He took the phone from her. "You're right. I thought it was odd, too, but my mind was somewhere else." He gave Anne a grin. "So I didn't ponder it for long."

Nelson jumped up, hitting buttons on his phone, and walked a few feet away. Loren and Anne both watched, questions evident on their faces.

"That's our FBI agent," Lucy said and took a big gulp of wine. "He's protecting us and has a big crush on Wendy."

Wendy shook her head. "No, he doesn't."

"He absolutely does," Kate said. "He's just pretending not to since he's on the job."

Wendy looked at Anne and Loren. "So he was wearing those paint coveralls? Makes me wonder if he's been staying here."

Vivian put down her wine glass. "I hope not. That freaks me out a little." She paused. "Actually, a lot."

"Agent Studmuffin looks like he's on it anyway." Lucy took another big sip of wine.

The Ridge's security officer met Nelson on the patio. Their conversation involved the officer nodding his head while Nelson pointed at the hotel, veins in his neck and forehead popping out. The security guy bowed his head and walked briskly back into the hotel.

Nelson walked over to the group. "Security is headed up to the fourth floor, Avon police are on their way back out, and we'll search the entire hotel again."

"Didn't y'all do that earlier today?" Kate asked.

"This time we'll go over the fourth floor more thoroughly. Somebody evidently missed something. A forensics tech with Avon is on his way as well."

"Geez," Vivian said and slumped back in her rocking chair.

Loren stood and poured the rest of the wine into the girls' glasses and picked up the empties. "Nice to meet you. I think we'll turn in for the night. We'll keep an eye out and alert security if we see…what's his name?"

"Craig," the girls all groaned in unison.

"Yes, if we see Craig again."

"Thanks for the pizza," Anne called over her shoulder as she hurried after Loren.

Everyone said their goodnights and goodbyes.

"Are you sure we're going to be safe here?" Kate asked Nelson.

He was about to answer when his phone rang. He looked at the display, then said, "We're going to interview all of the construction workers and issue special badges that will be required for entry to the property." He walked away and answered his phone.

"I can't believe Craig has been on the property and no one from the security team recognized him." Vivian finished her wine and put the glass on the ledge, but it was unbalanced and fell. The glass shattered. "Dammit!"

Wendy knelt down and picked up the pieces. "Calm down, Viv. Craig wouldn't have wanted to be seen. He probably snuck around and used side entrances and stuff." She tossed the broken bits into the trash.

Nelson walked back over, hands on hips. "There's been a development on the fourth floor. I'm going to take you to your room, where you need to stay."

Shit.

33

Vivian locked the deadbolt to their Presidential Suite.

"That'll stop him!" Lucy yelled.

"It's another layer anyway," Vivian said.

"Since we're not allowed to leave," Lucy said as she leaned against the kitchen cabinet, "I vote we hop our asses into the monstrous bathtub — not naked, though — and pretend like we're in one of the hot tubs outside."

"I'm in," Kate said. "I'll get my suit on."

Wendy grabbed one of their wine bottles and a camera. "I'll get everything ready for us."

Vivian looked out the sliding glass doors to the balcony and the hot tub down below. "I wish we didn't have to pretend. I'd rather be down there." She went to get her suit and yelled, "Damn that Craig!"

Suited up, Vivian joined Wendy, who was squeezing an entire mini-bottle of shampoo under the stream of water. A small mound of bubbles grew to a mountain.

Vivian stepped in and settled among the suds. "I need me a tub this big at home. This is fun!"

Kate got in, corralled some bubbles and blew them at Vivian. "That bottle made a whole lotta bubbles."

"We need more!" Wendy cracked open another shampoo and dumped it under the water.

Lucy came in and sat on the edge of the tub. She placed both feet in the water and started to stand up but slipped and landed on her butt. She disappeared under the veil of bubbles, which flew everywhere, and water sloshed over the edge of the tub.

Wendy reached down and fished Lucy out. "Good thing we're staying in tonight, but how about you not drown on us? That would really jack up our vacation."

Vivian did her usual point and laugh at Lucy. "You've got bubbles on your head and a bubble beard. You look like Santa with boobs."

Kate, always the sympathetic one, said, "Aw, Luce, you okay? That looked like it hurt."

Lucy wiped bubbles and water off her face and out of her eyes. "I'm fine, I'll survive."

This got Vivian to singing "I Will Survive," and the other girls joined in as Wendy handed everyone a plastic cup of wine.

"I've got to go get my suit on, I'll be back in a sec."

Vivian thought about her kids. "I'm going to have to steal some of this shampoo off the cart. The kids would love this. These bubbles are practically unpoppable!"

"Is bath time difficult with your crew?" Kate asked.

"Nahhhh. I line 'em all up in the tub. There's not enough room for anyone to go under and drown, unlike in here with Lucy. It's efficient for me and they have fun."

Wendy came in wearing her cowboy hat and holding everyone else's. "I think this is a photo op!" She passed out the hats, sat the camera on the counter and set the timer, then yee-hawed as she jumped in the middle of the tub.

That was the first of many silly pictures of the evening, some of which included bubble beards, sudsy legs all in the air and a hats-off salute.*

They continued on with good ol' tub time until they heard banging at the door.

"Oh my god, who is that?" Lucy said before ducking under the water.

"It's probably Agent Nelson," Kate said. "It's been a while since he left."

Vivian looked at Wendy. "You're closest. Go let him in!"

Wendy got out and ran to the door, not bothering with a towel and leaving a trail of bubbly water in her wake. She peeked through the peephole and saw Wade, phone to his ear. She unlocked the deadbolt and swung the door open.

He lowered the phone and stared at her. "What the hell? I was about to kick down the door. This was dead-bolted and you locked the door to my adjoining room."

"Sorry, didn't realize your door was locked. We are soaking in the bathtub, come on in."

He glanced down at her and then at the trail of bubbles leading out of the bedroom. His left eye twitched and he followed her to the master bath.

Vivian noticed his bulging jaw muscles and clenched fist and knew he was pissed. *Oopsie.*

"I've been calling you," he said.

"You have? I haven't heard it ring." She looked at her phone, and showed it to Nelson. "See, no missed calls."

He huffed, but there was nothing to be said. He looked down, noticing he was standing in water.

Wendy grabbed a towel and threw it onto the water-covered floor. "Lucy had an accident."

The girls all laughed.

After a moment Nelson brought them back to reality. "Listen, we need to talk about what we found on the fourth floor."

"Did y'all catch him?" Lucy asked.

"No, but we did find the painter's clothing he left behind. I doubt he'll be trying that stunt again."

"Is that where he spent the night?" Vivian asked.

"We found an empty bag of chips and a beef jerky package. The forensics tech will obtain DNA from the items and try to confirm identification, but it was likely him."

"It was. He loves that crap," Vivian said.

Wendy, a recent vegetarian convert, said, "Ick."

"Was he in a room?" Kate asked.

"He was hiding out in one of the rooms that had already been renovated. How he had access, we're not quite sure but are working on it."

Vivian shook her head. "I'm surprised with all you've done with hotel security and the local guys that he's just waltzing around the property. Who's in control here?"

Nelson stayed silent.

"So what's next?" Vivian asked. "What do we do from here?"

Nelson shook his head. "I recommend you either go home, or stay right here, in the hotel."

Vivian slapped at a bubble. "We have to do something. I'm not going home until Craig has been caught and I don't see how sitting around here all day is going to accomplish that."

Everyone was quiet for a minute.

"What about whitewater rafting?" Kate said as if Nelson hadn't protested. "I know we didn't have plans to do that, but if we plan it tonight we can have your team set up and in place along the route."

Nelson's face twitched. "I'm not going to get authorization for a team and I won't be able to raft with you."

Kate kept going. "We could do the Royal Gorge like Anne and Loren did today, though hopefully none of us will be swimmers."

Vivian was apprehensive. "I don't know. I've never rafted before, much less in whitewater with a stalker after me."

"There is no way you should even consider this," Nelson said adamantly.

Lucy's previous drunkenness seemed to disappear. "I've done that trip before. The water moves pretty fast, so it technically makes you a moving target, not easy to catch. Plus, we'll all be with you, Viv. What could happen?"

Vivian nodded, thinking it over.

"Craig could be waiting for us at the end," Wendy said.

Nelson walked off down the hall, then came back to the doorway. "This is not safe. It is absolutely not a good idea. Even if I was able to assemble a team, there's no way we could completely control the situation."

Vivian popped a bubble. "Fact is, you can't completely control any situation. Craig is totally unpredictable and he could choose to come after me tomorrow regardless of what I do and where I am, or he could be on his way to Rio de Janeiro. But either way, I'm not going to sit here and do nothing. I have to take calculated risks before I take this home with me. I am willing to risk rafting tomorrow in order to draw him out. The question is, will you be there to apprehend him if he shows up?"

Nelson's face was flushed and he looked like he could snort steam. He turned and marched off. The door to his adjoining hotel room slammed.

"I think he's officially pissed." Lucy said.

"Well, I am too. And I'm gettin' pruney," Vivian said, looking at her fingers. "I'm gettin' out." She grabbed a towel.

Kate popped the drain, and then Lucy got out, too.

They dressed, went into the kitchen and hit the snackage. They huddled around the coffee table, on the floor by the couches. They tore into fruit, cheese and crackers. Wendy poured them a last cup of vino.

As they rehashed the day, Vivian's emotions started to get the best of her.

"I've gotta do what I've gotta do to end this here," she said. "But I don't want to put y'all in any danger."

Wendy grabbed Vivian's arm. "Look, we're in this together, just like Mexico. That's what friends do."

Kate agreed. "None of us want him out there. Your sweet kids…I couldn't go home knowing something could happen around them."

"We're gonna catch that dirty rat bastard." Lucy smacked the table. "How dare he screw with my brakes, then screw with you. He's goin' down!"

Nelson opened the door to his room and walked over to the girls. "Agent Cervantes and I are strongly against you girls whitewater rafting tomorrow. We don't know to what extent Craig will go to get to Vivian."

The girls all started to protest at once and he held up his hand. "As with the bike ride this afternoon, the FBI can't stop you from going, only advise you against it. We won't be there should you come into any danger. In fact, I'm going back to Denver first thing in the morning. You need to pay extra attention to your surroundings at all times tomorrow, from the time you leave here in the morning to when you return. Get back here before dark. If at any time any of you think you're in danger, call me immediately."

Lucy looked at Nelson. "I'm familiar with where we're going and having rafted the Gorge before, I think it's one of the river trips where Craig would have the least access to her. We'll be careful."

Nelson got up. "As far as I'm concerned, Craig is a loose cannon." He looked at his watch.

Lucy took notice. "We better get to bed. We need to leave by 6 to make it to the rafting place on time."

"Holy crap, is that 6 in the morning?" Wendy asked.

"It's a ways away."

Wendy looked at Vivian. "You sure you want to do this?"

"As long as y'all are with me."

"We'll be there, Kate said, getting up from the couch.

Vivian looked at her phone, 12:02. She picked up the processed cheese can and squirted a last dab into a swirl on her finger. "I agree."

They said goodnight to Nelson and went to their various bedrooms.

After brushing her teeth and getting her jammies on, Vivian crawled into bed next to Lucy, who was already snoring lightly. The bed conformed to her body and the pillow was just right, but she couldn't relax.

Nelson popped his head in the door.

"I feel like I'm back on a band trip," Vivian joked, "and you're doing a room check."

Nelson opened the door a little more. She could only make out his silhouette.

"My priority is your safety and I have some concerns," he said. "Please call me as soon as you're off the river tomorrow."

"Will do and thanks," she said quietly, pulling the covers to her chin.

He pulled the door to where only a crack of light remained. Vivian squirmed and couldn't keep her eyes closed. Images of Craig flashed through her mind, and concern for her children kept her unsettled. The light that shone beneath the door went out, and finally, uneasily, she drifted off.

34

Day 5

L et's go, let's go!"

Vivian awoke to the overhead light being flipped on and off at a strobe-light, seizure inducing pace. Lucy was hollering for her to get out of bed. Then she moved to the blackout shades, tearing them open with the force the jaws of life ripping open an annihilated car.

"Time to rise and shine. We've got a criminal to catch."

Vivian's eyes felt like sandpaper; 5:30 a.m. sucked. She had slept fitfully and wasn't ready to start the day. Then, the thought of Craig and her kids propelled her out of bed. "All right, already, I'm up."

Lucy opened the door to Wendy and Kate's room and start clapping.

"Hup, hup, hup, hup! Mooooooooove it. We roll out in t-minus-20."

Wendy groaned and rolled over, then yelled, "Shut the hup up!"

The girls got ready and grabbed bananas, snack bars and trail mix. Before heading out the door, they found Nelson's note and map on the kitchen counter. He had highlighted the best route and written a note saying not to stop on the way there or back and to be careful. The door to his room was open and his belongings were gone.

Kate called the valet and the girls headed out the door. Lucy's SUV waited in the drive and they all got in.

She turned to Vivian. "You ready?"

Vivian slapped her palm on the dash. "Let's roll."

Lucy headed down the mountain and merged onto I-70 as the sun broke above the mountains in front of them. Light traffic left nowhere for Craig to hide, and Vivian felt good about their rafting adventure and the day ahead. She didn't think they'd be in any real danger, other than the rapids, but was betting Craig would surface at some point. Vermin were like that.

"Anyone need to stop?" Lucy asked as she exited to U.S. 9 in Frisco.

No one did, so they kept rolling.

Vivian and Lucy chatted quietly as they took the bypass around Breckenridge. Wendy and Kate were in the back, studying their eyelids. As they ascended Hoosier Pass, Lucy took the sharp curves like a pro, but it stirred the sleeping beauties and caused a firestorm of foul-mouth frenzy from Wendy. Vivian gripped the "oh shit" handle and added a few choice words of her own as they hit one of the curves hard.

"Ye of little faith," Lucy said, steering with one arm. "I managed to save us when the brakes went out. These turns are *no problemo*."

Kate opened her eyes and looked a little pale. She tugged her seatbelt tighter.

Vivian's ears popped as they crested the pass. She loosened her grip as Lucy cruised down the mostly straight descent. Soon the highway flattened out and the mountains were in the distance. As they approached the town of Hartsel, Vivian's bottle of water had caught up with her. "My bladder is speaking to me, and it's not saying very nice things."

Kate seconded the motion.

"I don't know," Lucy said. "Nelson said not to stop, and therefore this town isn't 'authorized.' "

Vivian looked at Lucy. "Unless you want my bladder to speak to your seat, you need to pull over."

She pointed out the Kum-N-Go sign just ahead. Lucy parked and Vivian ran for the door.

Post potty break, the girls loaded up on more water, powdered donuts, milk and coffee. They hit the road and it wasn't long before Lucy pulled to a stop in front of the Clear Creek Rafting Company. Lucy shut off the engine. The girls sat in silence for a moment.

Vivian broke it. "Look, I appreciate y'all offering to go with me to do this. You're the greatest friends ever, but maybe I should go alone."

"Hell, no!" Lucy said.

"We told you yesterday, we're all in this together," Wendy said, reaching for the door handle.

"Yeah!" Kate said. "Let's go bait that hook and reel 'em in!"

The girls woo-hooed and went inside where two tall guys were at the counter, signing forms and chatting it up with a blue-eyed, sandy-blonde girl. She had a big grin on her face. As Vivian walked up the guys slid over to make room. The blonde, Kirsten, blushed and then went over the highlights on the forms. Vivian snickered on some of the verbiage, holding the rafting company responsible for mishaps was the least of her worries, but she signed anyway.

Paperwork done, Kirsten went about getting the girls outfitted. Vivian stepped into a dressing room and got down to her swimsuit. She took off her necklace and wrapped it in her shirt. She went to work, tugging a wetsuit up her legs one at a time, then wiggled and twisted to get her arms through the holes. Zipping it over her boobs proved to be a problem so she wiggled and twisted some more. "This thing is tight!" she yelled out. Then she sat on the floor to pull on the dank boots and then wondered how she was going to get back up. She managed, then slipped on the bright blue splashguard jacket. *Craig oughtta be able to spot us in these!*

Once they were suited up, Kate gathered the girls into a huddle. "Keep your peepers peeled today for anything suspicious and let's stick together. No falling out of the raft, the water's going to be frigid."

"Do you think we'll need a code word if we see something?" Lucy asked.

The side of Vivian's mouth twitched. "I doubt Craig will be close enough to hear what we're saying. I don't think it's necessary."

"I want a code word!" Lucy said.

Vivian smiled. "Fine, have a code word. Ice cream?"

"Nahhh," said Lucy. "Let's spice it up. How about 'hot tamales.' "

They all agreed.

The girls walked out to an old, beat-up school bus where the rest of the group waited, ready for the drive to the river. Vivian did a scan of everyone before taking a seat. None of the five guys and two guides even remotely resembled Craig. The one other woman sure didn't resemble him.

As they drove along, the guide, a man with long, stringy, light-brown hair named Fast Eddie, explained they would be rafting through Bighorn Sheep Canyon this morning, stop for lunch and then continue on the Arkansas River through the Royal Gorge. They pulled to a stop in a gravel parking lot and piled out. Two bright blue, eight-man rafts sat along the riverbank.

Vivian giggled and turned away from the group.

"What's so funny?" Kate asked.

Vivian cut her eyes to a tall, lanky rafter. "His wetsuit is pretttttty tight and a little revealing." She covered her mouth to keep from laughing.

"Maybe his package is packin'," Kate giggled.

Lucy gasped. Loudly.

Wendy smacked her on the arm. "Shhhhhhhhh! No one's packing!"

Fast Eddie broke them into groups, taking the girls, Package and another guy, of whom all 6-foot-2 looked military down to his buzz cut, square jaw and muscular build. Vivian felt like she was in good hands between these two and the professional guide. Crazy Kendall, the other guide, took the two other guys and the older couple from Alabama. Eddie went over safety precautions, how to not die in the event they fell out of the raft, how to get a swimmer back in the raft, etc. "Does anyone have medication or anything else important that needs to go in the dry bag?" he asked.

Vivian held up her phone. "Sorry, I didn't mean to bring this." That was a lie. She had brought it for tracking purposes.

Eddie tossed it into the bag, then handed out helmets. "These do not come off unless you're at lunch. Or dead."

As they walked to their raft Vivian smacked Lucy on the ass with her paddle and started a paddle/sword fight among the girls. Kate lunged forward, her paddle clanking against Vivian's and knocking it to the ground.

Fast Eddie got between them. "Unless you'd like to be paddled by me, I recommend you stop."

The girls froze and looked at each other, knowing they'd gotten in trouble. He then put them in the raft on the side of the sandy bank.

Vivian reached to grab her paddle and saw Wendy turn toward the back of the raft.

"Whatcha lookin' for?"

"Dammit! Instinct! I was looking for the beer cooler."

Lucy shook her head. "This ain't the Guadalupe, honey. You won't find any beer on this trip. It's ill advised."

"I know, it's just ingrained in my river sense!"

"As if you have *any* sense by the time you get off the Guadalupe. Come on!" Vivian said.

Eddie hopped into the back of the raft and showed them how to secure themselves by sticking one foot under the side. Then he provided a paddling lesson. "Forward right two means that you three over here paddle forward two times. Together! Watch the person in front of you and get into a rhythm. Forward left three," he pointed, "means this side of the raft paddles three times." Then he went over back right, back left and together paddling.

"One last thing, people," Eddie said, then snarled, showing gaps in his teeth. He pointed to his mouth. "This here is what we call 'summer teeth,' as in some are here, some are in the boat, some are in the water and some are long gone. At all times your hand must stay on the t-grip of your paddle. All it takes is one slip, then WHACK! You've got summer teeth. Or, your neighbor does, and they won't be real happy with you."

They put on their life preservers and waded into the water and one by one jumped into the raft, getting to their designated spots.

"Holy crap, that water's freezing!" Kate yelled.

"It's melted snow," Lucy responded. "What'd ya expect?"

"And where is the sun?" Vivian said. "That'd help warm things up."

The gray skies showed no promise of sunshine or increase in temperature. The cool morning in the 50s would continue into a cool afternoon in the 50s. Brrrrr.

Vivian and Lucy sat in the front, Kate and Wendy in the middle, and Buzz Cut, who introduced himself to Vivian as Galvin Shick, and Package as Freddie Smith. Fast Eddie took his spot on the back of the raft, in the middle and started shouting out paddling commands.

The other boat launched soon after and pulled alongside. A burly guy in his fifties sat across from his wife, who snapped pictures as he posed with his paddle. Crazy Kendall shouted instructions, which the couple ignored. "Quit posing and get paddling." Kendall's chin-length, strawberry-blond hair curled up around his helmet and a few strands hung in his face.

Fast Eddie told them about their first set of rapids which were coming up. "This is a Class IV called Spike Buck," he said. "And if you don't listen to me, it'll buck ya right outta this raft."

The water moved faster, and the sound of rushing water grew louder.

"This is so fun!" Vivian said. "I need to pee again, though!"

"There's no potty breaks on this river 'til lunch," Eddie said, then he called, "Everybody forward three!"

They worked together propelling the raft through the rapids. As they hit the first big drop, a wave of water crashed the front of the raft. It washed over Vivian, taking her breath away, but the worst of it was the water that made its way inside the neck of her splashguard and trickled down her back.

Motherfudrucker! That's worse than the giant splash I just took.

Eddie yelled, "Back left, back left." But it didn't stop them from crashing into a car-sized boulder, spinning them around.

They all screamed, and were now going backward, but Eddie kept his cool. "Left back three," he yelled, "right forward three!" He steered them out of the rapids and into slower moving water.

He had them coast while the second raft went through Spike Buck. Crazy Kendall was yelling and screaming at the burly man, who had hunkered down in the bottom of the raft. "Get your ass outta there, you're going to pop us!"

The man steadied himself on the side. "I slipped."

Everyone safely through the first rapid, Fast Eddie started up again with the commands. The landscape transitioned from forest and flat to steep cliff walls and red rock.

The river narrowed and Vivian scanned both sides of the cliffs for Craig. She shrugged off an ominous feeling, then glanced at Kate.

"We got ya covered."

Vivian tried to relax.

"Listen up, people," Eddie called out. "We've got three big ones in a row, and one of 'em's a monster called Shark's Tooth. If you don't follow my instructions, I guarantee we'll be eaten alive."

35

Vivian steeled herself. She was ready for this, she could do this. *Yeah!*

Fast Eddie called out command after command and they sailed through the first set of rapids, no problem. The second set posed more difficulty, but with everyone working together, they made it without incident. Then came Shark's Tooth. The current grabbed them and slammed them head on into the pointed boulder. Out of the corner of her eye, Vivian saw someone become a projectile. They were long gone. The raft taco'ed against the boulder and everyone in it was the meat. The water continuously slammed against one side of their "taco shell" and had them stuck.

"Everyone get up on the rock side, up on the rock side!" Fast Eddie shouted and shoved Kate and Lucy that direction.

Shick helped Wendy move over and Vivian threw herself on top of the dog pile, which created enough leverage to dislodge the raft. Everyone rolled around, getting footing and back into place.

"Hot tamales!" Lucy said, adjusting her helmet.

"Little late for that," Wendy said.

"Who'd we lose?" Eddie asked. "I saw someone fly out."

"Smith went for a swim," Shick said.

"There he is!" Vivian pointed to a waterlogged Smith, who clung to a rock downstream.

As they approached, Lucy put down her paddle, braced herself against the side and reached down to grab him. She dunked him, then pulled with all her might, propelling herself backward, and he landed on top of her. He scrambled up, thanking her.

Shick handed Smith his paddle, which had been plucked from the river. "Way to go."

Smith's teeth chattered too much for him to make a remark.

Eddie called to Lucy. "That was textbook. He outweighs you by at least a hundred pounds, and you pulled him in like he was nothing."

Lucy nodded coolly, acting quite satisfied with herself. "I work out."

"Hey, man, you okay?" Eddie asked Smith, who just nodded. "Your ass flew. You're lucky you didn't do a header into the shark's tooth."

"I barely missed it," Smith said. "I'm good."

"Paddle's up!" Eddie said, raising his, and they did a group paddle high-five.

Vivian heard a whistle and looked over to the right bank. The group in the other raft had stopped for lunch. Crazy Kendall waded into the water and helped pull their raft ashore.

"I've heard of the raft taco but never seen it with my own eyes," he said. "That was freakin' awesome, man!"

"Yeah, that was great," Wendy said, following Lucy up the bank.

Kendall slapped Smith on the back. "And you, the human cannonball!"

Still shivering, Smith said, "That was my favorite part."

Eddie and Kendall started making super long submarine sandwiches for lunch and set out some fruit. The girls huddled together by a picnic table, freezing in the cool air, the sun still covered by clouds.

"Holy shit, I'm a Popsicle," Vivian said.

"Your lips *are* blue," Kate said.

"I'm not getting back in the front. I don't know who's getting up there, but it ain't gonna be me."

"I have hypothermia," Lucy said softly, hunched over, fists balled up to her chest. "I'm not getting back up there, either."

"We took the brunt of the splashage," Vivian said, "and it's just too damn cold."

"Let's make the guys get up there," Kate said. "That's sure to shrink things up!"

"Dammit, just when I'd quit thinking about it," Wendy said through chattering teeth. "Great idea on stickin' them up front, though."

"They can shield us from the splashes," Kate said.

Wendy glanced at the portable toilets. "I'm so cold right now. The thought of taking off this wetsuit in the cold air, nuh-uh."

Vivian looked down at the mud around her feet. "Just pee in your wetsuit like I did."

"What?" Lucy said. "When did you do that?"

Vivian laughed. "Sorry, I had to go and didn't want to take all of this off. It warmed me up for a minute, but now I'm cold again."

Lucy moved between Wendy and Kate. "How am I friends with you?"

"And you have to wear that all day," Wendy said. "Gross!"

"I was cold. I dare ya to get your ass in that Port-o-Potty and take it all off."

Wendy groaned. Kate, too.

Lucy handed Kate her life preserver. "I'm going in."

The other girls sat down at the bench and Kendall passed them plates. "Lunch is ready. Dig in."

For two guys with summer teeth, they prepared a nice spread. A watermelon bowl held an assortment of fresh fruit, baked chips, three kinds of sandwiches and brownies for dessert. Only water and lemonade to drink, though, nothing hot.

They served themselves and picked a picnic table. "I would die for a cup of hot chocolate right now," Vivian said, swinging her leg over the bench.

"Don't say that kind of stuff," Kate said, alarmed.

"What? I'm probably going to die of hypothermia anyway!"

"No, you're not." Kate put her arm around Vivian.

"Aww, you love me even though I peed."

Kate whispered in Vivian's ear. "I did, too!"

The two guys from the other raft sat down at their table. They introduced themselves as Brian Finck, a red-head, and Mike Hayes, a cute, brown-haired, blue-eyed guy. Brian needed to reapply sunscreen to his freckled face and Mike did his best to disguise the shivering in his 5-foot-8 frame.

"Having a good time?" Vivian asked.

"Freezing my ass off," Brian responded and Mike asked how they were enjoying the trip.

Vivian laughed. "A little less cold would be nice. It's been an adventure so far, that's for sure."

Smith sat down. "Yeah, yeah, I did that on purpose. Needed to cool off."

Everyone laughed.

"We're going to let you really cool off," Wendy said. "In the front of the raft. That'll put things in proportion."

Vivian nudged her with her elbow, but not before Kate spewed water across the table.

"Oh, I mean perspective," Wendy snickered.

Lucy rejoined them. "What'd I miss?"

"Shick and Smith have agreed to take our spots on the raft. We're in the back of the bus now." Vivian took a big bite of her sandwich.

Lucy slapped Smith on the back. "Good job, guys. Way to be chivalrous."

The girls finished their lunch and helped to clean up.

"Back to business," Kendall said, pushing his raft off the bank. "Big water awaits."

The groups got into their rafts, Vivian making damn sure she and Lucy were in the back, with Shick and Smith up front. Fast Eddie shoved them off and explained what was next.

"We've got a little bit of calm followed by a few rapids, but then we hit the Narrows. We have to hit it on the left side to enter the Boat Eater in the sweet spot. It's fast, it's furious, and it can be a total fuck-up if you fail."

Lucy lifted her paddle for a high-five. "To no fuck-ups!"

The rafters slapped paddles and turned their attention to the task ahead.

Eddie slapped his paddle on the water. "Make sure you smile real pretty for the camera. He's usually sittin' on a rock in the middle of the Boat Eater. Gets paid the big bucks to sit on his ass all day. Works his index finger real hard, snapping pictures of you folks trying not to die on the river."

36

The canyon walls closed in and the water moved faster as the rafts approached the Narrows. Crazy Kendall maneuvered into a calm spot behind a rock, giving Fast Eddie's crew first shot at this set of rapids.

"It's time for the ride of your life, so listen up, folks," Eddie said, then called, "Everyone forward three."

The raft rode the waves and everyone paddled forward per instructions. Vivian's paddle struck a rock, but she got back in rhythm on the next stroke. The raft bounced off boulders, and they continued to paddle through whitewater. They maneuvered through two more sets of Class IV rapids and then cruised underneath the Royal Gorge Bridge. Spanning more than 1,000 feet above, it signaled they were within the national park.

Halfway up the cliffs on the left, a gondola descended to the scenic overlook. People milled about on the platform and at the railing. *I wonder if Craig is up there,* Vivian thought.

Shick watched the overlook as they coasted swiftly past it. The whitewater started again and Eddie yelled more commands to keep the raft going left, toward the mouth of the Boat Eater rapids.

The group paddled in sync, and Vivian felt good about making it through. After the first drop, a curtain of water washed over them and unhinged that feeling, but their momentum and the continued paddling carried them forward. Next drop, they hit a rock on the left side but kept moving. A minute later, the right side of the raft slammed up against a boulder. Pop! Air hissed out the side below Vivian. She screamed as she lost her balance and fell in. Wendy also fell backward into the water, grabbing Smith, taking him with her.

Damn, this is cold! Speeding downstream out of control, Vivian's leg smacked into a boulder underneath the surface. *Ouch, that hurt! Don't panic, don't panic.* She remembered to face downriver and put her feet out in front of her, like Eddie had showed them. She tried to turn and look for the raft and the rest of the group, but the force of the water was too much. She tumbled over a three-foot drop and got sucked under, breathing in the Arkansas River.

I'm going to drown.

She churned, flip after flip, in the falls, unable to get above water.

No! I can't die, the SPS cannot raise my children.

A tug on the back of her life vest had Vivian's head above water. She sputtered and coughed, lungs burning from the influx of water.

"Swim left!" Shick was in her face, yelling above the roar.

Vivian kicked her legs and gasped for air. He hauled her up onto the bank and she collapsed on the sand. She heard a scream and saw Kate whiz past, holding her paddle. Wendy wasn't far behind, still clinging onto Smith.

Shick scrambled back into the water, yelling for them to swim over. He tried to reach them, but the current pushed them downriver too quickly. Kate crawled onto their side of the bank 30 yards down. Wendy and Smith wound up on the opposite bank even farther down.

Vivian sat up, still coughing up water. "Where's Lucy?" She scanned the river but didn't see her. "Luuuuuccccyyyyyyyyy!" She looked for a yellow helmet to pop out of the water but didn't see one. She stumbled back into the river. "Luuuuuuuccccyyyyyyyyyyy!"

"There, over there!" Shick pointed across to the other bank. Lucy stood on top of a rock, paddle in hand, waving it furiously.

Vivian fought off tears of relief and waved back. Then realization sunk in. How the hell were they going to get off this river?

Kate picked her way along the boulders, making her way to Vivian. "You okay?" she asked.

"I'm going to have a killer bruise on my leg, but I'm okay. You?"

"I'm fine, and look, I saved my paddle!"

Vivian looked across the river and heard shouting. Fast Eddie hung off the side of Crazy Kendall's raft, yelling at the group to paddle over to his crippled raft, which had wrapped around a boulder. Mike grabbed the rope of the semi-deflated raft and hauled it with them as they pulled to the right bank by Wendy and Smith.

Eddie went to work transferring what was left of the supplies from his dead raft to Kendall's.

Kendall called to Vivian, Kate and Shick, "Just hang tight. Another raft will be coming through soon. They'll pick you up."

Vivian pointed to Lucy sitting on the boulder. "What about her?"

"We'll get her. Eddie's gonna stay here until you're picked up."

Wendy and Smith crawled into the raft and sat on the center section.

They shoved off and went back for Lucy, who leapt off the boulder into the center of the raft, landing on the burly guy. Smith helped her up and she took a spot next to Wendy on the center tube.

As they floated past, Lucy yelled, "Are y'all okay?"

"Yes!" Kate said. "Guess we'll see ya later!"

Vivian sat down on the bank, the adrenaline wearing off and the freezing cold seeping into her bones. She wrapped her arms around her knees and started to cry. "I can't stop shaking. And I think I might throw up."

Kate sat and hugged her. "It's cold."

"Actually, she's most likely experiencing the effects of adrenaline," Shick said. "The body produces adrenaline in a fight-or-flight situation, releasing dopamine as a natural painkiller. It allows the muscles to perform respiration at an increased rate, which improves strength. Unfortunately, the post-adrenaline affects include nausea and emotional responses as well. Crying, anger…"

"Plus it's cold as shit," Kate said. "Adrenaline, yes, but she's probably hypothermic."

Vivian started to laugh. "I watched this show on TV where the guy fell into a frozen pond, so in order to survive he got completely naked." She reached for the buckle on her life preserver.

Shick stopped her. "I think he was most likely wearing regular clothes and not a wetsuit, which is designed to help you maintain warmth."

Vivian shook her head. "Well, this shit ain't working."

37

Vivian and Kate huddled together for warmth on the left bank of the Arkansas River while Shick did jumping jacks, pushups and sit-ups to keep warm. On the opposite bank, Fast Eddie passed the time by inspecting their deflated raft.

Vivian kept her eyes focused upriver, waiting for the first sign of a raft coming to their rescue. She didn't know how much longer she could stand Shick's exuberance, much less the cold. She looked away for a few seconds to check on Eddie and his progress when Shick ran splashing back into the river.

He had grabbed a paddle and used it to wave at an oncoming raft. This caught Eddie's attention, and he pointed vigorously toward his stranded rafters. The guide raised his paddle in acknowledgment.

Thank God. We're going to be rescued!

They all watched as the raft made it through the Boat Eater without tacoing, tumping or taking on too much water. Their guide steered toward Shick, who waited in the water to pull them ashore.

"I see you showered today," the guide said as he pulled up.

"We went for a little swim, but the hot water was out," Shick said.

"Pile in, river rats."

The four other passengers moved aside to make room. Vivian's teeth chattered as Shick helped her into the raft. "Thank you for picking us up," she said to the guide.

"Gotta share the river love."

"I'm all about the river love today," Kate said as she sat down in the middle of the raft by Vivian. "But I'll be happy when this love affair is over."

"But the fun was just getting started," Shick said as he pushed off and then jumped in the raft.

"Sorry 'bout my freeloaders, Jessie," Eddie called as they floated past. "Here's my dry bag." He tossed it over and Jessie caught it.

"Chicken Hawk is on the loose, he'll take you to the prom," Jessie responded, hitchin' his thumb over his shoulder.

Eddie gave a salute and the rafters turned their attention to the next set of rapids coming up, Lion's Head. Vivian braced her feet under the bench in front of her and was glad she didn't have to paddle anymore. Her arms ached from paddling and swimming, and her leg throbbed where she had whacked it. Her frayed nerves just weren't up to the task. The new crew performed like champs, and they were out of the rapid in no time.

"Suck it, Lion!" Jessie said, then slapped his paddle flat on the water. "Yeah!"

"I think he has his own way with words," Kate said with a laugh.

Shick shook his head. "He might be under the influence of a substance or substances."

"Whatever," Vivian said. "He's getting us where we need to go."

Jessie guided them through one last Class III rapid and then coasted a short jaunt to the exit point. Shick jumped out to help pull the boat ashore, and Jessie said, "River rock stars!"

Vivian was glad to out of the raft. The last few steps in the water brought fiery stabs of pain shooting up her leg. Craig spying on her was a faraway thought. All she wanted was warmth. Fast. And a couple of ibuprofen.

Crazy Kendall met them at the bank and led Vivian and Kate directly onto the waiting bus. Smith greeted them as they stepped on, and Lucy and Wendy cheered. Mike gave them a wave from the back row. Brian was behind the bus talking on the phone.

Vivian sat next to Lucy and asked the driver, "Is there a heater? I think I might die from exposure."

The driver shook his head and said, "We'll get you back to the shop soon."

Lucy looked even paler than normal, and Vivian didn't know that was possible. "You look almost translucent. I'm going to start calling you Casper."

"I'll start calling you Big Blue then, since that's the color of your lips."

"If I don't get warm soon," Wendy said from the seat behind them, "I think I'm not going to make it. I'm so cold that it hurts the blood vessels in my elbows to move my arms. They might shatter and I'll bleed to death."

Kate sat hunched in a ball. "Thank goodness I'm not pregnant. My body temperature over the last several hours would have been detrimental."

"It could have been your baby's first brain freeze," Vivian said. "But not in a good, ice-cream lickin' kinda way."

Shick hopped on the bus and sat down in front of Vivian and Lucy, slapping the seat back. "Hot damn, that was fun! You girls ready to do it again?" His smile looked like he genuinely wanted to get back on that freezing-ass, melted-snow river and raft again. Hell, maybe even swim it.

"It was fun until the raft deflated," Vivian said, "but there's no way you're getting me back out on that river today, or any other day, until the weather warms up at least 30 degrees."

"The cold is all part of the fun."

Okay, this guy might really be insane. Cold is part of the fun? Not this cold!

Lucy looked at Shick and laughed. "I'm all for rafting in cold water, but this was too much. If I don't get warm soon, I might start losing fingers and toes. I could really use some hot soup right about now."

"I could go for some dinner," Wendy said. "The stress of the raft deflating and subsequent swim has made me ravenous."

"I could go for a drink, or three," Vivian said. "A cup of hot chocolate spiked with peppermint schnapps and Baileys sounds perfect right about now."

"Chocolate," Kate said with a faraway look in her eye. "Yes, chocolate."

The bus bumped into the rafting company's parking lot and lurched to a stop. The girls got out and made a beeline for the door.

Kirsten met the girls and led them to where they could get out of their wet clothes and rinse off. Vivian wanted all of the above but fumbled with the Velcro on the splashguard and zipper on her boots because her hands were so cold. She managed to get down to her bathing suit and rinsed off with the hose. The water wasn't warm, but it was warmer than she was, so she went for it. She grabbed a towel and headed to a changing room. Finally in dry clothes, she ran her fingers through her curls, put on her necklace and slapped her cowgirl hat on her head. *Done.*

Vivian walked into the gift shop area and saw Shick, Smith and Mike outside examining the deflated raft with Fast Eddie.

The other girls had finished changing and were at the photo counter with Brian, scrolling through the shots at Boat Eater.

"That's where you fell out," Kate said, pointing to Vivian in the photo.

"And there went Wendy!" Lucy laughed at the next photo that popped up. "I love that you took Smith with you. That was hilarious!"

"It was an impulse grab. I didn't mean to drag him down with me."

They watched the progression of the raft deflating and everyone falling in. Brian asked Kirsten to stop on a few of them.

"We gotta buy these," Vivian said. "They're fantastic!"

Brian set his wallet on the counter. "I'm going to need digital and print copies of all these photos. How quickly can you have them ready?"

"I'll do it right now. Give me 10 minutes."

"You have that much fun today?" Wendy asked as Kirsten went to fulfill the order.

Brian gave a quick smile. "Yes, had a great time."

Mike came into the shop and pointed at Brian. "Need to see you."

Brian followed Mike out the door and they joined the other guys looking at the deflated raft.

"Wonder what's going on?" Vivian said.

Kirsten set a CD on the counter. "I talked to Kendall when y'all first got back and he said it was weird the raft popped. They're made to withstand slamming into boulders on the river."

Lucy headed toward the door. "Let's go see what this is all about."

The girls walked outside and the men quit talking.

"What's going on?" Vivian asked Kendall, who looked at Shick.

Kendall slipped away and Shick looked at the other guys before answering. "It wasn't a boulder that popped the raft."

"What do mean?"

"You'd better talk to Agent Nelson."

38

Vivian's head swam and she wasn't sure she'd heard Shick correctly. "Did you say talk to Agent Nelson?"

"Yes, it'd be best for you to speak to him directly."

"Who are you?"

"Agent Galvin Shick with the FBI."

"I knew it!" Lucy said. "You were too excited about the cold-ass rafting to be normal."

Wendy looked at Smith, Brian and Mike. "I presume you are agents, too?"

Smith nodded. "I'm Agent Freddie Smith, and you've met agents Finck and Hayes."

Brian and Mike nodded.

Kate, hands on hips, asked, "Where is Agent Nelson?"

"Will somebody please tell me what the hell is going on here?" Vivian cut in. "Has Craig done something? Why didn't you tell us you were with the FBI? And yeah, where the hell is Agent Nelson?"

Shick turned her toward the door of the rafting company. "I think we'd better get you inside."

Vivian stopped. "I'm not going anywhere until you tell me what's going on."

Smith gently touched her shoulder. "It really would be best, ma'am, to get you inside."

Hayes held the door open. "Nelson should be here any minute. He was coming from the Fremont County Sheriff's office close-by."

Vivian and the girls went inside the shop. A few minutes later Nelson arrived. He conferred with Shick in the parking lot and inspected the raft, before walking to the shop.

Vivian met him at the door. "What's going on with the raft? Why are you here?"

171

Nelson let the door close before explaining. "I know you're surprised to see me, but I wanted to make sure you would be okay. Your raft did not deflate due to a rock or boulder."

"It didn't?"

"No. It was shot. Twice."

Vivian's eyes grew wide and she took a step back.

"Once on the right rear and again, eight inches farther back. The trajectory was angled, indicating the shooter was in front of the raft at approximately 45 degrees."

She was having a hard time comprehending all of this. "Shot?"

"I understand one bullet's entry was very close to where you were sitting."

"I…I don't understand why…"

"Craig is wanted for more than credit card and wire fraud. He's wanted for a high-profile burglary."

Vivian reached for the bumblebee pendant dangling around her neck.

"Exactly."

39

Vivian's knees almost buckled, and she grabbed the counter for balance. "I'm going to pass out."

Wendy walked Vivian to a chair by the register and leaned her forward. "Here, put your head between your knees."

Nelson stepped closer to Vivian. "Craig stole several pieces of jewelry, estimated at more than a million dollars, from a Thai diplomat three years ago."

"How was he able to pull off a theft like that?" Kate asked. "This is unreal."

"She was in D.C. for a State dinner and we believe Craig and an accomplice broke into her hotel room and stole jewelry and cash."

Lucy fanned Vivian with a brochure. "Why would they travel with those kinds of valuables? Seems like poor judgment."

"They had it in the room safe. But it wasn't enough."

"Why didn't Agent Tucker in Fort Worth know this?" Wendy asked. "And how do you know about it?"

"I was friends with one of the agents on the original case and she showed me pictures of the pieces taken. It bothered her that the leads had dried up. The team identified a suspect right away, a hotel employee, but hasn't been able to prove he did it. The pieces never surfaced on the black market and an accomplice hasn't been identified until now. Until I saw Vivian wearing the pendant."

Vivian sat up. "So it's real?"

"Actually, the one he gave you was real, but I switched that out yesterday when you went for the bike ride. What you're currently wearing is a fake."

"Oh." Disappointed.

Lucy leaned close to Vivian and looked at the pendant. "How'd you get a fake made so quickly?"

"We didn't. Replicas of all the jewelry came out shortly after the theft. It's typical in a case of this profile. I simply had Cervantes deliver one to me that was in FBI custody."

Wendy looked out a front window. "But why send these guys down the river with us and not tell us? I think I can speak for all of us when I say we've been a little stressed about Craig today."

He looked at her and his eyes softened, ever so slightly, at the corners. "We did not believe Craig was violent and had hoped to catch him while he was attempting to catch up with you. But this is a high-profile case — stealing money from a foreign dignitary — and now that we know Craig is tied to the crime, this investigation has now been kicked into high gear."

Vivian's stomach flipped. "I think I'm going to be sick."

Wendy reached around the counter and grabbed a trash can. "Can we get some water over here please?" she shouted.

Vivian stared into the white plastic bucket. Snippets of torn receipts and old chewing gum stuck to the bottom. She took a few deep breaths and handed it back. "I'm okay. I'm okay."

Kirsten came over with a bottle of water.

"Thanks," Wendy said, cracking the cap open and handing it to Vivian.

"So what do we do now?" Lucy asked. "He has escalated about as high as you can in terms of dangerous."

"I've got people searching the area near those rapids, but it's been more than an hour since the incident," Nelson said. "I doubt they'll find anything."

"But what do *we* do?" Kate asked.

"Right now I've got to collect some evidence, then make some calls. Shick and Smith will stay with you for the time being. Hayes and Finck will be close by. I don't want you going back to the hotel until I can be there."

"How long will that be?" Wendy asked.

"At least an hour."

"I need a drink," Vivian said, standing up. "And I'm still freezing."

Wendy and Kate flanked her.

"There's a burger joint down the street about a block," Kirsten said, then handed Agent Nelson an envelope containing the rafting pictures. "You could totally walk, it'll probably help warm you up." She handed another envelope to Vivian, smiled gently and winked her bright blue eyes. "On the house."

174

They walked outside, where Shick and Smith were waiting. Nelson pulled his colleagues aside and spoke to them quietly while the girls got their purses from the SUV.

Smith shook his head when Vivian started to walk away from the SUV. "No walking. Take the car."

The girls piled in and followed Shick and Smith for the two-minute drive, then they parked next to Hayes and Finck, who stayed in their car.

"I can't believe this is the same Craig I know," Vivian said, kicking a rock in the parking lot. "He's way worse than I could have ever imagined and now he's trying to kill me."

"Maybe he missed on purpose," Kate said. "And he's just trying to scare you."

Wendy stepped around a pot hole. "He wants that necklace, that's for sure, and it'd be harder to get if you were dead. Besides, he wants you to run away with him."

Vivian saw Shick cut his eyes to Smith. She kicked the rock again.

Wendy linked arms with Vivian. "Let's not think about it anymore. They're going to find him, I know they will. Wade is not going to let anything happen to you."

Vivian, Kate and Lucy all stopped walking.

"Ooooohhhh…Wade." Vivian said.

Wendy pulled her along and opened the door. "I meant Agent Nelson."

"Mmm hmmmm, sure you did," Lucy said.

The small restaurant was nearly empty, and a sign at the door told patrons to seat themselves. The girls took a booth away from the windows near the back. The two agents sat adjacent to them at a square table.

A woman who looked to be in her 70s ambled over. Her hair was pulled up in a bun, and she wore a blue and white checked cotton dress and apron that pictured one hand holding a rolling pin, smacking the other hand. It read, "Don't kiss the cook, he's mine."

"What can I getcha?" Her dentures flapped a little.

"I'd like a double rum and Coke, please," Vivian said.

Wendy ordered a draft beer. Lucy and Kate got water.

"I'm not really hungry, but maybe we should get cheesy fries or something," Kate said.

"That sounds good," Vivian said. "Can we get some fried pickles, too?"

"Mmmm, yes," Lucy said.

Kate looked over the menu. "I think I'll get a salad, but I'll share."

"Yippee!" Vivian joked.

The lady brought their drinks and took their order, then went over to Shick and Smith.

Vivian listened as they ordered burgers with the works. She took a long sip of her drink and grimaced. *That's strong.*

"This trip is getting worse and worse," Vivian said. "Maybe we *should* go home."

Wendy slammed her beer down. "And risk dipwad going back to Fort Worth? No way."

"Yeah, we're going to get him here," Lucy said.

"I just feel so bad. Y'all could have gotten hurt, hell, even killed, out there today. I can't ask you to do this anymore."

"Listen, Vivian," Kate said, "there's no way we're letting you go home to deal with this by yourself. We have the chance to catch this asshole, and dammit, we're gonna do it."

Strong words from Kate.

Vivian didn't say anything for a while. The other girls talked about their adventure on the river until the appetizers came.

"Holy crap, the fried pickles are fantastic," Lucy said as she dunked one in the homemade ranch dressing. "Mmmmmm."

"Damn, they are good," Wendy said and doused a pickle slice in Tabasco.

The burgers were delivered and Vivian ordered another double.

The door opened and a young couple walked in. Vivian watched as Shick and Smith eyed them, then went back to work on their burgers.

The door opened again and Agent Nelson appeared. He sat at the table with Shick and Smith, talking to them briefly, then he grabbed a few fries and walked out the door.

Vivian slid out of the booth and walked over to Shick and Smith's table. "What'd he say?"

Smith wiped his mouth with his napkin. "We're to meet him back at the hotel when we're finished. No stops."

"Did he say anything about what he found?"

"He'll debrief you back at the hotel," Smith said, then took another bite.

Vivian sat down with the girls and picked at the remnants in her basket.

"What'd Agent Nelson say?" Wendy asked.

"*Wade* said he'd see us at the hotel and give us the LD there."

Wendy ignored the jibe and finished her beer.

"Let's pay out and hit the road," Lucy said. "I'm watchin' you two yahoos drink and I can't cuz I'm drivin', not to mention I'm under constant FBI surveillance. I'm ready for a glass of wine."

Smith walked over, apparently hearing Lucy's comment. "I'll be driving your car, actually. Nelson's orders."

"You mean I could have been drinking this whole time?"

"Looks like," he said.

They paid their waitress and gave her a nice tip.

"I hope she's workin' cuz she wants to and not cuz she has to," Lucy said.

"I have a feelin' she's working because the cook kisses her," Kate laughed.

They gave Hayes and Finck a five-minute head start, then left the restaurant.

Smith adjusted Lucy's seat all the way back, cramming Vivian's space. Lucy and Kate were in the back with her, Wendy having claimed shotgun.

"You'd have more room back there if one of you wanted to ride with Shick," Smith said.

"Nah, we're all about togetherness, thanks," Lucy said, propping her feet up on the console between him and Wendy.

Smith kept up with Shick, who drove fast, even through the hairpin turns. A little too fast for Vivian's heart.

They were about 10 miles from Breckenridge when Vivian's phone resonated with "When It's Love" by Van Halen.

"I didn't program this ringtone and it's a number I don't know," she said.

Smith glanced at her in the rearview mirror. "Answer it."

"Hello?"

"How was your rafting trip today? That water looked awfully chilly."

40

Vivian's heart raced and all she could do was hit Smith's seat in front of her.

"You know I was only trying to teach you a lesson, right? Just show you that I'm in control here."

Vivian tried to stay calm, but her voice shook. "Yes, Craig."

Smith waved his right hand in circles, indicating she should try to keep him on the phone. "I know you wouldn't hurt me."

"Good. I'm glad we've got that straight."

She couldn't think of what to say and blurted, "We should talk. Seeing you in the spa, it brought back...uh, I... I miss you."

"Finally, you're beginning to come around."

"Yes, and I want to see you." She looked at Smith in the rearview. "Can we meet?"

"There's a place in Breckenridge called Boarders. Be there in 20 minutes."

"Sure. Okay, Boarders."

"And wear your pretty necklace."

"I have it on."

"You need to be alone."

"Craig, you know I'm here with my friends. They're with me in the car right now. I can't come alone."

He was silent.

"But I'll talk to you alone when we get there, okay?"

He hesitated, then said, "Fine."

"We'll meet you there in 20 minutes." She waited for his response.

"Vivian?" he said.

"Yeah."

"I love you."

She didn't have a response to that and hung up.

Smith immediately went to work, calling Shick first, since he was only a few minutes ahead, then Nelson. Smith put him on speakerphone.

"This is not a good idea," Nelson said. "There's not enough time to prepare."

"It's all we've got right now," Vivian replied. "This may be the only chance we have to catch him. We leave the day after tomorrow."

"It's too dangerous. He *shot* at you today."

Vivian took a deep breath. "He'll be checking my whereabouts with my phone. It's our only option."

A door slammed and Nelson cursed. "We don't have enough time or manpower. I can't guarantee your safety."

"I'm not asking you to guarantee my safety," Vivian said. "I need to guarantee my children's safety, and in order to do that, we need to catch this jerk. Agents Smith and Shick are with us, and Hayes and Finck are probably almost to Breckenridge by now. Can we do this or not?"

The line was quiet. Finally, Nelson said, "Smith, take me off speaker."

Smith had a series of "yes, sir" and "understood, sir" answers, then "10-4."

Smith gave instructions to the girls as they zoomed toward Breckenridge. "It's got to look like the four of you are arriving by yourselves, so I'm going to pull over in a few minutes and get in with Shick. We need to get there and into position before you show up. Lucy, Boarders is on Main Street on the right side."

"I know where it is."

"Good, then take a few wrong turns in Breckenridge getting there, about five minutes worth, then go to the restaurant. Park as close to the front door as you can and hurry inside. Finck will cover the door, and Shick will cover the back. Hayes and I will be at the bar. Do not acknowledge us in any way. Sit at a table close to the bar but where you can see the front door. "

He looked at Vivian in the rearview mirror. "Nelson is on his way and should get to the bar shortly after you do. Our plan is to apprehend Craig outside or in the bar before you get there. In case that doesn't happen, when he arrives, don't go up to him. Hayes and I will secure him. You're not to have any interaction with him."

"Sounds like a plan," Vivian said. The butterflies in her stomach felt like they were being dismantled by a swarm of praying mantis.

"Nelson wants you to text him the number Craig just called from. He's going to try and trace it."

"Okay," Vivian said, and did as instructed.

Smith pulled up behind Shick on the side of the road and hopped out. "See you soon. And remember to get lost!"

Lucy got back onto the highway and followed them into Breckenridge. As they drove around "getting lost," the girls tried to reassure Vivian.

"Nelson is pissed," Kate said. "The orders to catch Craig must come from high up in the FBI's organization."

"Yep," Wendy said. "Must be some political thing with Thailand."

"Can't say I blame them. That's a chunk of change," Vivian said, moving the fake pendant back and forth on the chain.

"Let's go get our man," Lucy said as she pulled into the Boarders parking lot.

They were not greeted by smiling agents and a shackled Craig, as Vivian had hoped. She got out of the car and looked around, then made her way to the door.

Hayes and Smith sat at the bar, and the girls took a table close by. A waitress asked what they'd like to drink.

Vivian shivered, unsure if it was still from the frigid waters or her nerves, and ordered a hot chocolate and Baileys.

Kate and Wendy did the same. Lucy added peppermint schnapps to hers.

Vivian glanced around as they sipped their liquor-laced cocoa, looking for Craig in disguise. He could not have blended in with the Generation Y crowd. For that matter, the girls didn't fit in either, and Hayes and Smith stood out like two Aggies in an Austin blues bar.

The "dude, you totally crushed it," "hammered it on that kicker" and "that was so dope" conversation was getting on Vivian's nerves. Young and carefree she was not tonight. She was a woman on a mission, and on edge.

With the last sip of her hot chocolate the Van Halen ringtone started back up. Nelson walked in at the same time.

Vivian glanced at him and answered on speakerphone. "Hello?"

"You fucking bitch. Fucking slut. Did you think I wouldn't know you're there with cops?"

"Craig, I—"

"I see your pretty boy just walked in. You fucking him? You fucking all of them?"

180

"No," Vivian tried to interrupt again but was cut off.

"You set me up, you bitch. It's over."

"Craig, just listen, please."

"Say goodbye, Vivian." Click.

Vivian's hand shook as she stared down at her phone. Tears welled in her eyes.

"He knows you're here," Vivian said to him as he pulled up a chair. "All of you, actually, and he saw you come in."

"Stay put." Nelson hopped up and gave rapid instructions to Smith and Hayes, who ran out the front door. He sat down again. "Tell me. All of it."

Vivian sighed and gave him a rundown of the last two conversations. "I think he's lost it. Totally nuts."

Nelson picked up her phone. "That's it. We're done with this. You're going home."

He had pulled up the app screen, and Vivian knew what he was about to do. She tried to snatch her phone from him but he was too quick and held it out of reach.

"It's too dangerous," he said. "We cannot let him track you anymore."

"That is why we need to catch him. I can't go home with him out there, somewhere, biding his time to come after me and he will." Vivian slapped the table. "I won't risk something happening to my children."

"We'll set up a security detail at your house, your children's day care…"

Vivian stood up and leaned into Nelson's face. "No. It has to happen here. You and I both know this is our best chance." Vivian grabbed her phone, picked up her purse and slung it over her shoulder. She ran outside. "Here I am, you fucker! Come and get me! And your stupid necklace!"

She grabbed the pendant and was about to rip the chain off her neck when Nelson ran up behind her, grabbed her arm and pulled her back inside. "Don't be ridiculous."

The girls were by the entrance, ready to take on whatever.

Vivian burst into tears and dropped her purse, contents skittering across the floor. Wendy and Lucy scrambled to pick things up with help from a nearby snowboarder.

Kate hugged her. "It's going to be okay."

Nelson stood back while Vivian came unhinged. Purse contents collected, Wendy went to work finding tissues while Lucy went to the bar and got Vivian a shot of tequila.

After a few minutes, and the shot, Vivian's sobs quieted and her tears stopped. She had needed to vent the fear and frustration, but now she needed to channel her emotions into jailing that lunatic.

He's going down, she thought just as Nelson pulled out his car keys.

Addressing Lucy, Wendy and Kate, he said, "Smith will drive you in Lucy's car." He pointed his key at Vivian. "You're riding back with me. Let's go."

41

Vivian couldn't remember a quieter car ride. No music, no conversation, *nada*, the entire way back to The Ridge. Hayes rode up front and kept the silence as well. She was glad to be reunited with her friends and fell into a group hug just inside the front doors. Though she had calmed down, she was still upset. It felt good to have their support.

They whisked her off to the elevators, Smith in tow, but Nelson stayed in the lobby. She caught a glimpse of Shick and Finck in the great room, in front of the fireplace. Finck gave her a wink.

The girls left Smith in the living area of the suite, went into the master bedroom and closed the door. They needed to chat, in private.

"Oh my gosh," Vivian said as she sat down in a high-backed chair. "I didn't mean to go off that much on Agent Nelson. I was just so pissed."

"It's okay, Viv," Kate said. "It was your momma bear instincts coming out."

"He'll understand," Wendy said.

Lucy flopped onto the bed. "He's Mr. Tough FBI Agent Man. He can take whatever you dish out. Whatever jackass Craig can throw our way, too."

Kate paced in front of the balcony doors. "We need to know what Nelson's team found out along the river."

Vivian sighed. "I guess I'll call him. Nobody said a word on our ride over." She started to look around for her phone. "Actually, I don't want to call him. Wendy, you have his number?"

Wendy's cheeks flushed as she pulled her phone out of her purse and dialed.

They went back into the living area to wait for Nelson. Vivian met him at the door.

"I'm sorry for earlier, but I need you to know how serious I am about catching Craig."

"Got it," Nelson said and gestured to the dining table. "Sit down. We'll talk."

Vivian complied. "What did you guys find at the river?"

"And did y'all find any trace of him earlier around Breckenridge and Boarders?" Wendy asked, sitting down.

Nelson stood at the head of the table, gripping the back of a chair. He glanced at all of them before explaining, "The search for Craig along the river didn't turn up much. However, we think we found the spot where he took the shot." He let that sink in. "Footprints led to a cliff in Royal Gorge National Park where we found a wrapper from some beef jerky.

"We made a cast of the footprints and collected the wrapper as evidence. Motorcycle tracks were found about half a mile away down the road, and we took casts of those as well. We can compare them to ones we took near The Ridge."

"That's good, right?" Lucy hadn't fully sat down and had one knee in a chair.

Nelson ran a hand over his face. "Yes, but there's more. We think he took several shots."

Kate sat next to Vivian, patting her arm, but stopped. "Several, as in more than two?"

Nelson nodded. Lucy slumped in her seat.

"We found rifle casings on the cliff with the beef jerky wrappers."

"Jesus." Vivian covered her mouth with her hand.

"How many?" Wendy asked.

"We found four, but I suspect he took more shots and the casings either fell off the cliff or he picked them up."

"Fuck." Vivian closed her eyes and willed herself not to cry anymore. She was done with Craig making her cry, but it was hard. "What about in Breckenridge this evening?"

"While we discussed the situation in the bar, I had Smith, Shick, Hayes and Finck check the immediate perimeter, and they couldn't find any trace of him."

Vivian let out a big sigh. "He's vanished again."

Nelson continued. "I pulled them in to come back here with you, but Breckenridge PD is working to canvass the town and facing mountainside. I also have a team coming in from Denver, and if there's something to find, they'll find it."

No one had a response to that.

"Any luck tracing the number Craig called from?" Kate asked.

"Burner phone bought two months ago in Fort Worth. No other activity on it."

Vivian fidgeted in her seat. "So he must have programmed that number and ringtone into my phone while we were dating. That's creepy."

Nelson drummed the chair back. "You can see why I didn't want you to bike ride or whitewater raft? Now he has escalated the violence beyond what we predicted. We don't know what he's capable of."

Vivian crossed her arms on the table. "I understand, but I want to do everything possible here in Colorado to draw him out, set a trap. It scares me to death, but I need this to be over. I need to know he can't come back and hurt me or my family. I'm trusting you to help me with that."

"I won't put your life at risk to catch Craig. No more adventures."

Vivian stood. "I don't think you understand. I will not be held captive here. I will go out, with or without your permission, with that app enabled on my phone and try to draw Craig out. I will do everything in my power to keep him from following me back to Fort Worth."

Nelson looked her in the eye for a long moment, then nodded once.

"So what do we do now?" Kate asked.

Nelson pushed back from the table. "For right now, you four sit tight. I need to make some calls."

"Have you let Agent Tucker know what's going on?" Vivian asked.

"That's one of the calls I'm going to make."

Lucy wrapped her arms around herself and shivered. "I'm still not warm."

"Let's go down to the grotto," Wendy said. "I'd love to fully submerge myself in some *warm* water."

"Yeah," Kate said.

"Awesome idea," Vivian said.

They all looked to Nelson for approval.

He nodded. "I'll send Hayes and Finck down to check it out. If they feel like there's no threat, we'll go."

"Thank you." Vivian pushed back her chair.

"We?" Wendy asked.

"I'll be on the men's side of the spa and checking into the grotto from time to time."

Her cheeks and chest burned bright red. "Oh."

"Will the other two agents be hanging out with us the whole time?" Kate asked.

"They'll leave you alone and look like they're there separately, but I insist they be in there."

"They're cute, I don't mind," Lucy said and went into the bedroom to change.

The girls got ready and met in the living room. Nelson had already changed into swim trunks and T-shirt, playing the tourist part. He checked a text message on his phone and then said, "We're clear. Let's go."

"Ummm, Wade," Wendy paused before walking to the door. "Did you have Shick or Finck search our room just now, before we got back, because the toilet seat in our bathroom was up."

Nelson rolled his eyes. "I'll speak to them about that."

"So gross," Lucy said and walked out the door.

42

The group took the elevator down to the spa, and Vivian took in a deep breath of whatever that wonderful scent was. It helped calm her nerves.

"Try to relax, the agents will be around," Nelson whispered because Suri was at the front desk.

"Hi, Suri." Vivian waved. "We're just going back to the grotto for a bit."

"Enjoy yourselves," she replied.

Vivian opened the door to the grotto and steam greeted them, full on. Hayes sat on the ledge in the hot tub, close to the waterfall, and Finck sat in a lounger. The grotto was otherwise unoccupied, and neither agent looked up or paid them any attention.

The girls dropped their robes on two loungers and got into the hot tub quickly. Hayes moved a little farther down the ledge.

"I think I'm finally defrosting," Vivian said. "This feels so good." She went under for a few seconds, letting the heat envelope her. When she sprang above water, Hayes had moved a bit closer. He looked at her, then moved back to where he had been. Finck pretended to read a *Cycle Sluts* magazine, but Vivian caught him checking them all out.

She turned her back to him while Lucy opened a bottle of wine and poured the girls a plastic cup each.

"Here's to warming up," Lucy said as she stepped back into the hot tub.

They cheersed to that.

They sipped their wine and enjoyed the water for a few minutes, then Lucy waded up next to Hayes and asked, "So have you ever investigated the mob? Cuz we met this guy on our last trip, named Al, and we think he might have been in the mob. We can't *prove* anything, but he sure disappeared quick when the *policia* showed up." She touched Hayes' arm and lowered her voice. "He was into something with that Shorty, I just know it. Oh, and Shorty went to jail. They wouldn't tell us why, but you...you could probably find out for what and for how long. We rode on his boat, you know. We thought we might become fish food, but we didn't." She picked at a piece of cork floating in her glass.

"Not my area of investigation," Hayes said. "Sounds like one helluva trip, though."

"Oh, lemme tell ya, Vi—"

Vivian splashed her. "It was an interesting trip and we met lots of, uhhmmm, charismatic people. Let's leave it at that." She gave Lucy the look.

Nelson popped his head in and looked around. "Good?"

Vivian nodded. He stole a glance at Wendy, who was under the waterfall, top on this time. "The spa closes in 10 minutes. You guys ready to head back to the room?"

"Uh, yeah," Vivian said and walked up the steps in the hot tub. "To change before we go to the fire pit. There's wine to drink and s'mores to be had."

Nelson walked into the grotto and closed the door behind him. "I'm not sure that's the best idea."

Vivian wrapped herself in a towel.

"I have four, *four* kids who need me. Their dad's not an idiot, but the thought of him raising them without me is too much. You do your job. You do it well, and I know I'll be fine."

He looked at Hayes and Finck who both got up and walked past him, toward the men's locker room. "I'll be waiting for you in the spa gift shop."

The girls and Nelson ran up to the room, dried their hair and layered up. Lucy grabbed their s'mores-making stuff and two bottles of wine.

"If I'm gonna die, I'm gonna die happy," Lucy said, stuffing marshmallows into a bag.

"Great philosophy," Vivian said, reaching into the bag and popping a marshmallow into her mouth.

Nelson escorted them downstairs to the fire pit. He threw a few logs on and sparks flew into the air. Then, he took the empty chair next to Wendy. Vivian sat with her back to the great room, Lucy and Kate on either side.

Shick and Smith sat at opposite ends of the large patio, one in front of Felix's and the other by Timberline. Vivian didn't see Hayes and Finck but figured they were out there somewhere.

"It's so quiet here," Kate said and leaned her head back on her chair. "Look, it's a waxing moon. Perfect time to cast spells for new beginnings, progression and growth."

"Cast what?" Vivian asked. "Do I need to get you a pointy hat and a broom?"

Kate smiled. "I get it from my mom's side."

"Steve and I could use a new beginning," Lucy said. "But I don't know any spells."

"Me, neither," Vivian said. "But I could damn sure use a new beginning! Cast something my way, would ya?"

"Ouuuuuuuuu, ouuuuuu," Wendy sang out, stretching her legs and propping her feet up on the ledge.

"Witchyyyy," Lucy sang.

"Woman," Kate finished.

"I love the Eagles," Wendy said.

Nelson shifted in his chair.

"I don't actually know any spells," Kate said and picked up a skewer. "But who wants a marshmallow?"

All of the girls did. Nelson didn't respond.

She pointed a skewer at him. "It's probably not illegal for you to partake, Agent Nelson. We won't tell your superiors."

He looked at the Hershey's and caved. "Yeah, I'll take one."

The night was perfect, not too cold, and the fire warmed Vivian just enough. A sliver of moon peaked in and out of the clouds that rolled across the mountaintops. The smell of the roasting marshmallows and melting chocolate mixed with the surrounding evergreens helped. She closed her eyes and took a deep breath, enjoying the peacefulness.

Kate and Lucy passed around some s'mores and they roasted more marshmallows. Lucy caught hers on fire and ran around the fire pit, singing the Olympic theme. She stepped back onto the ledge and blew out what was left of the charred mess. "Who wants this one?"

"It's a throwback," Vivian said. "Toss it in the fire."

Wendy sang, "Burn, baby burn," and the girls joined her in singing "Disco Inferno" by the Tramps.

Vivian resumed her peaceful state, sipped her wine, ate her s'more and put her feet up on the ledge.

"So why the FBI?" Lucy asked Agent Nelson.

Nelson wiped the graham cracker crumbs from his lap. "Finished school with a masters in criminal justice. I can speak seven languages, and I have an extensive information technology background." He smirked a little.

"What does that mean, extensive IT background?" Kate prodded.

"As a teenager I was mischievous. For fun, I'd hack into company networks. I never did anything malicious, but I shouldn't have done it."

"You little criminal you," Vivian teased.

"I never got caught, thank god. You have to have a squeaky clean record for the FBI, you know."

"Then what?" Wendy asked.

"My senior year I got lucky. I had a computer science teacher who figured out that my skills outmatched his own by a long shot. His brother worked in the FBI, and he got me connected to the FBI's honors internship program. For 10 weeks I worked alongside agents at FBI headquarters in D.C. After that, I was hooked. I figured out what I needed to do in college, including take a lot of languages, then got my masters."

"Seven languages, geez!" Lucy said. "How do you say 'overachiever' in Farsi?"

Vivian heard a sound off to the right. She leaned around her chair and looked but didn't see anything. Then she heard it again, a rustling, scratching in the darkness.

Nelson got up and put his hand on his holster.

"What?" Shick stood up.

"I thought I heard something over there." Vivian pointed into the night.

"Go inside. Now!" Nelson jumped in front of her, shielding her from the invisible threat.

The girls grabbed their wine and Lucy grabbed the chocolate (priorities), and they hustled into the great room. Hayes and Finck rushed past them, out the door, guns drawn.

Nelson sent the agents in different directions as Vivian and the girls watched from behind the windows.

"Should we hide behind something?" Wendy asked.

"Maybe," Kate said.

"What did you hear?" Lucy asked Vivian.

"Something moving, for sure."

They crouched down behind one of the couches, but continued to watch the action outside. Nelson used his phone as a flashlight, holding it in one hand and his gun in the other. He scanned the outer seating area surrounding the fire pit. He flashed the light toward the ski lift. One of the chairs was swinging back and forth. He moved in that direction as Shick flanked him. They moved around either side of the lift and came back together.

Finck and Smith had gone in opposite directions, Finck toward the cabana and pool, Smith toward a grassy, open area that led to condominiums.

Hayes walked close to the fire pit and then stopped, listening. He turned his head to the right and glanced at the trash can. When he reached to remove the lid, a raccoon jumped out at him, hissing, causing Hayes to yell and throw his gun in the air. The other agents trained their guns on the little animal, only to pull back once they saw it scurry away.

The girls walked outside to the fire pit, laughing at the scene.

"Bandit get ya?" Finck said to Hayes.

"Girly man, afwade of a wittle animal," Smith teased.

"Both of you shut up," Hayes said, picking up his weapon. "I've had no sleep the past 48 hours." He jerked his thumb toward Finck. "You try sleeping in the same room with this snore machine."

Finck shrugged. "Earplugs." He fell into one of the chairs around the fire pit. "May I?" He pointed to the s'mores fixings.

"Sure thing," Lucy said.

"I think this calls for Buttery Nipple shots," Kate said. "Wendy, I don't really know what's in those. Will you go up to the room and get it. Please?"

"Buddy system!" Lucy chimed in, then nudged Nelson in the shoulder.

43

Wendy and Agent Nelson made their way to the elevators.

"So I guess you were assigned Craig's case because of your mad computer skills?"

"That's part of it."

"What's the other part?"

The elevator doors opened. Wendy tapped the 12.

"I think the other part was luck," Nelson said. He moved in close as the doors shut, wrapped his arms around her and kissed her deeply.

She let him.

The doors opened and closed on their floor, but neither moved to step off. Wendy reached around him, feeling his muscular form, and moved her fingers up and down his back. He caressed her face and ran his hand through her long, brown hair.

"God, you're beautiful," he said, then kissed her again.

He felt amazing to her. Her breath quickened and she pushed him against the wall, wanting to feel all of him. Her hands slid over his chest and down to his waist. She was tugging on his shirttail when the door opened and she heard an "Oh!"

Lucy and Kate.

"Oh, errrr, sorry to interrupt," Kate said. "We were going to grab another layer, it's getting chilly."

Wendy's cheeks, already filled with crimson, flushed an even brighter shade. She couldn't speak but moved away from Nelson. In the corner of her eye she saw him adjust his shirt.

Kate hit the 12 and everyone was quiet until Lucy started tapping her foot and humming Aerosmith's "Love in an Elevator."

The doors opened, and they all got out. Lucy continued to hum as they walked down the hall and Kate giggled.

Wendy grabbed Lucy's elbow. "Okay, okay, enough."

"What, I'm just singing about an elevator. And loooooove."

"Cool it!"

Lucy winked at her. "Okay, you naughty girl."

Agent Nelson let them into the suite and waited by the door as they gathered their stuff.

"Do you need a jacket?" Kate asked Wendy. "Or are you pretty warmed up without it?"

Wendy went into the bathroom. *What the hell am I doing?* she thought as she looked at herself in the mirror. She took a moment to brush her hair, then went into the living area and put on her red suede coat, then grabbed the shot stuff.

"Didn't think you'd need that," Lucy said, tugging her jacket as they walked out the door.

Wendy didn't say a word, only led the way back to the elevator, smacking the down button several times.

As they walked out to the fire pit, Vivian could tell that something big had gone down. Lucy's eyes were wide open and she shifted them from Wendy to Nelson. Kate looked at Vivian and winked, then tossed her a coat and scarf. Wendy took her same spot and started making shots.

She poured herself one first, slammed it back, then made four more, passing them out to each of the girls. She held her second one high.

"To whatever tomorrow brings," she said.

They drank their shots and warmed themselves by the fire.

"What'd ya do down here all by yourself with these big boys?" Lucy asked playfully.

Vivian's face lit up. "I called mom. She said the kiddos were in bed but had been doing great. Audrey painted a picture out on the back porch of a bumblebee, and Lauren's been having fun playing games and reading books with Nana. Mom said the twins were doing great, being big eaters, and that Ben and Olivia had been playing together, rolling a ball to each other. And she had gotten video of it! Yay, Mom!"

"Aw, how sweet," Kate said.

"Does your mom know what's going on?" Wendy asked.

Vivian kicked at the fire pit. "I told her about what Craig did to the house before I left, just in case he showed up."

"You kinda had to, I guess," Lucy said. "It's safer that way."

"Yep, even though it freaked her out."

"What's on tap for tomorrow?" Kate asked changing the subject.

Vivian looked toward Nelson. He was speaking to Finck near the Timberline. "Guess we need to ask him."

Lucy couldn't resist. "Wendy, maybe *you* should go ask?"

Wendy shook her head and crossed her arms. "I'm stayin' right here."

"What the hell happened up there?" Vivian asked her.

"Agent Nelson got frisked," Kate giggled.

"I'll tell you later," Wendy whispered. "We can't talk about it right now."

Nelson walked back to the fire pit.

"Any developments?" Vivian asked.

"Afraid not."

"We need a plan for tomorrow. It's our last, full day here. We're running out of Craig-catching chances."

"I'm aware of that, but because he's notching up the violence and completely unpredictable, I'm not using you as bait."

"Agent Nelson, we've been over this and you know how I feel," Vivian said as she picked up a skewer and pointed it at him. "He's going to continue to come after me, and I'm not going home until he's caught."

"By putting yourself in danger, you're putting your friends in danger. Do you understand that?" Nelson stole a glance at Wendy, then looked at Lucy and Kate. "Do you guys understand the seriousness of the situation?"

Kate moved from her chair and sat on the ledge, close to Vivian.

"We understand he's unpredictable right now, but we're sticking with her until Craig is caught."

Wendy touched Nelson's arm, then quickly pulled it back. "She'd do it for us." Wendy laid her hand on his arm this time. "And we trust you completely to keep us safe."

Nelson looked at her but was quiet, an internal war waging.

"I have an idea," Lucy said, reaching for her wine. "We could go snow tubing. It's still open in Frisco."

"What's that?" Vivian asked.

"Oh my gosh, it's super fun. I did it last year when my sister was here. You go up the mountain on this conveyor belt thingy, then come down on these trails made just for the tubes. You go really fast, well, not going up, but coming down. There're bumps and humps and they'll spin ya around. It's awesome!"

"What do you think, Agent Nelson?" Kate asked. "This sound like something we could try?"

"I'm familiar with the Frisco Adventure Park."

Vivian tried to form an image in her mind of Nelson having fun snow tubing. Didn't work.

"I'd have to set up a team to act as employees and I'm a little concerned about manpower. I can work with local police to establish a perimeter." He crossed his arms, then tapped a finger to his cheek. "And I like the fact that you're moving quickly going down. It's the slower trip up that worries me."

"We could go for a hike," Kate offered. "We haven't done that."

"Again, manpower is the issue."

"I can snow tube like a mad woman or hike the shit out of Colorado," Vivian said, handing Wendy her shot cup for a refill. "Let's set something, *anything* up."

44

As they wrapped up their night by the fire pit, Nelson excused himself to go upstairs to make calls and do some paperwork. He said he'd have an answer about tomorrow's activities before they went to bed. He instructed the four agents to stay outside, close by.

Vivian saw him linger in the great room for a minute before disappearing toward the elevator. *I bet he was waiting for Weeeeendy!* She sang in her head.

"So what the heck happened upstairs?" Vivian asked Wendy, who groaned.

"I'm out of control. Oh my god, I cheated on Jake."

Lucy giggled. "Actually, it wasn't up any stairs at all, it was love…in an elevator."

"What are you talking about?"

Wendy leaned forward and spoke quietly. "I kissed Wade in the elevator. Well, actually he kissed me first, but then I went completely passion crazy."

"She was goin' for the goods!" Kate said.

"Shhhhhh! I was not! His shirt, well, just came untucked…accidentally."

"Mmmmmmmmmmm," Vivian said. "That's mysterious."

"Accident my ass," Lucy said. "She was goin' for the gusto. She had him pinned to the wall and was takin' that bull by the *horn!*"

"Wow!" Vivian said. "So unlike you!"

Wendy slapped her hand to her forehead. "I know. I know. I'm a bad person."

"Geez Louise, calm down. It was only a kiss. It's not like you did the nasty or anything." She paused and looked at Wendy. "You didn't, right?"

"No!" Wendy screamed. It echoed through the mountains.

Smith looked over at them with concern. Vivian waved him off.

"Yeah, cuz there wasn't time!" Lucy said. "We interrupted their livin' it up while they were goin' down session."

"And thank god you did because apparently I can't control myself with him."

"He is awfully cute," Kate said. "And you said you were going to break up with Jake. Maybe this is a sign that you should."

"Dammit. I did say that, didn't I? But I haven't, and now I've kissed another guy. God, I'm a terrible person."

"Chillax, it was a moment of weakness," Vivian said. "That song has caused many a normal person to go for lovin' in an elevator. With strangers even!"

"Speaking from experience?" Kate asked.

"No comment." Vivian said.

"Who's the naughty girl now?" Lucy laughed.

Vivian smiled sweetly and changed the subject. "I'm cold, are we about done here?"

"Yep, I'm ready," Wendy said and started gathering up the liquor bottles.

They packed up everything and let Smith know they were ready. He escorted them to their suite and saw they got in safely. Agent Nelson was in the living area, laptop open and on the phone when they arrived.

"I understand that, yes sir," he said. "I'll ensure that's done. Okay, I do appreciate the assistance. Yes sir, goodnight."

Lucy saluted him. "Sir, we are ready for duty, sir."

Agent Nelson half-smiled. "Are you drunk?"

"Sir, no sir!!" Lucy grinned. "Well, maybe a little, but not a lot, sir."

Nelson tried to cover up a grin. "Okay, sit down. Let's talk."

The girls jumped onto the couch and Nelson stood in front of them, pacing. After a few moments he spoke.

"That was the chief of police for Frisco. She's aware of the situation and willing to help provide manpower for the snow-tubing operation. I've gotten more details—"

Lucy raised her hand.

Nelson sighed. "Yes?"

"Did you just call a lady 'sir?' "

"Yes. That's what she prefers."

"Weird."

Nelson continued. "We will have agents acting as employees outside on the tubing hill and a couple selling hot chocolate outside. We're set to leave at oh-nine-hundred. That should give us enough time to get there, have you get checked in and be in the first round of tubers, which, from what I've been told, is the least crowded. "

Lucy raised her hand again.

"Yes," he said, annoyed.

"We didn't really bring the appropriate clothing or shoes to do this type of activity, I'm afraid."

"Do you have jeans?"

"Yes."

"Do you have tennis shoes?"

They all nodded.

"Then that's good enough for me. It's only 50 minutes. Just don't fall out or flail about in the snow. Now, may I continue?"

"Yes. No wait," Lucy turned to the girls. "Maybe we can rent snow boots there."

The circles under Nelson's eyes seemed to grow bigger and darker with each interruption. "Moving on. We'll have every vantage point covered. The area around the snow tubing hill is pretty flat. There are snow dunes here and there, but there's not higher elevation from which he could shoot."

A chill surged through Vivian, causing her to shiver. She wrapped her arms around herself.

Nelson stopped pacing, knelt beside the coffee table and turned a map to face the girls. "Here's Frisco and here's the tubing hill," he said, tapping two places. "You'll park and go inside the main building. After you pay, they'll direct you into an igloo-type hut to receive instructions from staff and pick up your tube. From there, you'll ride the conveyer belt up the side of the hill and go tubing over and over, as many times as you can. Some of the employees on the hill will be undercover agents and cops. We'll do surveillance and keep a close eye on you and the surroundings."

"Sounds easy enough," Kate said.

"What do you think the chances are he'll do something?" Wendy asked.

He looked at her for a moment, then to Vivian. "Honestly, I don't really know."

45

Day 6

Vivian thought she heard something beyond the door. She pulled the covers up to her nose and listened, heartbeat loud in her ears. She looked around the dark room. The clock read 4:42. The doorknob turned slowly and the door cracked open.

"Hello? Who's there?"

"It's me, Kate."

"You scared me!"

"I figured you'd be asleep but wanted to check on you. I had a dream."

"I'm awake. Having a hard time sleeping. I'm nervous."

"I understand. I think we're making the right choice, though, trying to catch him here instead of sending you home to deal with a potential problem around the kids."

"Yeah, I know."

Kate sat next to Vivian on the bed. "My paw-paw came to me in a dream. He was young and spry, not like when he died. He looked handsome and fit."

Vivian sensed a calmness in Kate's voice that made her feel better.

"Did he tell you anything?"

"We never spoke in the dream, but he was holding a picture of the four of us from our Playa trip. It was torn and Wendy's piece of the picture was dangling, about to be torn off completely."

"Then what?" Vivian sat up.

"He got a piece of tape and fixed the picture. Then he handed it to me, waved and walked away."

"Wow. That's kinda freaky."

"It was actually very peaceful. I never felt bad in the dream, so I'm guessing things are going to work out. We need to follow Agent Nelson's instructions and everything will be fine. I know it. Now you try to get some rest."

"Okay." Vivian scooted down in the bed and said goodnight as Kate closed the door.

Eventually she drifted off, only to be wakened by sunshine peeking through the curtains. This time the clock read 7:11. She rolled over and found Lucy was already out of bed. *Always the early riser.*

Vivian kicked off the covers and found Lucy on the balcony, wrapped in a blanket, sipping on orange juice and eating a banana.

"It's a glorious morning," Lucy sang out around a banana chunk in her cheek.

"Mornin'. Chillaxin' out here, I see."

"It's just so pretty. Wanna share my blankie?"

"Sure." Vivian scooted her chair over by Lucy's and huddled under the blanket.

A few minutes later the door opened and Wendy and Kate joined them, both with a steaming cup of coffee.

"Y'all ready for some snow tubing action?" Lucy asked. "I just know you're gonna love it!"

"I am, especially if we can catch Craig in the process," Vivian said as she pulled the blanket closer.

"Let's get busy. We've got inappropriate clothing to put on," Lucy said, "and I don't mean inappropriate like what you're thinking, Viv!"

"You got me." Vivian smiled. "I was imagining us flying down the hill in our skivvies!"

They all went inside and got ready, putting on jeans, tennis shoes and layers of shirts. Vivian unclasped the necklace with the bumblebee pendant and hung it around her neck.

There was a knock on the internal dividing door. Nelson said they needed to be ready by 8:15, which was creeping up fast.

Vivian scarfed down the last remaining donuts and drank a glass of juice. "I'm thoroughly sugared up," she announced to the room.

"It's about that time," Nelson said, walking to the door. "I've called the valets and your car is pulled around."

The girls were quiet in the elevator, their nerves high. When they reached the lobby, Nelson went over the plan one more time.

"Everyone's got it, right?"

They acknowledged, went outside and got into the SUV.

"You'll get a text from me about Phase 2 should we need to go to that," Nelson said. "Good luck." With that he closed Vivian's door.

Phase 2 was lunch in Vail at Lucy's previously suggested Hail-Yeah. If there was no Craig activity during snow tubing, they'd get lunch while Nelson formulated Phase 3, a hike.

Lucy drove down the mountain and took the interstate to Frisco. She knew exactly where she was going, parked and turned the car off.

"Y'all ready?" she asked, looking at Vivian.

Vivian nodded. "Yep, let's do this and have some fun while we're at it!"

They made their way inside the building to check in, signed their life away like they had at the bicycle and rafting places, and were told to head out to the igloo.

"Do y'all rent snow boots?" Lucy asked the college-aged kid behind the counter.

"No ma'am, sorry, we don't."

Lucy turned away from him, sad.

"It's okay, Lucy, we'll make do," Kate said.

"I'm not upset about that. Did you hear what he said? He just called me ma'am."

They girls laughed and headed to the igloo. Only a few others waited, some of whom Vivian guessed were undercover cops. She was glad there weren't any children around.

A staffer introduced himself and asked that they watch the safety video. It was a bit corny, little penguins with body parts that didn't touch. Oval body, round head, narrow arms and no feet. Vivian watched as the disjointed penguins demonstrated the right and wrong way to go down the hill.

Butt in was the only acceptable way. No belly flops allowed. The penguins demonstrated the "magic carpet" and how to enter and exit properly and not take everyone else with you in a big snowball. The video ended and the staffer opened the back door of the igloo and passed out tubes.

Vivian's shoes didn't offer much traction so she slipped and slid in the snow as she pulled her tube by the leash. She was glad the tubes had a bottom — the ice would be cold and wet on her butt. On the Guadalupe

River, no bottom meant rocks hitting your butt. Either way, she was a with-bottoms kinda girl.

The girls waited at the magic carpet as those in front of them stepped on the slow-moving conveyor belt.

Vivian looked around, wondering if Craig was watching. She drug her tube up to the edge of the carpet, took a deep breath and stepped on.

Come out, come out, wherever you are!

46

The wind whipped, cutting through Vivian's three layers of shirts, as she waited her turn to go careening down the hill. She held the tube upright behind her, trying to block the worst of the wind. Kate waited with her, but Wendy and Lucy had opted for a different course to their right.

The hill offered eight route options. Vivian and Kate had picked the one with the most humps. Lucy and Wendy went for the one with fewer, but bigger, humps. None of them wanted to go down the lazy river.

When it came her turn, Vivian asked the muscular, buzz-cut tube pusher if she and Kate could go together. He said yes and helped them settle into their tubes, then he gave Vivian Kate's tube leash and vice versa.

"Don't let go," he told them as he gave a push. "And once on the bottom look out for people coming downhill as you cross the lanes."

"SPIN US!" Kate yelled right as he was about to give a final shove. He did and they flew over the humps, going round and round, laughing and squealing the entire time. The wind whistled in Vivian's ears, and bits of snow and ice flew into her face.

At the end of the run, they bumped along what looked like an industrial-sized rubber kitchen mat, then went halfway up an incline that slowed them down. At the tip of the incline, orange plastic safety netting pinned across metal stakes kept them from zooming off the hill.

"That was awesome!" Kate said, hopping up easily out of her tube.

"Woo-hoooo!" Vivian yelled. Her shoes slipped on the snow and she flopped out of her tube on her hands and knees. Kate helped her up.

They stood at the bottom of the hill and watched as Lucy and Wendy churned their way down the path next to them. They, too, went about halfway up the incline toward the plastic netting.

"I told you!" Lucy said. "That rocks, right?"

"I loved that," Wendy said, getting up. She slipped in the snow, too, and landed back in her tube. "My hiking boots really aren't cutting it out here, but it's worth it!"

Vivian gave her a high-five and all of them made their way across the lanes, back to the magic carpet, and loaded up, one at a time. As Vivian rode uphill, she looked at the parts of Frisco that lay beyond the adventure park.

It was a quaint town, not too big, not too small, with numerous family-owned businesses. She scanned the windows of those stores but couldn't see Craig. No rifles pointing out any windows, no crazed man behind the glass. She knew that was extreme, but couldn't help it. Or was it? He could be hiding anywhere.

"Let's see if they'll let all four of us go together," Kate said as they stepped off the magic carpet at the top.

They went to a different lane, one with medium moguls, and asked the tube pusher if they could go as one. He glanced around and shrugged. "Not a problem."

Kate got out her camera while they waited their turn and took pictures of the girls with their tubes and the snow-covered Rocky Mountains in the background. A lady tuber offered to take the four of them together, so they playfully posed.

Vivian pretended her tube was a big donut and took a bite. Lucy held hers up like a giant halo, and Wendy and Kate stood back to back, holding theirs out in front as they kicked their legs like drill team girls.

"Have fun and be safe," the lady said as she handed over the camera to Kate.

"Is she…" Wendy said and took a few steps forward in line.

"Probably," Vivian answered.

When it was their turn to go, Kate flipped the camera to video. They loaded into their tubes, everyone taking the leash of the person to her right.

"Spin or no spin?" tube guy asked.

"Spin!" they all yelled.

He shoved them off, sending them down the giant snow hill swirling and twirling. Kate got all of the action and the screams on video.

When they neared the end, their momentum kept them going right up to the orange netting, too close for Vivian's comfort. "How far's the drop on the other side?" she asked the girls as they slid down the incline and came to a stop at the bottom of the lane.

"Ehhh, not that far." Lucy waved her off. "Plus, you're on a giant air cushion. Couldn't hurt that bad!"

Right. I'm not sure my back would agree with that.

They gathered up their tubes and hit the slopes several more times, once each individually, but going down together was faster and more fun. Other tubers from their igloo video class rode the slopes time and again, too.

An announcement blared through the slopes saying that time would be up after one more run. The girls went back to their original foursome slope and told the tube pusher to spin 'em with all his might.

"Go get 'em," he said and let out a grunt as he released their tubes and they flew down the hill spinning as wild as a Texas twister. At the end of the run they hit the orange netting, and Kate and Lucy teetered on the edge before coming back down the incline.

"That was a close one!" Kate yelled. "We almost went over!"

"Nah...not with me as an anchor," Vivian said. "Y'all weren't going anywhere!"

They returned the tubes to the drop-off and went inside to warm up. They got their stuff out of the locker and pretended not to know Shick, who stood close by doing a good job of being incognito.

"I'm soaked," Vivian said, looking down at her jeans.

"Yeah, we really needed to wear ski pants," Lucy said, putting on her scarf. "Next time!"

Kate bought everyone a hot chocolate and they huddled near the fire. Vivian checked her phone. She had a message from Nelson.

No indications of Craig's whereabouts.

Proceed to Phase 2.

Will maintain surveillance at restaurant.

They sat for a few minutes, drying off before going back into the chilly air. Finally warm inside and out, they grabbed their stuff and headed to the car.

Lucy drove to the Hail-Yeah and lucked out with a spot by the entrance. The parking lot was packed.

"Okay, remember what Wa— uh, Agent Nelson," Wendy stammered, rosy-cheeked. "We go in and ask to sit upstairs."

"Ten-four," Lucy said and opened her door.

They shuffled inside and Kate followed Nelson's instructions. The hostess grabbed four laminated menus and sets of silverware.

"Follow me."

As they were halfway up the stairs, something crashed at the top. Vivian ducked, shielding herself behind the wooden handrail.

Kate gently grabbed Vivian by the shoulders. "It's okay, Viv. It was just a waiter dropping a tray of plates."

Vivian's eyes watered. "Jeeeesus hell. I'm a nervous wreck. I need this to be OVER."

47

I need another cup of hot chocolate with a little sumthin' sumthin' mixed in," Vivian said as she scanned the menu. "Damn, maybe a double." Her hands still shook from the scare on the stairs.

"It was really loud," Kate said. "I jumped, too."

"Yeah, but you didn't duck and cover," Vivian said, hanging her head.

"I almost did, though," Lucy confessed. "And for good reason. I mean, it's not often you're stalked by a man who's wanted by the FBI. He has tried to kill you, Viv. And us. You have every right to be on edge."

A waitress walked up in a Scottish plaid short skirt and tight button-down white shirt, boobs busting out of it.

"Hey there, welcome to the Hail-Yeah," she said in a high, cutesy voice. "My name is Barbie. What can I get you to drink? We have our house-brewed draft beer on special today, $3 pints."

"Do y'all have a hefeweizen?" Wendy asked.

"Sure do," she chirped.

"I'll take that."

Kate ordered a glass of tea, Lucy a soda and Vivian a hot chocolate spiked with amaretto and crème de cocoa.

Barbie bounced off.

"I think she's supposed to be a trashy little schoolgirl," Vivian giggled.

"At least she can pull it off," Kate said. "I couldn't fill that shirt out if my life depended on it."

"Reminds me of our good ol' Flying Dutchman days, Viv," Wendy said. "But we were sailors, not schoolgirls. And *way* cuter."

"And those outfits weren't nearly as trashy," Lucy said. "Y'all didn't have your boobs poppin' out like Barbie doll, there."

"True, but we did show some tummy," Vivian said, playing with the salt shaker. "Can't do that anymore, compliments of the twins."

"They're worth it," Kate said.

"I know, but it does suck having twin-skin. Maybe one day I can have plastic surgery and get it nipped and tucked."

"Do it," Lucy said.

"You can't do that," Kate said. "It's like a badge of honor."

"Screw that. If I could afford it, hell yeah, I'd do it. Hey, I just used the name of the restaurant in a sentence. Wonder if I get a discount?"

Barbie flounced back with their drinks and took their order, then flitted off to a table of guys, sticking all her humps and bumps out a little extra.

The girls watched the videos Kate had taken on their snow tubing descents and laughed at themselves laughing. Lunch arrived and Vivian was surprised, but pleased. Barbie had gotten everything right, including making her burger plain and dry with cheese only. She had a thing about hot food touching cold food. Lettuce, tomatoes, onion or pickles (the worst) should never touch her meat and buns. Ick!

Vivian was enjoying being with her friends, secure in the fact that Nelson was on watch, keeping them safe. She was just about finished when Smith came through the heavy wooden restaurant doors. He was on the phone, serious look on his face.

He headed upstairs to their table and clicked off the phone. "The team is in place."

"Where's Nelson?" Vivian asked. "I assumed he'd be here."

"That's who I just got off the phone with. He felt like it was pertinent he be on the trail today so he's up there already. Here's the deal." Smith pulled a chair up to the end of their booth and sat down. "You are to drive to the trailhead in Lucy's SUV and park in one of the few spaces, then start up the trail. Officers with Vail PD will have the parking lot covered and will be posing as other hikers on the trail."

"How will we know who are real hikers?" Wendy asked.

"You won't."

"But what if we get in trouble and need help?"

"I'll be monitoring you from the back of a van in the parking lot. You will all have ear buds and microphones so that no one misses anything."

"What if I have to take a trail pee?" Lucy asked. "It never fails; I always have to take a trail pee."

The corner of Smith's lip turned up. "Use the restroom here before you leave. Once you're on that trail, there will be no privacy."

"Where are these microphones going to be exactly?" Vivian asked.

Smith glanced fleetingly at her boobs before focusing on her face. "Agent Nelson called in Agent Cervantes to help with the operation. She'll be here shortly and will connect the transmitters to your waists and tuck the wire here." He indicated his breastbone. "Agent Finck is in one of the buildings from an old mining camp. Agents Nelson and Shick are at the cabin at the end of the trail."

"Cabin?" Kate asked.

"The trail ends on private property, and the old homestead cabin is open year 'round for skiers and hikers."

"I've heard of that," Lucy piped up. "It's called the Bighorn Hilton."

"Agents Hayes and Cervantes will hike up after you to cover the rear. Take your time but hike straight to the cabin. Don't stop at the old mining camp or at Bighorn Falls. Don't take the side trail to the cliff. Go to the cabin."

Smith asked and looked at each of them. "Are you ready?"

"Heck yeah."

"You know it."

"Absolutely."

"We're takin' this jerk-ola down today."

48

A gent Cervantes walked in and indicated the girls should meet her in the restroom, where she got them suited with ear buds and microphones. She called Smith in the parking lot and conducted a sound check.

Everyone could hear and be heard, so Smith took off to the trailhead.

The girls got into Lucy's SUV.

"We need some rock," Wendy said. "We gotta get pumped up!"

Lucy fiddled with her iPhone as she drove. "I have just the song. This band opened for Soundgarden recently and they were great!"

"Guilty Pleasure" by Gone For Days blasted through the speakers, and the girls rocked out on the short drive to the trail's parking lot.

Lucy pulled into the last available space and Vivian had to carefully open her door to not hit the navy blue van parked beside them.

"The package has arrived." Smith's voice came over Vivian's ear bud.

Vivian giggled. "He called us the package."

The girls snickered.

"Come on up," Nelson greeted them from 10,788 feet.

"We're gettin' to it," Wendy said and grabbed her jacket and Lucy's backpack full of supplies. Then they headed to the trail.

Kate stopped to read the map at the marquee.

"Way to use those taco skills Buck taught you," Vivian said.

"It's *topos*, Viv, you goofball. And I'm glad we had that course," Kate said, still studying the map. "Those skills could come in handy today."

"We have fresh water, thanks to Lucy," Wendy said and took a sip out of the CamelBak Lucy had the foresight to pack. "No filters for us."

"Just shared germs," Vivian said and reached for the tube to take a sip, too.

"Eh, whatcha gonna do?" Lucy shrugged.

Satisfied, Kate turned from the map and caught up with them. "I just had to get my bearings."

They hiked only a short distance before the trail became a steep incline. Vivian did okay at first, but after five minutes she had to stop to catch her breath.

"Wait up!" she called to Lucy, who was way ahead of the rest of them.

"Some of us aren't used to the altitude," Kate said, wheezing a little.

"Or the excursion," Wendy said between deep breaths.

"Stick together at all times," Nelson said into their ears.

Lucy walked back to them but marched in place. "Come on, girls, let's go. You can do it. Gotta keep that heart rate up!"

"Oh no," Vivian said, "drill instructor Lucy is back."

"You know it. I'm in my element." She kicked her right leg up on a boulder and stretched, then her left. "Your body will eventually figure out that you aren't going to die from lack of oxygen and you'll hit a groove. In the meantime, keep moving."

Taking another deep breath, Vivian started back to it. The trail continued the incline, leveling out for only short jaunts between switchbacks.

Kate stopped and rested on a boulder. "I wasn't," she took a few breaths, "expecting it to be this difficult."

"Geez," Wendy said, panting. She stopped for a second and twirled each ankle in a circle. "Is it going to be like this the whole way? I'll never make it. Ankle surgery, remember?"

Lucy accepted no excuses. "You finished your physical therapy didn't you? Come on! Work those cleaned-up ligaments! You're like the bionic woman now, right?"

Wendy gave her a look but pushed ahead.

Nelson beeped in their ears, "It becomes a gradual ascent in another quarter-mile. Hayes and Cervantes have you in sight. You need to keep moving to keep the distance."

They followed his orders and made it through the first grueling half mile. The last switchback led into a grove of aspens where the girls stopped to rest and breathe. Each took a turn with the CamelBak before starting out again.

Vivian felt fairly safe as she walked through the trees but continually looked around now that she didn't have to concentrate on each foot placement. "Checking in," she said to Nelson. "Any news?"

"Negative. No reports from anyone."

A couple in their twenties approached, each with a large backpack and bedroll, a German Shepherd trotting alongside. "Hi. Great day for a hike," the girl said as she passed them.

"Hey," the girls called to her retreating back.

The aspens stopped at a creek with a waterfall in the distance. The girls took a few minutes to shoot pictures, then Lucy walked up and down, looking for the best place to cross.

"Looks like if we step on this log, then that one and then this rock," she said, pointing, "we should be able to cross without getting wet."

"And this is melted snow," Kate said. "I've had enough of that for one trip."

"I second that," Vivian said as she took a tentative step on the first log. It didn't budge so she placed a foot on the second log.

Lucy was at the rock and held out a hand, helping Vivian the rest of the way across. Kate went next and crossed the stream without incident.

Wendy didn't have a problem on the first log, but once she had both feet on the next, the rock it had been on gave way and the log rolled out from under her. She landed in the creek with a splash and a yelp.

"What's happening?" Nelson boomed.

"Wendy slipped on a log," Vivian reported. "We're okay."

Lucy jumped in the creek and put an arm around Wendy's waist. "I've got you."

Wendy wiped water off her cheek. "I think I screwed up my non-bionic ankle."

"Oh no," Kate said, stepping onto the large rock she had used getting across.

Wendy hobbled across with Lucy and Kate's help. Back on solid ground, they helped her to a butt-sized boulder and she eased down.

"Thanks, Lucy, for sacrificing your dry feet for me," Wendy said.

Vivian carefully removed Wendy's hiking boot and sock. "Doesn't look too bad, yet."

"Do you think you can keep hiking?" Nelson asked.

"Yes," Wendy said and flexed her toes. "I think if I wrap it and take a couple of pain relievers I can keep going. I don't want to turn back now."

Lucy dug in the CamelBak and pulled out their first-aid kit. She handed Vivian an Ace bandage and tossed Wendy two ibuprofen pills and the tube for the CamelBak.

Smith beeped them. "You ready to move? Hayes and Cervantes are coming up."

"Almost done," Vivian said, trying to hurry and wrap Wendy's ankle. When she finished, she put Wendy's sock and hiking boot back on.

Wendy stood up gingerly, testing weight on her left foot. "I'm okay. It's tender but I'll live. Let's go."

They started out again, and it wasn't long before the girls reached the old mining camp.

"Finck's here, right?" Vivian asked the team.

"Affirmative," Smith answered.

Lucy, going against orders, ventured over to one of the shacks and poked her head in the door. She gasped, then hollered, "AHHHHHH!" She turned tail and hauled ass up the trail.

49

Lucy's scream carried through the valley and reverberated off the mountain faces. Vivian figured the people down in Vail could hear it. Finck ran out of his hiding place in a shack, gun drawn, and Nelson shouted question after question in the girls' ears.

Vivian, Wendy and Kate had run after Lucy. If Lucy screamed and ran away from something on a trail in Colorado, it was a good idea to follow suit.

Vivian finally turned around and saw what she had fled from. A mountain lion ran at full speed across the meadow toward a pine grove.

"Holy Jesus...oh my gosh...mother of a son of a sailor," Lucy said between pants, hand on her chest. "I thought I was going to be mauled. You should've seen its teeth. Fuckin' A!"

"Damn, that thing was huge!" Vivian yelled.

"We wouldn't've let you become a kitty treat," Wendy said, giving Lucy a one-armed squeeze.

The tension and fear in Vivian gave way to a burst of uncontrollable laughter. She bent over, she was laughing so hard. The other girls joined in, her hysterics being contagious.

Hayes and Cervantes ran up the trail and met Finck, who didn't look happy. The girls walked back down the trail to them.

"That's one heck of a set of lungs you've got," Finck said to Lucy, putting his gun back in the holster.

Cervantes shook her head. "I thought it was Craig."

"Or a raccoon," Hayes said with a grin and gave Lucy a light punch on the arm.

She rolled her eyes. "Yeah, yeah. I'd like to see what any of y'all would do if a mountain lion bared its fangs to you."

Finck made a gun with his finger and thumb and did a pretend shot.

Wendy shifted from foot to foot. "Holy crap, my ankle. Think any of these places have a chair I can sit in?"

Finck shook his head. "The closest thing to a chair is that rock right there." It was not much of a rock.

She laughed, then looked at the girls. "Screw it. Y'all ready to keep going?"

They were, but Lucy bent down to tie her shoe.

"We'll hang back in one of the shacks for a few minutes," Hayes said and indicated Cervantes. "We need to stay behind you guys."

"Got it," Lucy said, standing and then walking up the trail.

Finck went back to his post.

They didn't get far before Vivian said, "Uh oh" and fiddled with her shirt.

"What?" Nelson beeped.

"My mike has come undone," she said into the abyss that was her cleavage. "I don't see it."

"Go back to Cervantes and have her fix it," Nelson instructed.

They walked back to the mining camp and Vivian leaned into the cabin Hayes and Cervantes had gone into.

She caught them in full make-out mode. Lips locked, hands in inappropriate places, moans and groans.

Vivian let an "oh" of surprise escape before she could stop it. She covered her mouth and Cervantes looked up at her, horrified.

"Oh, uhhhh … we, we were—"

Hayes scrambled to his feet and helped her up. "We were just playing the couple-in-love-out-for-a-hike part."

Nelson said in Vivian's ear, "What's going on? I can't hear you."

They must have their microphones off, she thought, then turned from the shack and said loudly into her shirt, "That was Hayes and Cervantes. The reception must not be good in there since you couldn't hear them."

Vivian turned back to the agents, who had straightened their clothing. "My mic needs to be re-stuck. It's gone missing."

Cervantes got right to it and Hayes politely stepped out of the shack.

"Well, he is cute," Vivian said with a smile once she was done.

Cervantes' cheeks went from pink to full-on crimson. Nelson coughed in her ear. Smith laughed.

The girls got back to the trail, working their way toward the old homestead. A little way down the path, ferns grew in lush patches and the pines began thinning out.

Vivian stopped at a side trail. "Is this the way to the cliffs?" she asked the girls. "I bet it has great views of the mountains."

"Don't take that," Nelson said. "No detours, stick to plan."

Vivian sighed, knowing she was missing a magnificent picture opportunity, but kept going. A few minutes later the pine trees gave way to a meadow and she didn't feel too bummed about missing the cliff view. The mountains rose around a meadow full of wildflowers, and she felt like she should hold out an imaginary skirt and twirl around like Julie Andrews in *The Sound of Music.*

"This is amazing," Kate said and whipped out her camera.

Lucy got out her cell phone. "We need one together. Huddle up, girls." She snapped a picture holding her cell phone as high above them as she could, which wasn't very high. The picture had a small bit of each of the girls — Vivian's curls and chin, Lucy's left eye, Wendy's chin, Kate's right eye.

Keeper.

"Look at that." Vivian pointed to one of the mountaintops that was more rounded than peaked.

The peak sort of resembled a thumb or other body part according to Vivian's trashy imagination. Lucy held her hand in front of it, in a grip, and moved her hand up and down. All of the girls cracked up and Kate lined up a picture.

"I think this wins the trashiest of the trashiness award on this vacation," Wendy said through her laughter. "This is worse than the grotto pictures."

Vivian tried her hand at it, and Kate got her handy picture, too.

Nelson said something, but Vivian couldn't hear him over their laughing.

Wendy quit giggling enough to reply to Nelson. "You don't want to know what we're doing, but I promise it's not dangerous."

"I know where they are and probably what they're doing," Smith said to Nelson. "They're coming your way." He coughed, trying to cover a laugh.

Nelson sighed audibly in everyone's ear.

It was just a mountain peak, but it looked a little too much like something else. While they were taking pictures, a thin white cloud drifted above the rock. Vivian doubled over.

216

"Keep moving!" Nelson finally shouted. "You're out in the open and it makes it harder for us to cover you. You're sitting ducks."

"We couldn't help it," Vivian said to him. "You'll see why later."

Playtime over, they did as instructed and were soon enveloped again by pines and aspens. Though the temperature was in the low sixties, Vivian started to perspire and the knots on the aspens started to look like big, gaping eyeballs. A twig snapped off to her right and she picked up her pace, making Lucy, who was in front, hustle along.

"What is it?" Lucy asked.

"I just have this creepy feeling all of a sudden."

The trail curved ahead and a dark-haired, bulky man about 5-foot-10 appeared, hiking at a brisk pace. He kept his head down and wore a baseball cap so Vivian couldn't see his face. He reached into his pocket and fiddled with something.

"Run!" she yelled and dashed into the overgrowth.

She hauled ass, running for her life.

50

T hat's him! That's him!" Vivian yelled to Nelson as she ran through the aspen and pine trees off the trail. Lucy was beside her, Kate and Wendy right behind.

Nelson shouted orders at the other agents on the trail, and Vivian heard running and crashing as the team took action.

She spotted a thick stand of spruce trees and ducked behind them. She sat against the thickest tree, shaking from fear and adrenaline.

"Did they get him?" she asked Nelson and the girls. There was too much commotion and chatter coming through the earpiece to make sense of anything.

"Oh my gosh," Lucy said, sitting down next to her. "Do you think that was really him? He found us?"

"It was his build and height. It looked like he had dark hair and he had the muscular shoulders. It was hard to tell exactly because he was looking down, but I'm pretty sure it was him."

Kate waved for them to be quiet. "Shhh, somebody's coming."

The girls knelt down, trying their best to hide among the foliage. Vivian kept her face down and her eyes squeezed shut.

"It's Agent Cervantes," Wendy said with a sigh. "She's by herself. I think it's safe."

"We're over here," Lucy called to Cervantes, who made a beeline in their direction.

She patted Vivian on the shoulder. "False alarm. The hiker you ran from is with Vail PD."

"Oh Jesus," Vivian said and wiped a tear of relief from her eye.

"But he reached in his pocket to pull something out," Kate said. "What was it?"

"His walkie-talkie. He's not mic'ed up like the rest of us."

Lucy took a deep breath and put her hand to her chest. "He about scared the pee out of me." She tapped her foot for a moment. "Speaking of which, I

218

gotta take a trail pee. Since you're here with us, can I take off this microphone so Nelson can't hear me?"

"NO!" Nelson answered before Cervantes could answer.

Cervantes grinned. "Just cover it with your hand. We'll wait for you over there." She indicated a spot a few feet away.

Lucy walked behind some fir trees and started singing to the tune of "Twinkle, Twinkle Little Star."

"Pee, pee coming out of me,

Into dirt and by the tree.

Down the trail so fast you go,

Where to, I don't really know.

Agent Nelson, don't you agree,

You're glad you didn't hear me pee."

The girls cracked up at Lucy's song. Cervantes tried to keep a straight face but had a hard time with it. Nelson, however, started coughing during the first line and went completely silent after that. Vivian could only assume he was either rolling on the ground laughing or completely horrified. Judging by his response, it was the latter.

"Cervantes, get them back to the trail, please," he said evenly. "Girls, no more singing. I couldn't hear anything else, and that is unacceptable!"

Wendy wagged a finger at Lucy. "Ummmm, you got in trouble."

"Trail. Now!" Nelson barked.

The girls followed Cervantes through the forest. She consulted with the team and got an all-clear before leaving the girls. She went left to meet her lover-boy, Hayes, and the girls went to the right, toward whatever awaited at the cabin.

They hiked along without issue before coming to another steep section on the path. The switchbacks kept them huffing, and Vivian stopped to rest halfway up.

"I thought this was supposed to be one of the easier trails around Vail," she said after she had caught her breath.

"It is," Nelson said. "Can you keep moving?"

"Yep." Vivian took a swig out of the CamelBak and they set off again.

At the top of the last switchback Vivian paused, causing Kate to bump into her. Two hikers approached, one brown-haired and about the same height as Craig. He looked up and waved, and Vivian could breathe again.

"Hey," he called as he got near. "It's not much farther to the top and it's so worth it."

"Thanks," the girls said at the same time as they walked past.

"Watch out for the two guys up there in the cabin," he called over his shoulder. "They've been hanging around up there awhile, and it feels like they're up to something."

"Thanks," the girls said again, and Vivian had to work to hold in the laughter.

"There ain't no tellin'," Wendy said once they were out of earshot.

"Any sign of Craig?" Kate asked the party line.

"Negative," Nelson said.

They walked past a pond where a busy little beaver had created the Hoover Dam of beaver dams. Sticks, twigs and decent-sized logs barricaded a stream, creating beaver paradise.

"Wonder if Beaver-Snatch from Beaver Liquors used to live here," Lucy said and shook her head.

"That thing was so ugly, it's hard to imagine him living, much less out here," Wendy said and tossed a twig on the dam.

Upstream, patches of snow remained beneath fir trees and wildflowers grew in an alpine meadow.

Kate stood in awe. "Nature is incredible. And beavers are nature's hardest-working architects, especially considering they use their choppers to cut down their building materials."

"Well said," Nelson beeped in their ears. "Now get moving to the cabin."

They rounded a bend and the expanse of wildflowers continued. Nestled far back in the field underneath a grove of spruce and fir sat a log cabin, a beaten path leading to the door.

Vivian looked around the open meadow. "We see the cabin," she told the team.

"Clear," Shick said.

"Proceed," Nelson answered.

Vivian picked up the pace. The trail continued past the cabin, farther up the mountain, and she got a weird vibe. She dismissed it as too much openness but was glad when Kate reached the cabin.

Lucy stopped in the meadow to pick a handful of yellow flowers. "Avalanche lilies, my favorite."

"Quit your pickin' and pick up the pace," Vivian called to her and stepped inside.

Agents Nelson and Shick stood at opposite ends of the one-room, two-window cabin. Gaps between the logs provided peepholes and gun muzzle clearance. It also allowed for ample airflow, which was not what Vivian desired at the moment since a chill ran up her spine.

"Home, sweet home," Shick said and swept his arm around the room.

Nelson took his rifle out of the wall and repositioned it to the front left window. "Welcome to the Bighorn Hilton, where skiers, hikers and attempted murderers are welcome."

51

Nelson sure did know how to make a girl feel welcome. The dank cabin was bad enough, but hearing "attempted murderer" brought the day back into focus. The hike up had been nice, but Vivian was here on a mission and this was her last shot.

"So what do we need to do now that we're here?" she asked.

"Sit down and relax. Make sure your cell phone is on," Nelson answered, glancing at his watch. "We still have several hours before dark. I want you to stay here and give Craig enough time to pin down your location."

Poking her head out the window, Wendy asked, "Hayes and Cervantes are out here, right?"

"Yes, and Finck as well," Nelson said. "Several Vail PD will come and go on the trails connecting to the Grand Traverse but will not stop at the cabin."

"What's the Grand Traverse?" Vivian asked. "That trail running up the mountain from here?"

"Yes," Shick said. "Remember you came up on the Bighorn Creek Trail, which ends right here. And if you look through this crack," he indicated a three-quarter-inch gap in the logs, "the Grand Traverse Trail picks up from here."

Nelson went outside to do his periodic perimeter search. "We need you to stay here for a while. I'll be back in 10."

The girls sat in the dirt and settled in for the wait. Vivian tossed a small rock in the air she had found lying on the ground. She grew bored with that and started a game of toss the rock through a cabin wall crack.

Wendy sat next to Vivian and began to pull the petals off one of the flowers Lucy had picked.

She barely whispered, "He loves me," pluck, "he loves me not," pluck.

After de-petaling three flowers, Lucy grabbed the rest of the bunch. "You're killing my bouquet. Why don't you just ask him!"

Wendy shrugged and tossed the stems aside. Still whispering, she said, "Two out of the three ended with he didn't love me, anyway."

Kate patted her shoulder. "What does your heart tell you?"

"That he loves me."

"Flower power," Vivian said, picking up some of the pulled petals and tossing them in the air.

"Whew," Shick said. "Glad that's settled!"

Lucy had four flowers left and stuck one in Vivian's ponytail, one in Kate's barrette and one behind her own ear. She held the last one in front of Wendy. "No more petal pulling. Stick it, sista."

Wendy tucked it behind her ear. "For decoration only."

"I have to... uh... you know," Kate said and stood, crossing her legs.

"Trail pee!" Lucy chimed.

"Yes."

"I gotta go again, too," Lucy said, then looked at Vivian and Wendy. "And you know what they say."

"What who says?" Wendy asked.

"They."

"I guess not," Vivian said. "What do they say?"

"Go when you can, not when you have to!"

"Sound advice. I'll go," Vivian said.

"Me, too." Wendy stood up.

Nelson opened the door. "I've got an escort on her way up. She'll take you."

A minute or so passed until Cervantes walked up the trail and met them behind the cabin.

"No peeking through the gaps," Wendy said to Shick and Nelson before they walked beyond the clearing.

"Yeah, no crack gazing through the cracks!" Lucy said and laughed.

"And no singing," Nelson commented.

Cervantes made a fist around her microphone. "Cover it like this. I've peed twice and you didn't hear me, did you?"

Vivian had not. She wanted to ask what else had she covered the microphone for but decided against it. Cervantes was friendly enough, but the girls didn't know her that well. Best not to push it when they needed her covering their back, literally at the moment. Plus, she had a gun.

Lucy passed out tissue, then the girls got their business out of the way, without singing, and returned to the cabin. Nelson peered through a gap, watching the trail leading to the Grand Traverse, and Shick leaned against the front wall, watching Cervantes hike down the path.

The girls sat on the floor and leaned against the back wall. Vivian checked her phone, the signal wasn't the strongest, one bar, but it was there.

"So where should we go on our next trip?" Kate asked.

"Bali. Fiji," Lucy suggested. "Thailand."

Kate coughed and Wendy laughed. Vivian gave Lucy an 'are you crazy?' look.

"Okay, maybe not."

"Spain, Italy and Portugal would be nice," Wendy said.

"They sure would," Vivian said. "But how about somewhere more affordable? I'm on a budget here."

"We all are," Wendy said. "But we can dream, and one of these days we'll make it there."

"What about the Adirondacks in the fall," Lucy said.

"You just want to get close to Canada and Pierre," Kate teased.

"Vegas!" Vivian said.

"Nah, we'd never get you out of the casinos, and that would defeat the purpose of traveling to spend time together," Wendy said.

"If I'm on a lucky streak, yep!" Vivian said.

"New Orleans is one of my favorite cities," Wendy said.

"That's a good one," Kate said.

Lucy interrupted. "My hair does not like New Orleans. Frizz-a-rama."

Wendy laughed. "San Francisco and the wine country?"

Lucy nodded. "That would be a great trip!"

"How about a dude ranch?" Kate suggested. "Like on our high school band trips!"

"Ouuueeeeee, ride 'em, cowboy," Vivian said, rubbing her hands together. "I could do me a dude. At a ranch."

Wendy laughed and started to stand. "I don't know about y'all, but I'd like to giddy-up outta here about now."

Vivian was tired of being cooped up, too, but disappointed Craig hadn't showed. "Think we could get out of the cabin for a bit? Maybe hike up the trail just a short way to the Grand Traverse?"

Nelson checked his watch and peeped out a gap. "I'd like you to stay right around here in the clearing, don't go up the trail. Pick more flowers or something." His eyes cut to Wendy.

Wendy coughed, blushed and reached the door in three strides. The girls followed, and they all walked to the middle of the meadow. Vivian covered her mouth and fought to contain a giggle.

Kate picked a lily and handed it to Wendy. "I bet this one ends up with 'he loves you.' "

Lucy wandered toward the tree line. "Let's move around, warm up our muscles for the hike down."

Vivian walked in a circle. "I need him to show. Where is that crazy jerk? Doesn't he see I'm wearing the damn necklace?"

"We've been on this trail for hours," Wendy said, bending to the side, stretching. "If he was going to show, I expect he would have by now."

Lucy stopped and turned to face them. "He's probably long gone to Mexico or other parts south."

Kate walked toward the trail leading to the Grand Traverse. "Maybe he just hasn't made his presence known."

"If he doesn't show, I'm going to have to learn karate like Karate Kid Kate over there," Vivian said, arms raised over her head, right foot up, knee bent at 90 degrees. She did her best Daniel-san impersonation. "Hiiii-ya!" she said, kicking her left foot at an imaginary Craig.

"No karate for now," Nelson said over the airwaves. "Are you ready to go?"

Vivian was torn but finally said, "Yes, but I'm going to karate chop every hiker we pass on my way down. Be prepared." With that, she did a wax-on, wax-off, ending with Daniel-san's memorable knee-up, kick-the-sky move.

225

52

The sun was getting low on the mountain behind them and the air chillier. Even so, Vivian wiped sweat off her brow. More and more of her curls had pulled free from her ponytail and hung in unruly ringlets. Her legs felt pretty good since the trek was on the downhill, but her knees ached.

"Are we there yet?" Wendy bellowed from the back of the pack. She'd been complaining more about her ankle in the past 20 minutes.

"We have a ways to go," Lucy said. "Do you need help?"

"Not yet, but crossing that creek again is going to suck."

"We'll just have to cross that bridge then," Lucy said.

"If only there was a bridge," Wendy moaned.

Music rang out from Vivian's jacket, startling her. *Figured I had crap for coverage,* she thought.

She fumbled with the pocket zipper, yanking it upward to open, and pulled out her phone.

"Not a number I recognize," she said.

"Answer it," Nelson said in her ear.

Wendy, Kate and Lucy were right by her, yet she hesitated. *What if I don't want to?*

Then she thought of her kids. Audrey, Lauren, Olivia, Ben. *They must never be in danger.*

The phone sounded a repeat chorus. She hit the button.

"Hello?"

No sound on the other end.

The girls stared at her. None of them said a word.

"Hello?"

"The signs of spring…a bumblebee and a flower…"

Vivian couldn't speak. She touched the pendant and then her ponytail and felt the flower Lucy had put there not an hour ago. The girls stood by her, no doubt seeing the fear in her eyes.

"No, don't take it out." The words were cold and deliberate. "I like it."

She slowly covered the phone and whispered, her voice shaking. "He can see me. He saw me touch my hair. The flower."

"We're all on our way," Nelson said. "Don't panic. He's toying with you."

I'm seriously about to panic. Vivian's heart rate shot up. She uncovered the phone.

"Craig, let's talk this out." She turned her head to the left, searching for any sign of him. Nothing, just trees.

"You can stop looking, Vivian. You'll never find me. I'm invisible."

She looked the other direction. A large boulder and more trees. Lucy grabbed her arm.

"Hayes and Cervantes are almost to you," Nelson said.

Vivian heard rustling. She knew they were close. Or was it Craig?

Hayes and Cervantes came into view but Vivian's relief was short-lived. Craig dropped out of a tree, knocking them to the ground. Cervantes struggled to get out from underneath Craig, and Hayes reached for his weapon. Craig kneed Hayes in the face, and then with a zap, Cervantes went limp. Hayes tried to raise his gun, but Craig was too fast. Zap! Hayes twitched alongside Cervantes.

Craig was dressed in camouflage from head to toe and had painted his face to match. He smiled at Vivian, white teeth shining through the dark paint. His eyes were bright green and wild. Terrifying.

"Run!" Vivian yelled to the girls.

They dashed from the path toward a large boulder, but Wendy's ankle gave way and she went down. Lucy reached to help her.

Craig ran directly toward them.

"Keep going, don't stop! Go! Go!" Wendy swatted Lucy off. "RUN!"

Wendy used her good leg to push herself behind the boulder and watched as Vivian, Kate and Lucy ran through the trees — zigging, zagging, ducking under limbs. Pain seared through her ankle and she fought off tears.

She heard someone coming from the other side of the boulder. There wasn't time to crawl into the forest and hide. She couldn't walk, much less run. Her ankle was busted.

Pop! Pop! Pop!

Gunshots rang through the forest. Agent Nelson appeared from around the boulder, ducking down, gun drawn. "Stay down!"

Wendy covered her head with her arms.

Shots pinged off the boulder and Nelson leaned out from behind it, firing at Craig, who had taken cover in a clump of trees.

"I can't move. My ankle. I might have torn something," Wendy told Nelson.

"Assailant is wearing full camo. I can see Hayes and Cervantes. Both are down," Nelson reported to the team. "I have Wendy with me. The other three ran west, off-trail through the woods."

Nelson peeked out from the boulder and another shot rang out, striking the rock. He returned fire, crouching and running to the tree closest to the rock. "Assailant has multiple weapons," he said as he cut behind another tree. He fired, missed and skidded behind a log. He popped out from the tree and squeezed the trigger three times, then scurried back behind it. "Can't get a clear shot!"

Craig sprayed the boulder and tree with bullets. Rubble rained down on Wendy. She covered her face and screamed.

Nelson gave up his cover and ran in her direction while shots rang out. He lunged for the boulder, grunted and fell onto Wendy.

She panicked and tried to roll him over. His head wasn't bloody, nor was his chest. "Are you okay? Where are you hit?"

Nelson ignored her and shouted information to the team. "I'm hit. Assailant running after the girls. Get here!"

He sat up, dragging his left leg and using the boulder for support. Blood gushed from his thigh. Wendy threw off her fleece jacket, hesitated for a moment as Nelson groaned in pain, then gave it to him. He pressed it down, cringing a little.

"Do we need to make a tourniquet?" Wendy asked.

"No, I don't think it hit anything major." Sweat covered his pale face.

Wendy didn't quite believe him. She spotted Lucy's backpack on the trail and tried to stand. It wasn't easy, but she used the boulder as leverage and hobbled to her feet. Managing to hop to the backpack and back to Nelson, she fumbled with the zipper but got it open. The contents spilled to the ground and she picked up the first-aid kit.

Footsteps pounded down the trail in their direction. Wendy tried to scoot to see who it was, but Nelson held her in place.

He shakily lifted his gun. "Keep your cover."

Finck ran down the trail and checked on Cervantes and Hayes, both of whom were still down. "They should be okay." He started to run to Nelson, but Nelson waved him away.

Nelson pointed in the direction Craig had run. "Take that asshole down."

"Yes, sir." Finck took off.

53

Vivian, Lucy and Kate ran as fast as the terrain allowed, breaking branches and jumping over fallen trees.

"Should we try to hide?" Kate said.

"Keep going," Lucy yelled and ducked under a limb. "Keep going!"

Vivian ran faster, looking for a clearer route. Her legs burned and she could hardly breathe but she knew if she stopped it could be over.

The trees around them thinned out and the ground sloped. Then the earth ended.

Vivian skidded to a stop just before the edge, holding her arms out to either side. Lucy stopped, too, but Kate's momentum careened her forward and she almost went over.

"Whoa!" Vivian said, reaching for her.

Kate caught her balance and they stood there, frozen for a beat, looking straight down. The cliff dropped 50 feet to a swiftly running stream.

Vivian got a little dizzy and took several steps back. "That was almost bad." She looked around. They didn't have many options. "We need to keep running or find somewhere to hide."

"There is no more running." A malicious voice came from the woods.

Oh my god. There's nowhere to go.

Craig took slow, deliberate steps, staring at Vivian as he advanced. His bright green eyes flared against the paint on his face. Gun in hand.

"We're meant to be together."

Kate and Lucy were on either side of her, holding onto her arms.

"Craig, this isn't how it's supposed to be."

"We will be together." He tapped the gun to his chest. "Even if we die together."

Lucy tightened her grip.

"Let's talk, Craig. I know you love me. No one needs to get hurt."

"You shouldn't have listened to your boy toy, Brandon. None of this would have happened." Tap…tap tap.

Vivian took a step back, toward the cliff.

"You should have come with me at the hotel." Craig pointed the gun at Vivian. "It would have been much easier."

She held her hands up in defense. "I wasn't ready, but I am now. It's not too late for us to be together, Craig. We have this," she yanked the pendant off her neck and held it up, "and we don't need anything else. Let's just go."

A twig snapped behind him and he turned.

Finck took a defensive stance. "Drop the weapon! Drop it!"

Craig made no move to do so. Instead, he let out a deep-throated laugh. "I'm not giving up on my girl now. She needs me."

Finck took two steps forward. "It's over. You're surrounded. Now drop the weapon."

Craig, still laughing, said, "Make me."

Finck fired two shots in front of Craig's boots.

Craig quit laughing. "Okay, okay." He held his arms out to his side, then dropped the gun.

"Kick it away," Finck yelled.

Craig kicked it back, toward the ledge.

Finck approached, gun pointing at Craig's chest. "Hands on your head. Get on your knees. Slowly."

Craig dropped to one knee, then the other.

As Finck moved in, Craig's hand slid down his neck, into the back of his shirt. A blur of black appeared above his head.

"Gun!" Vivian yelled, but it was too late.

***

Wendy crept up behind a tree. Her ankle throbbed, but the adrenaline kept her moving. Nelson had passed out. Hayes and Cervantes were still out, and Shick had been the last to leave the cabin and wasn't there yet. She knew Vivian, Lucy and Kate needed her.

Then she'd heard gunshots and screams. It was up to her.

The girls were huddled together, inches from the edge. Craig was laughing like a maniac, waving his gun in the air.

"You see, Vivian? You see?" More laughing.

Wendy looked down at the only weapon she had and flicked the tab off. She closed her eyes for a second, opened them, and moved toward Craig.

***

Finck was down, bleeding from his shoulder and holding his knee. Craig kicked Finck's gun away, then searched him. He removed a gun strapped above Finck's ankle, then turned his attention back to Vivian.

She was paralyzed with fear. She, Kate and Lucy remained at the cliff's edge.

"I told you, we're meant to be together. Everything is going my way. I can't be beaten. I'm smarter than these yahoos."

Behind him, movement in the trees. A flash of blue.

"You know now, right?" Craig aimed the gun at Vivian. "You know we're supposed to be together forever."

She glanced behind him and couldn't believe what she saw.

"Craig, this isn't you. Look at yourself. I know this isn't who you are." Vivian spoke as calmly as she could, hands clasped in front of her. "I know you love me, and I... I love you so much, too. We'll start over. Forget about everything that's happened."

It was the time Wendy needed. She jumped from behind Craig, aimed and mashed down the trigger. Bear spray hit the side of Craig's face.

"Get out of here, now!" Finck yelled.

Lucy dragged Vivian by the arm away from the scene, Kate on their heels.

Craig, yelling obscenities, waved his gun in Wendy's direction. She moved behind him but kept the bear spray trained on his head. When he spun around, she got him full in the face. He screamed, clutching at his eyes, and dropped his gun.

"Run! Go! Go!" Finck said.

Kate had other intentions. "Hiiiiiiiiiiiiiiiiiii-yaaaaaaah!" She karate kicked Craig right in the nuts. "Take that, you monster!"

He doubled over, then fell to the ground. Tears, snot and slobber streaked his camo-painted face. He howled in pain.

That was enough for Wendy, who kicked his gun over the cliff, then turned and hobbled away. Kate wrapped an arm around Wendy for support, and they hurried after Lucy and Vivian.

Craig's unintelligible screams carried through the forest, and it wasn't long before Shick crashed through the trees. Passing them, he yelled, "Keep going. Help is by the trail."

Vivian wanted to watch Craig go down. Literally, over the cliff would have been perfect, but arrested would suffice.

Shick, gun in hand, descended on Craig. He grabbed his legs and dragged him away from the cliff. Shick attempted to flip Craig on his stomach and pull his right hand behind him, but Craig maneuvered onto his side, clawing at him like a wild animal. Shick shielded himself as best he could, then punched Craig in the face with a hard right.

Lights out.

Shick flipped Craig over and handcuffed him. He stood up and kicked Craig in the ribs.

Vivian and the girls hustled back to the trail as quickly as Wendy's hurt ankle would allow.

"Is everyone okay, well, except for you, Wendy? I know you aren't okay," Vivian asked as she helped Wendy hop over a log.

"My sinuses burn," Kate said. "I got a whiff of bear spray. That is what that was, right?"

Wendy smiled despite the pain. "Yep. Bought it in Aspen after seeing those trash cans. Gotta be prepared."

The hiker couple with the German Shepherd ran past them. The guy pulled medical supplies out of his backpack, handing it to the girl as they ran.

"Keep heading straight that way," Lucy said. "They're at the cliff."

They continued on.

"You've had that spray the whole time?" Kate asked Wendy.

"In my jacket pocket."

Vivian held a branch back for the girls to pass. "Where's your jacket?" she said to Wendy.

"I gave it to Wade. He got shot in the leg."

"We heard," Kate said, pointing to her ear bud. "Is he going to be okay?"

"I don't know. He didn't think it hit his femoral artery, but he was bleeding pretty good. He passed out right before I came to help y'all."

"Oh god, that sounds serious."

They made it back to the trail and found Hayes glassy-eyed but sitting up. Cervantes was leaning against a tree, hair frizzed out to epic proportions. A couple of Vail PD hikers attended a pale-faced Nelson.

He looked at Wendy and shook his head. "Don't ever do that again."

She smiled. "He's going to be okay."

"We need some help over here," Lucy said, helping Wendy hobble over to Nelson. "She busted her ankle."

One of the officers attending Nelson came over and sat Wendy down, then took off her shoe and unwrapped the bandage job that Vivian had done. Her ankle was bruised and swollen. "We'll get you some real help when the medics get here."

Vivian sat down next to Wendy and pulled her knees up to her chest. The scene at the cliff caught up to her and she began to cry.

Kate sat down next to her and put an arm around her shoulders. "It's okay, it's all over now."

"I know, but I can't believe this. Wendy's hurt, Agent Nelson and Agent Finck are both shot, you almost fell off the cliff."

Kate sat there for a few seconds, then said, "Wendy has crap for ankles. It was probably ready to blow anyway. Agent Nelson won't be dancing any time soon, but he'll be okay. Finck, well, he'll need a new knee but hopefully his shoulder wasn't too terribly injured. As for me plunging over the cliff, nah, I wasn't going over. I was just trying to make things exciting."

Vivian laughed through the tears. "Make things exciting, huh? You're right. We do need to add some excitement to our vacations."

Lucy walked over in time to hear Vivian's last remark. "If this isn't exciting enough for you, I can't wait to see what the next one brings."

54

The girls waited on the trail until help arrived, including EMTs and fire/rescue personnel.

An EMT attended to Wendy's ankle. She turned it this way and that, flexed her foot up and down. She didn't think anything was broken, but a ligament was most likely torn. "You need to go to the ER and have them do an MRI to determine the extent of damage."

Wendy sighed. "All they're going to do is wrap it good, right?"

"Yes."

"Then wrap it good for me here. I'm not spending my last night of vacation sitting in an emergency room."

The paramedic started to protest but Wendy cut her off. "I'd rather my doctor do surgery on me if needed, and I'll see him as soon as I get home, okay?"

Placated, the EMT re-wrapped her ankle and told Wendy to ice it and stay off it as much as possible.

Shick, face scratched and rubbing one eye, hauled a handcuffed and red-eyed Craig through the forest and down the trail. Two other officers were on hand for the hike of shame. Craig stumbled over a rock and fell face down in the dirt. Shick helped him stumble a little more as he jerked him up.

Hayes and Cervantes were finally able to stand and walk around, uneasy at first, then mostly recovered. Cervantes ran her hands through her hair, but there wasn't much that could be done for the frizz-ball.

Lucy offered her a ponytail holder. "Bumble and Bumble De-Frizz is the only thing that will help what you've got goin' on."

Cervantes grinned, said thanks and put her hair up. It looked like a giant pom-pom sticking out of the back of her head.

Nelson was transported to the cliff, where he and Finck waited for airlift to arrive. It wasn't long before the whoosh of the chopper rotors could be heard. Vivian stood up and watched as a basket was lowered and then raised a few minutes later with Finck. The process was repeated for Nelson. Agents securely on board, the helicopter flew off into the twilight.

Vivian turned to face the girls. "Y'all ready to go? I don't want to hike down this mountain with flashlights."

They were ready and Wendy was helped down the mountain by two burly firemen. She seemed pretty okay with that.

The old mining camp looked eerie in the dusk, and Vivian had no inclination to stop or peek inside the shacks. She picked up the pace to keep up with Lucy.

They got to Bighorn Creek and the firemen splashed across carrying Wendy. They sat her down on the other side, then helped Vivian, Kate and Lucy across. It was much harder, in the fading light, to see the rock and logs they had used in crossing that afternoon.

The switchbacks were easier to manage going down, and for that Vivian was thankful.

Once at the bottom of the trail, they gave individual statements to Agent Smith. Their stories were the same. Craig jumped out of a tree, zapped Hayes and Cervantes, shot Nelson, shot Finck twice, Wendy bear sprayed him, he clawed the crap out of Shick before being handcuffed.

Smith walked Vivian over to Lucy's SUV where the girls waited.

"Is there anything else we need to do?" Vivian asked him.

"What time is your flight tomorrow?"

"It's at 4:40, so we need to head down the mountain by noon. Wendy and Kate fly out about that time, too. Lucy, who lives here in Boulder, is dropping us off."

"Nothing for now," Smith said. "We'll probably be by tonight to wrap things up, or it could be in the morning. For now, drive safely back to the hotel. I recommend picking up some crutches for 'Grace' here." He nodded to Wendy.

"Yeah, good idea," Kate said.

They got into Lucy's SUV and she cranked up the engine.

"I can't believe it's over," Vivian said as they left the parking lot. "Talk about a bad breakup."

"That's not the only thing that's over," Lucy said, putting on some Beaver Balm. "Our vacation is over as of tomorrow."

"So not fair," Vivian said. "I could use another day, or four."

"Let's not get all blah. We need to celebrate!" Kate said and patted Vivian on the back. "You are free from drama, and we have one more crisp, cool night at The Ridge."

"True. Let's do it up right," Wendy said. "Maybe hit Beaver Liquors, grab some champagne. I need to drink for medicinal purposes."

Vivian looked at her. "Need some natural anesthetic?"

"Yeah, sure. Grapes are natural. Anyway, back to my master plan. We go back to the hotel and y'all can take a dip in the grotto while I relax in a lounger, and then we can enjoy the fire pit and chow down on s'mores."

"Okay, but I'm buying the champagne," Vivian said. "As long as we don't buy it at the hotel. It'd cost me a small fortune! Or maybe a small child."

"You're not lacking in those," Lucy laughed.

"Let's book it to the beave!" Wendy said.

Lucy drove into town where they stopped at a pharmacy and grabbed Wendy some crutches. Then they were off to Beaver Liquors for natural anesthetic — two bottles of wine and a bottle of champagne. They didn't stop at the novelty section this time. They were women on a mission.

Once at the hotel they stopped by the front desk and told Trey about the hike and the takedown. He was impressed, especially with the bear spray and karate kick. Seeing Wendy using the crutches, he sent for a wheelchair.

"I'm pushing her," Lucy said and got into place behind the wheelchair the instant it arrived.

"She's a little too excited about this," Wendy said, hesitantly sitting down.

"I'm an excellent driver. Cars, wheelchairs, you name it."

"I dunno." Wendy propped her feet on the two rests. "How many accidents have you been in?"

Lucy shushed her and pushed her to the room without running into anything. Vivian deemed Lucy worthy of wheelchair duty.

Three of them changed into swimsuits, robes and slippers and Wendy kept on her hiking clothes. No sense in sweating in anything else, she reasoned.

Wendy hopped to the wheelchair and sat down holding a bottle of wine and four cups. "I've got us set in the beverage department. Let's jet."

They walked and wheeled to the elevator, taking it to the spa.

"I could get used to this," Wendy said as Lucy wheeled her into the grotto.

"As if this place doesn't spoil you enough, now you want to be carted everywhere!" Vivian said, depositing her robe on a lounger.

"Would it be your pleasure to do that for me?" Wendy asked Vivian sweetly as she opened the bottle and poured everyone a cup.

Lucy gave the toast. "To our last night in our Rocky Mountain paradise. May it not be full of surprises!"

Clink!

Before getting in the hot tub, Kate grabbed everyone two slices of cucumbers. "We deserve to pamper ourselves."

"Amen to that," Lucy said, sitting on the ledge in front of Wendy's lounger. Kate sat down next to her.

Vivian sat on the ledge close to the waterfall and put the cool cucumber on her eyes and leaned back. Warmth and bubbles enveloped her, a million tiny air massages, working out the stress. The cucumber chill soothed her eyelids. She wanted to float like that forever.

"Viv. Viv." Lucy was pushing on her arm. "Wake up."

"What? Huh?"

"You fell asleep! I've never seen anyone crash that fast. Ever."

Vivian peeled the cucumbers from her eyes. "I've had a rough week. Guess I needed a nap."

Kate was already out of the water and toweling off. "We were getting pruney, so we decided it was time."

"Besides, I need more natural anesthetic," Wendy said, dropping into the wheelchair.

Lucy slipped on her robe. "I'm getting hungry."

Vivian was, too, so she dried off and threw on her robe and slippers. "I'm ready."

They went back upstairs, freshened up, changed into warmer clothes and decided to celebrate at Felix's.

"Should we go ahead and pack up the champagne and s'mores stuff?" Lucy asked.

"Probably a good idea," Kate said. "I'm sitting by the fire pit right after dinner. No more moving. No more worrying. No more anything, except for the calm movement of my hand bringing to my mouth warm, melted chocolate and lightly roasted marshmallow mushed ever so gingerly between two graham crackers. Mmmmm."

"Maybe we should have those first," Vivian said.

"I need some real food. We can splurge, but nobody order the $500 margarita!" Wendy said, wheeling herself to the door of the suite.

55

M att, the host, greeted the girls in Felix's and escorted them to a lovely table. Wendy asked for the wine list. Matt made a few suggestions, and she ordered a bottle of Archery Summit Red Hills Estate pinot noir.

"It's nice to sit here and not worry that someone's watching," Vivian said, opening her menu, her back to the wall. She had a great view of the restaurant and the mountainside.

"True that," Lucy said, flipping a page in her menu. "Now what do I want?"

"I know what I'm having," Kate said without even cracking her menu open. "I want a big-ass steak. Medium rare. On the side I want the scalloped potatoes and glazed carrots."

"Ditto," Vivian said. "Except do they have mac and cheese? I do love myself some good mac and cheese. And I want mine medium. I don't do blood."

"Are you getting that instead of the potatoes?" Lucy asked.

"Nope, instead of carrots. I want carbs with my carbs. Bring it on."

Lucy shook her head. "I think I'm having the Hawaiian roasted pork tenderloin."

"I can't decide," Wendy said. "I'm torn between the blackened trout and the venison stew. I'll ask which is better."

Matt returned with the wine and Wendy went through the sniffing, swirling and tasting before approving. The waiter arrived to take their order and Wendy asked for a recommendation. He said both the venison and the trout were good, but he went on and on about the trout, so trout it was.

Matt and the waiter left, and Lucy held up her wine glass. "To the capture of Craig, compliments of Wendy!"

"And karate chops!" Wendy said, slicing her hand through the air.

"And bear spray!" Kate added.

"And to my brave, loyal, very best friends," Vivian said. "I couldn't have done this without y'all."

They cheersed and had just put down their glasses when the waiter arrived with a crab cake appetizer.

"Compliments of Felix's," he said.

Lucy drizzled the white wine butter sauce over the crab. "Score!"

Vivian took a bite and did a little dance in her chair. "Oh my god, this is good."

This called for another toast. "To Felix's!"

Clink.

"It is so nice here," Wendy said, looking out the floor-to-ceiling windows. The moon glowed against the mountain and glittered off the pool. "I can totally understand why you love living in Colorado."

"It is a nice place," Lucy said. "And I love that the community does things to promote a healthy lifestyle, like bike paths. In Boulder they're everywhere. Try to ride your bike anywhere in Texas and you're highly likely to become road kill."

"We're getting better," Vivian said in defense. "In Fort Worth our mayor is an avid biker and a proponent for bike lanes. But others in city government had started the campaign even before she was in office."

"Even so, it's not like Colorado," Kate said. "Austin is better than most cities in Texas, but pedestrians and bikers are still likely to get run over."

"It's damn hot in Texas in the summers," Wendy said, taking a sip of water. "So I'll stick to getting around in my Trans Am."

"I wouldn't mind living in Colorado. Maybe one day," Vivian said. "Until then I'll have the stationary bike at my gym. I do have a good view sometimes, though."

"Oh really?" Kate said.

"No one in particular, but there's some good eye candy."

Wendy's phone rang and she looked at the display. It rang several times but she didn't respond.

Vivian leaned across the table. "Who is it?"

"Jake."

"You gonna answer it?"

Wendy clicked on and rolled away from the table. This was one conversation she didn't want to have in front of the girls. She tucked the phone between her ear and shoulder and said hello. She made her way into the great room and pulled up by the fireplace.

"How's your trip?" Jake asked, sounding upbeat.

Wendy laughed. "Just peachy. I'm in a wheelchair."

"You're what?"

"Blew out my ankle today running from a crazed stalker. Had to give my jacket to an FBI agent who got shot in the leg. The Ridge is fabulous, though, and I'd love to come back."

"What the heck are you talking about? Do you need me to fly up there? Are you okay?"

She sniffled a little. He still cared. "Nothing's broken, I'll be fine. I survived falling out of the raft that had been shot while we were whitewater rafting through the Royal Gorge and Lucy got us stopped safely in the runaway truck ramp when her brakes went out."

"Brakes out? Falling out of a raft? Can you please tell me what's going on?"

Wendy went over the past six days, highlighting some details, but not all. She did mention the five FBI agents, hard to leave that part out, but she didn't mention the grotto incident. Or the elevator.

When she finished, Jake said, "Why didn't you call me?"

"For what?" she said, instantly pissed off. He hadn't been around much lately, why did he think his presence would help now? "We've been in good hands. There isn't anything you could have done."

"I'd just like to be there for you."

"Really? It sure hasn't felt like it lately." She hung up the phone, her hands shaking. She hadn't had the heart to break up with him over the phone, he deserved better than that, but if he really cared about her, he needed to show it. She was on the verge of thinking his caring only went so far, as in "let's just be friends" far.

She regained her composure and rolled back to the dinner table. Their food had arrived, and she gave a quick recap of the conversation as everyone dug in.

Lucy ate a bite of grilled pineapple and said with a full mouth, "So, are you breaking up with him?"

Wendy teared up a little but was determined to forget about the Jake situation for now. She wanted to have a great time on her last night of vacation.

To lighten the mood, Vivian went over the high school roster, updating the girls on who was where, who'd gotten married, who'd popped out a kid or two.

Lucy and Kate had a few updates, but Wendy, sticking around the Get Down, had the most.

"Did y'all hear Pete Montoya is a plastic surgeon now?"

"Really?" Kate looked surprised.

"Has a practice in the Houston Medical Center. I used to party with him in high school. I knew he was a smart guy, but I just can't picture him doing something so serious."

Vivian stabbed a piece of steak. "Is he single and if so, do you have his number?"

Wendy laughed and they continued their scrumptious dinner. A time or two, Vivian caught herself looking around for psycho stalkers and had to remind herself that Craig was locked up.

She took one last bite of mac and cheese and pushed back her plate. "My name is Vivian Taylor, and I'm a carboholic."

"Yes, you are," Lucy said as she reached over and scammed a bite of mac and cheese. "Damn, that's good."

"Too good."

Kate pushed back her plate. She had wiped out the steak and most of the potatoes but left the carrots. "I was just trying to look healthy."

Wendy loved her trout and Lucy finished her tenderloin. They sat for quite a while, chatting and polishing off the wine.

"Not sure I have room for s'mores," Vivian finally said.

"Come on, there's always room," Kate said. "Marshmallows are mostly air anyway."

Vivian tried to stand. It took her a second. "Are they? ARE they?"

"We'll pretend like they are," Kate said, linking arms with her.

Wendy rolled back from the table. "After this meal, I don't mind being carted around."

Lucy grabbed the handles on the wheelchair. "I'll push your ass to the fire." She stopped and put on the brake. "Actually, I can sit on your lap and let's have a Ridge person push us."

"I bet they would!" Vivian laughed and looked around for assistance.

"Uh, no!" Wendy shoved Lucy's butt away. "I'm injured here!"

Lucy sighed and unlocked the brake. "Fine, I'll push. But someone else is pushing you back to the room later."

They made their way to the fire pit, which they had to themselves.

"Mud season rocks," Vivian said, collapsing into a chair.

Everyone agreed.

The fire was perfect. Peaceful. Warm. Safe.

Vivian had just closed her eyes when she heard a familiar voice.

"I knew I'd find you here."

56

V ivian couldn't believe it. Rodney, her masseur from Playa Del Carmen, was standing beside her.

"Oh my gosh, what are you doing here?" She jumped up and hugged his neck.

He squeezed her back, holding on to her with his tall, lanky frame. He whispered in her ear, "I'm sorry you've had such an awful time. Trey told me what happened." He squeezed her again, then let go and said to the group, "Trey emailed me. He told me that some crazy Texas gals had checked in who had been referred by yours truly. I knew exactly who he was talking about."

"You came all the way from Mexico?" Kate asked.

"My sister got married this past weekend, so I was in town, but I couldn't go back to Mexico without a visit to my old stomping grounds."

"I'm so glad you're here," Vivian said. "Join us!"

"I plan to," he said. "But first..." He held up a couple of liquor bottles. "Rodney Specials all around!"

They girls cheered as he mixed, swirled, shook and poured five of his infamous Mexico concoctions, complete with the "kiss" of grenadine. He delicately handed each of them a martini glass, then held his high.

"To friends reunited, wrongs that are righted. May the rest of your vacation be fantabulous!"

They clinked glasses and sipped their lovely beige drinks.

"Mmmmm, just like I remember," Kate said, licking her lips. "You've got to teach me how to make these things."

"Sure thing, honey. The secret's in the shake." Rodney sat in the chair next to Vivian and put his legs up on the stone ledge. "I hear that things haven't been exactly perfect during your stay."

"You can say that again," Wendy said. "But it's over now, thank god."

"So what'd you hear about our crazy vacation?" Lucy asked.

Rodney swirled his drink. "I heard that Vivian was being stalked by her ex but that he's been shackled, like all of us at Shorty's party!"

"You were the only one who got shackled," Vivian said. "We got lucky!"

"It's all coming back to me. Of course, give me a few more of these and I'll forget again."

"Did you hook up with the trainer guy you saw at the party?"

Rodney shook his head. "Not long term. He was too immature for me." He pondered that for a moment, then put his drink on the ledge. "So guess what?"

"What?" they asked.

"I have an even bigger surprise for you than me!"

"You're full of surprises!" Vivian laughed.

"First thing tomorrow morning, I've lined it up for you all to have massages, and I promise, no weirdo stalkers will crash your comfort."

"Rodney, you're the best!" Lucy yelled, standing and giving him a hug.

"Really, Rodney," Vivian said, holding her glass high. "You're our Rodney Special!"

They reminisced about Mexico, Al and Adrienne, the big party bust and Jon.

"Lucy still talks to Pierre," Vivian said.

"He was the bald guy, right?" Rodney asked.

"Yep," Kate said. "We thought he looked like Mr. Clean."

"He was a hunk," Rodney said, then looked around the group. "Who's ready for another?"

They all lifted their glasses, and Rodney started mixing and shaking.

Vivian looked up to see someone walking toward them. Her skin prickled and her heart pounded for a beat until she recognized the man.

"Well, well, well, what do we have here?" a scratch-faced Shick said as he joined them.

Only one eye looked back at Vivian, but she pretended not to notice. "Agent Shick, this is Rodney, our friend from Mexico."

Rodney stepped forward, seemingly quite happy to meet Shick, and they shook hands.

Kate and Wendy said hello and also ignored the scratches and one eye.

"What's up with the eye patch?" Lucy asked, then gave him a hug. "Thank you, by the way."

"That fucker clawed me like a rabid wolverine," Shick answered, touching the patch. "It's not permanent. Doc says I have to wear it for two to three weeks."

"It's pretty sexy if you ask me." Lucy gave him a high-five.

"I concur," Rodney said, taking a seat while holding up his drink so it didn't spill.

"I'm just glad you didn't lose your eye," Vivian said. "Those scratches look pretty bad."

Shick traced a deep cut that started somewhere under the eye patch and ended at his earlobe. "I turned my head just in time. A split second slower…"

Vivian shuddered and decided it was time to change the subject. "Way to take Craig down."

"The bear spray helped," Shick said and laughed. "I may have to start carrying that."

"Yeah, yeah," Wendy said, shoving his shoulder.

"Seriously," he said "it really was instrumental in bringing him down. You probably saved your friends' lives."

"I have no doubt," Vivian said, going over to Wendy and hugging her shoulders. "Thank god somebody in this group is Captain Safety. She keeps us supplied in bandages and bear spray."

Wendy rolled closer to the fire pit and propped her bad ankle up on the ledge. "I know my role in this outfit. Somebody's gotta keep y'all healthy. Or at least drugged."

"And you do a greatastic job of that," Kate slurred, then plopped down. "Oh oh. I think I'm a little messedrunk."

"You never get drunk," Vivian said. "It's about time!"

Kate smirked and leaned her head back in her chair.

"I'm not drunk," Vivian said. "But I'd like to be. Rodney, pour me up another, will ya?"

He'd already mixed and shaken, so he topped her off. Wendy and Lucy also got refills.

Shick sat on the ledge in front of Vivian. "Craig won't be able to bother you for a very long time. He has been transported to a maximum security facility in Denver and charged with attempted murder, premeditated murder, burglary, multiple counts of assault to a federal officer, violating a restraining order and international wire fraud."

Vivian stopped rocking in her chair. "Well, hell. That's enough. How could I have misjudged his character so much? He's an evil person."

Shick nodded his head. "In fact, there's more. I understand the man that died at your hotel in Aspen may have been Craig's partner in the credit card skimming operation."

"Please don't tell me…" Vivian said.

Shick sighed. "We don't know for sure yet, but we suspect Craig was involved in his death."

"Holy shit!" Wendy yelled. "We've been the bait for a murderer!"

"We didn't know," Shick said. "We just confirmed the identity of the partner a few hours ago."

Vivian snapped in the air. "Rodney, help here! This is too much to take!"

Rodney filled her glass.

Shick leaned forward, touching her knee. "Vivian, Craig was very good at deception."

Vivian started rocking again. "That doesn't make me feel any better, but thanks."

Everyone was quiet for a minute.

Rodney stood and took the floor, waving his drink around. "So Shick, you're telling us…Craig was a credit card skimming schemer, buddy off the balcony bumper, sail away with me stalker and all around asshole?"

"That's what I'm saying."

Rodney lifted his glass. "Well, here's to his happy ending. Giving and receiving them. In jail."

Everyone lifted their glass high and cheersed to that.

"How's Wade?" Wendy asked Shick. "Any updates on his condition?"

"The doc was able to remove the bullet from Nelson's thigh. It didn't hit anything major, but he lost a lot of blood."

She cringed. "What hospital is he in? Can I see him before I leave tomorrow?"

"I'm not at liberty to disclose that, sorry."

Wendy nodded, then stared off into the fire.

"He has your number, you'll likely hear from him." Wendy perked up at that. "In fact, all of you might be hearing from someone involved in the investigation and prosecution of Craig. We have evidence of his crimes and audio of today's events, but you still may be needed to testify against him."

Vivian didn't know how she felt about that. She didn't want to see Craig again, ever. Maybe they'd let her do a deposition.

"I'll be happy to go to court and tell the judge what a good-for-nothin' scumbag Craig is," Lucy said, waving around her Rodney Special. She then switched gears. "How's Finck?"

Shick smiled at Lucy's righteousness and said, "Finck got really lucky. The shot through his shoulder was just that, but his knee will need some reconstruction. He'll be out for a while."

"Bummer," Lucy said.

"It could have been worse," Shick said. "Nobody died."

"Thank goodness for that," Wendy said.

"What about Smith?" Vivian asked.

"He took all the credit," Shick smirked, then continued. "He's the one who got the bastard booked and settled away, dammit. The rest of us were being patched up."

"We really appreciate all y'all did to help Vivian, and we give all of you credit." Lucy held up the last of her drink.

"Yes, we do," Vivian said, lifting her Rodney Special. "To the FBI and everyone else who helped capture Craig."

Everyone cheersed except for Kate, who had passed out in her chair, soaking up the warmth of the fire pit.

"Looks like it's time for bed," Wendy said, handing Rodney her glass. "Sleeping Beauty here may need her own wheelchair to make it upstairs."

They said goodnight to Agent Shick and gave Rodney big hugs goodbye.

"Thanks in advance for tomorrow," Vivian said.

"Honey, you deserve every minute of relaxation, celebration, master—"

"Okay, okay, I get it. Thank you Rodney! You're a gem!" Vivian and Lucy heaved Kate up from her chair, and with Wendy rolling behind, they went up to bed.

57

Day 7

Vivian's head hurt. And the light…dear god, the light was beaming directly at her eyeballs through the crack in the curtain. She groaned and rolled over.

"Morning, glory," Lucy said quietly as she put a fresh glass of water and two ibuprofen on the nightstand. "Wendy brought these over."

Vivian opened one eye and looked at the white, chalky pills. She wanted to take them, but her arms, which didn't hurt, were warm and comfy under the covers, and the thought of taking them out was too much. "Uhhhhhhhh."

"Oh come on now," Lucy said. "You can do it."

Vivian's pounding head took precedence over the warm covers and she reached for the pills.

"That's a good girl," Lucy said as she closed the curtain so no light shone through. "Now we have about an hour and a half before we need to leave for the spa. Lie back and take a happy nappy."

"Okay," Vivian muttered and closed her eyes. She was snoring before Lucy had left the room.

***

"Feeling better?" Lucy asked, pulling open the curtain just a bit.

Vivian stretched her arms above her head. "Oh my gosh, yes."

"Good. We have to be in the spa in 10 minutes, so brush your teeth, throw that hair back into something semi-tame and let's go."

"Where've you been?" Vivian asked, looking at Lucy's workout outfit.

"I did the circuit downstairs."

Vivian threw the covers off and tried to stand. She swayed a little.

"Then Wendy and I grabbed a small breakfast. I had oatmeal."

The thought of oatmeal was not appealing. Vivian walked to the bathroom and closed the door. She looked at herself in the mirror.

Wow, I've got a lot of gray, she thought, running her fingers through her hair. She'd had a few strands before her first daughter was born, but now they were running rampant. She pulled the magnification mirror away from the wall and turned it on, looking at her skin.

Screw a massage, I need a facial. I think I'm getting a new wrinkle. She pushed at the skin next to her nose, right under her left eye. *I've got to stop sleeping on that side of my face.*

Lucy knocked on the door. "Two minutes!"

"Okay, okay," Vivian said and pushed the mirror back to the wall. She brushed her teeth and washed her face with a washcloth, careful not to scrub too hard. Then she looked through Lucy's array of products. She plucked out an expensive-looking facial moisturizer and slathered it on. *Damn, this is good stuff.*

Lucy always had the best products. Hair stuff, face stuff, skin stuff, you name it. Vivian, on the other hand, was lucky to get out the door with her teeth brushed in the morning, much less hair or makeup done. She'd recently perfected the art of drying her hair with the minivan heater while driving to the hospital. Her wonderful sitter, Miss Margie, was only a few blocks away from her house so she could scrunch in silence. There were just enough lights and traffic along her route that she generally walked in looking decent, which was good because there were lots of cute residents at the hospital.

"Time to go!" Lucy knocked on the door again. "Free massages! We don't want to be late!"

Vivian pulled her hair back in a clip and slipped on Ridge slippers. "Ready."

"You're looking much better than you did earlier this morning," Lucy said.

"Thanks for taking such good care of me."

"It was mostly Wendy's doing."

"Thank you both, then."

Wendy and Kate had emerged. Wendy, who was able to walk with a slight limp, looked rather perky. Kate looked green.

"You okay?" Vivian asked Kate.

"I'll make it."

"Let's work together," Vivian said, linking arms with her.

Kate complied and put her head on Vivian's shoulder. "I think I drank too much."

"We all drank too much, thanks to Rodney," Vivian said, patting her head. "Let's go get those nasty toxins worked out, c'mon."

The girls rode the elevator down to the spa. A new girl was at the counter, not Suri, but she greeted them warmly. They went to the locker room and changed into the luxurious robes, then went into the lounge.

After a few minutes of mostly silence, a female masseuse came in, calling for Kate. Then one for Wendy and another for Lucy. Before following her masseuse out the door, Wendy looked back and smiled as the door closed behind her.

Vivian was alone.

She sat in the lounge, a little uncomfortable. She picked up a magazine, then put it back down. *It's because I'm so rarely alone. And because last time I was in here things didn't go so well. Geez, relax!*

She watched the fire and scrunched down into the softness of her lounger. The soft music playing overhead and the warmth of her blanket forced her eyes closed, but only for a moment. Her masseuse touched her on the shoulder gently, introduced herself, then escorted her to the Blizzard Room. Vivian undressed and slid onto the warm table. *These linens feel and smell amazing.* She positioned her face into the smushy, round cutout.

The masseuse knocked on the door, then entered.

"Everything good?" she asked.

"Perfect."

Finally.

Vivian's massage started with her scalp and ended at her tippy toes. It was magical.

"Take your time getting dressed. I'll get you some water." The masseuse closed the door behind her.

"Mmmmmm mmmmm," was all Vivian could say. After a long moment she slowly peeled herself from the table and wrapped up in the robe. She opened the door and the masseuse pointed to her feet.

"Oops, you forgot your shoes."

"So I did," Vivian said lazily. She shuffled to them and stuck her feet in, then trailed behind the masseuse to the ladies lounge where Lucy, Kate and Wendy were waiting.

"How was it?" Kate asked.

"Fantab," Vivian responded, dropping into a lounger. "I don't want to leave."

"Too bad your first massage didn't go like that." Wendy stood at the beverage station, dipping a teabag into a steaming to-go cup. "Want one?"

Vivian waved her off. "No thanks."

Wendy snapped a lid onto her tea and walked toward the door. "Ladies, I hate to say this, but we have a plane to catch. Well, not you, Lucy, but you have to get us there."

Groans.

"I know, I know, but I speak the truth. Let's get upstairs and pack it up, pack it in."

They forced themselves from their loungers and made their way back to the room. Vivian threw clothes into her suitcase as Lucy neatly folded and placed.

"Are those all clean?" Vivian asked.

"No," Lucy responded.

"Then why are you folding them?"

"You just focus on cramming and stuffing, I'll handle my own packing."

Vivian shook her head and threw another sweater into her bag. "You need therapy."

"Twenty minutes," Wendy yelled from the other room.

Vivian picked up the tossing and stuffing pace, did a final sweep of the bathroom and grabbed her razor. *Need this baby!*

She zipped up her burnt orange bag and hauled it off the bed. "I'm ready!" She then started packing up the bar. "What time is it?"

"11:45," Lucy called from the bedroom.

Close enough, she thought, and poured herself the last of the rum with a splash of Coke. *Gotta get ready for that flight.* She swirled her drink around with her finger, took a taste, then added more Coke.

"Look who's starting early," Lucy teased and picked up an unopened bottle of tequila. "Should we tip the luggage guy with this?"

"Definitely," Vivian agreed. "I can't believe we have extra."

"I think wine was our beverage of choice on this trip, but don't be fooled, we drank a lot of everything else."

Vivian finished packing the bar and Lucy called down for a bellman and for the valet to bring her SUV around.

"Did y'all do one last check of your room?" Kate said, rolling her luggage to the door.

"I did," Lucy said as she peeked around the bedroom door. "I think we're all set."

Wendy emerged with her suitcase and purse. "I'm sad to leave."

"We'll just have to come back sometime," Vivian said. "*Sans* stalker."

"Amen to that!" Wendy said. "All of it."

"Let's take one last ride to the spa, just to smell it," Vivian said, hitting the B button in the elevator.

The doors opened and they all inhaled the fabulousness of the spa before the doors closed again and they were taken to the lobby. Trey greeted them and had their bill ready to review.

"Guess it's time to settle up," Kate said.

"Can you divide the total by four?" Wendy asked.

"Of course," he said with a smile.

Vivian tapped her credit card on the marble countertop. "Wish we didn't have to leave. Just when I'm finally beginning to relax!"

Trey handed each of them a leather bill presenter.

Vivian flipped hers open and started to slip her credit card inside. "Something must be wrong. Mine has a zero balance."

"Mine, too," Lucy said, handing it back to him.

Trey gave them a big, broad smile. "We've comp'ed the entire stay. Food, room, spa services, all of it. I'm sorry things didn't go the way we intended, but we'd love it if you came back to see us another time."

"Shut the front door!" Vivian yelled.

Trey nodded.

"Y'all rock!" Lucy said, digging in her purse. "I can't believe it." She tried to hand him some cash, but he declined.

"It was our pleasure."

"Thank you so much!" Kate said, smiling at him. "Truly."

Wendy shook Trey's hand. "Thank you. And we'll be back, you can count on it!"

"I'm just glad everything turned out well."

They said goodbye and headed to the SUV. The bellman had it skillfully loaded, leaving a space for Lucy to see out the rearview. She handed him a tip and hopped in. Vivian got into the passenger seat, and Kate and Wendy slid into the back.

"We need some good goin' down the mountain tuneage!" Vivian said and plugged Lucy's phone into the radio jack. "What are y'all feeling?" She scrolled through about 50 songs before they decided on James Brown's "I Feel Good."

"Cuz you know what…I *do* feel good!" Vivian squealed, dancing to the music.

They zoomed down the mountain, passing the Continental Divide and rocking out to a variety of upbeat music.

Around Idaho Springs, Lucy looked at Wendy in the rearview mirror. "You said on the drive out here that you'd make a decision about Jake. Did you?"

Wendy fiddled with the cooler lid before answering. "I think he and I need to talk when I get home, but I think it's over. He likes his new job and being back home and I don't think I'm factored into that."

"I'm sorry, Wendy. I know you really liked him," Vivian said.

Kate patted Wendy's shoulder. "He's losing a great girl. Hang in there."

"What about Nelson?" Lucy asked.

"It's the long distance thing again, and I'm guessing with his job, that would be next to impossible to make work."

"He sure did have the hots for you, though," Kate said.

Wendy sighed, then changed the subject. "We never did decide where we are going on our next trip. We need to start saving."

Vivian got the map out of Lucy's console. "New York City… Miami… Vegas!"

"Not Vegas, but New Orleans has a casino…" Wendy tempted.

"Then New Orleans sounds *great*!" Vivian said.

Lucy shook her head. "You may have a problem. Do I need to get you that 1-800 number?"

Vivian ignored her. "Any other suggestions?"

Kate leaned toward the front and pointed to the West Coast. "What about something like Washington? Seattle?"

Lucy got excited. "Yeah, we could hike Mount Rainier."

"Dear god, you're killing me," Vivian mumbled.

"I don't mean hike to the top! I mean hike around the back country. Geez! It's actually a volcano, you know."

"Great, we can get lava'ed to death *while* we hike," Vivian joked.

"It's not active like that, but snow doesn't build up around the rim."

"I'd like that," Kate said. "Whatever we do, we need to look now."

"Before you're lost to motherhood," Lucy said. "You know it's coming."

"We won't lose her," Vivian said, patting Kate's knee. "She'll always still go. Look at me. I *need* these trips to maintain my sanity."

"Yeah, how's that working out for ya so far?" Wendy smirked.

"True, so far they've only raised my blood pressure, but hey, at least we were together, right?"

"Right!" they chimed.

The trip down the mountain flew by, and before long they emerged on a long downhill straightaway.

"I can see Denver," Kate said, pointing to a hazy clump of buildings.

They hit some traffic along the way, but nothing too crazy. Lucy announced they'd be there in 10 minutes.

"The airport is so isolated," Kate said.

"Probably won't be for long," Wendy responded. "If you build it, they will come, and all that."

"True." Kate nodded her head and looked out the window.

Lucy followed the signs to short-term parking.

"I figured you'd just drop us," Vivian said.

"Nah, I want to make sure you don't have any issues. Plus, I can help Wendy if she needs it."

Wendy laughed at that. "I'm able to walk today, and I'm not the one with the oversized, overstuffed suitcase here. I'll manage just fine."

"Oh goody, you can help me then!" Vivian said.

They parked and Lucy helped unload everyone's stuff. What remained of the backseat bar she was taking home as a thank-you for driving.

"One last hoo-rah, ladies," Lucy said, sticking the cowboy hats on everyone's head, then putting on her own. "Or should I say, yee-haw?"

The wind whipped up, and Vivian pushed her hat down and tucked some of her curls behind her ears. They made their way to the check-in kiosks at their various airlines, handed over luggage to screeners and then reconvened in the center of the concourse to say goodbye.

Vivian was just about to give Lucy a hug when a deep voice took her by surprise.

"I heard a rumor I'd find you here."

58

Vivian couldn't believe her eyes. Agent Nelson hobbled toward them using a wooden cane and looking a bit pale.

Wendy rushed up to him as quickly as her ankle would allow and threw her arms around his neck, knocking her hat to the floor.

Vivian scooped it up and stuck it back on Wendy's head after she let go. "Looks like the patient has escaped."

He nodded and exhaled. "They tried to keep me there, but I was ready to go. Things to do, you know." He glanced at Wendy.

"Oh, I know," Vivian grinned, then she gave him a big hug. "Agent Nelson, thanks for everything you did for us. Really."

"It's my job. And please, call me Wade."

"I know it's your job, *Wade*, but still."

"You're welcome," he said and bowed his head gracefully.

Lucy and Kate took turns hugging his neck and thanking him, too.

"You really should be in the hospital," Kate urged. "I can't believe you aren't."

He shifted position and winced a little.

"Do you need to sit down?" Wendy asked.

"That's probably a good idea."

Vivian checked her phone for the time. "I really need to get going. My flight's in 45 minutes."

"Me, too," Kate said.

Nelson looked at Wendy. "You have a few minutes? I'd like to talk to you."

"Sure, my flight's not for an hour and a half."

The girls started to say goodbye.

"Oh, wait, I have news," Nelson said.

"What's up?" Kate asked.

"There's a reward for the jewelry."

Vivian's mouth dropped open. "You're kidding."

"Nope, not kidding. It was for the capture of the thieves, and I'm going to recommend it go to you." He pointed at Vivian. "It's a bit of an approval process, but I imagine in a few months you'll be receiving a check."

Lucy jumped up and down, clapping. "Oh my god, how much?"

Nelson smiled. "$50,000."

The girls started screaming and hugging. All but Wendy jumped around in a big circle. Vivian tried to compose herself. "Holy crap, that's freaking fantastic! We need to set up the Getaway Girlz Traveling Trust Fund and use that money for our girls' trips!"

"Woo-hoo!" Lucy yelled.

"*Aye ya yai ya yai!*" Wendy chanted.

Kate stopped jumping. "Are you sure, Viv? You might need that money to help with the kids."

"Seriously, Vivian," Wendy said. "That is a lot of money for us to travel on. Why don't you take most of it and leave some in the trust fund?"

"We brought down Craig together, so we should share the money. How about we each take $7,500 and leave $20,000 to travel with?"

"I'm pickin' up what you're puttin' down," Lucy said.

"Let's break out the map!" Wendy said.

Kate gave Vivian a shoulder squeeze. "Thank you, I need these trips, too!"

They did another round of jumping, cheering and screaming.

Lucy looked at her watch. "Y'all better get to security. Sometimes the line sucks."

Vivian and Kate gathered their things, gave goodbye hugs to Lucy, Wendy and Wade and headed happily toward security. Vivian turned to look behind one last time and saw Lucy headed out of the concourse. She didn't see Wendy or Wade anywhere. *Guess they found a spot to sit and "talk."* She grinned.

Vivian and Kate boarded the tram, and it wasn't long before they arrived at Kate's terminal. Vivian gave her another hug as she headed out. Once the tram started up again she took off her cowboy hat and set it in her lap. *I'm so glad I bought these!*

The final stop was her terminal so she gathered up her carry-on and walked to the gate.

"How long 'til we board?" she asked the airline employee.

"Not long, five minutes maybe."

Vivian took a seat by the windows and pulled out her book. When she did, the adorable porcupine she'd bought in Aspen peeked out at her. She had brought all of the kids' stuffed animals with her as carry-on, just in case something happened to her checked luggage. She patted it on the head and started reading.

Before long, she'd boarded the plane, turned her stream of air on full blast, closed her eyes and fallen asleep. She awoke as the landing gear went down and they approached the tarmac. *That was my kinda flight.* She hurriedly went to baggage claim, got her suitcase and made her way to the car. She drove as fast as traffic would allow and was excited to see her cute little house on the cul-de-sac. She carefully pulled into the side-entry driveway, making sure no little ones were playing in the large space, a favorite, protected spot for tricycle riding and wagon-pulling.

She turned off the car and pulled out the four gifts. *I'll get the rest later.* She opened the car door and heard her favorite word echoing joyfully through the garage.

"MOMMY!"

***

Guess it's time to get to this, Vivian thought as she lugged her suitcase onto the bed.

It'd been a week since she'd been home from her girls' trip, and though she'd unpacked the essentials, most of the items were still crammed inside. Her phone buzzed on her nightstand. She picked it up and read the display. *What in the world?*

It was a text message from Wendy, and she couldn't believe her eyes.

Next girlz trip is in The Big Easy!

My bachelorette party!

Love ya!

Appendix

Just a few of the jokes we made at the fire pit about the butt crack girl:

Blue moon, Moon Lighting, moonstruck, moonwalk, fly me to the moon, howl at the moon, moon pie, moons over my hammy, Moon River, Moon Dance. Wonder who the first man was to walk on the moon? Full moon tonight? Why yes it is!

Flying Buttress. Butt...what are you talking about? Sure is cold and breezy out here, I'd go inside, butt, I like the fire.

Ass-tronomical, ass-cot, ass-inine, another word for a donkey, ass-pen, kick your ass, your ass is grass, creav-ass, ass-plosion, assholio. Assuming she can't feel her back side. I could use some assistance over here.

Crack whore, smokin' crack, step on a crack. You're cracking me up. Does that window have a crack in it? Say no to crack. Pass the graham crackers. I love peanut butter crackers.

And finally...
Anyone know a good plumber?

This is the life!

Golden Head is just the right height.

The ugliest beaver snatch ever.

Five Girlz in a tub!

"Oh god, she's doin' the wine goggles!"

In Bachelor Gulch with our Girlz.
Yeeeeeeeeeeeee-haaaaaaaaaaaaaaww!

Acknowledgments

We'd like to thank:

Our favorite Girlz, Lea Bass Rogers (cover design, story input), whose creative spirit and keen eye never ceases to amaze us. And Angela Wenk (story input, all-around antics), whose whirlwind of adventure provides us a ton of laughs. Thank you both for the continued support!

Thank you to the rest of our Getaway Girlz! Beth Zimmerman, our fan club Prez, Laura Trujillo, our unpaid promoter, Stephanie Surendran, our unpaid accountant, Vikki Shelton, our unpaid entertainment, Gretchen Hoover, our favorite dentist who makes us smile ten times bigger, Ellen Young, our perky cheerleader, Christine Moreno, our world traveler and Gerri Ybarra, Debra Baity, Claire Skold and Rose Benavidez, our new recruits.

John Dycus, the best editor in the world, for continuing to make us better writers and for the wittiness that keeps us looking forward to your next email (JK Rolling down the hill, F and replace…truly, where do you come up with this stuff?).

Janet Neff continues to amaze us with her uplifting personal, professional and never-ending support. Thank you Janet, for your friendship!! And Mr. Bill, for the sustenance and fine (naked) artwork. Keep that man cookin'!

Kimi Phillips, who, besides being a great photographer also took care of Johnell after her cliff-diving incident. Thanks also to the Hamilton ER folks. Y'all did a great job, too!

Kyle Phillips for your help with the book trailer. It turned out great!

Our beta readers – Jackie Meeks, and Janet Neff (again)!

Chris Broome, self-appointed CRM with Barnes and Nobles in Pasadena, TX. Your one question got us on the right path. Thanks for that, and for keeping *Getaway Girlz* stocked on your shelves!

Christina Judge, Alicia Jenkins and April Ciccarello for being our Fort Worth launch party girlz!

Steph, Vik and La for being our Get Down launch party girlz!

Brian Simons for your law enforcement expertise and making our bad guy worse.

Robbyn's brother, Steven, for the faulty brakes insight.

Johnell's brother, Reid, who is a great seller of books and full of ideas (like the dude ranch)!

Luis Estrada for your book trailer brain-picking.

Rose Epler for the fashion advice.

Riley, server at Brownstone, for his T-shirt quote: "I'm not Santa, but you can sit on my lap anyway."

Jono Ayala for designing the fabulous shadow box for *Getaway Girlz* that graces the wall at Chuy's.

Thanks to our favorite writing spots across Fort Worth, not only the free electricity, but also the great happy hours. Special thanks to Chuy's on W. 7th for hanging us up (and sometimes they come crashing down nearly taking out patrons, but we won't mention that!).

Johnell would like to thank:

Thank you to my kidlets, Danielle, Sadie, Cayce and Cameron. Thanks for being so supportive of my whimsical endeavor, for never complaining when I have to take you to a book signing and for being all-around, darn great kids! Love you guys!

Mom and Dad, thanks for always being there! You're willingness to keep a bag packed, car gassed up and ready to roll means a lot to me!

I'd also like to thank Robbyn for making me do this. I joke about you being a whip-cracker (which you are), but first and foremost you're a wonderful friend. Heart you!

Can't forget my Cook Children's family who've been so supportive during all of this! Especially my boss, James Eagle, who puts up with my clowning around on a daily basis, poor guy! And Susan Caskey, who helps me maintain my lottery habit! Thanks, all of you!

Thanks to Robbyn's husband, Dave, who puts up with our late (and occasionally wild), nights. I appreciate you sharing Robbyn with me!

Robbyn would like to thank:

Thank you David, for supporting my passion. And for putting up with the late nights when I'm out writing. I love you!

Mom, thanks for being the best mom I could've ever asked for. And yes, I know I shouldn't say "fixin' to" but I can't help it. It just comes out of my mouth.

Dad, thanks for the trips you took me and Steven on as kids. We always had a blast and they instilled the travel bug in me. I'm thinking Ouray... twenty years later!

Thanks Johnell for taking this crazy journey with me. I knew we could do it, but yep, somebody's gotta be the whip-cracker! Cheers to two down and many more to come!!

Thanks to Jason and Con with Envoy Mortgage. You guys are the best bosses ever! If you need a mortgage in Texas, call me! Need one in California, Colorado or Arizona - contact Kelli Fitch. Need one in North Carolina - contact Jason Pitarra. Need one in Illinois or Oregon - contact Con Browne. www.envoymortgage.com

Watch for the next book in the Getaway Girlz series:

Big Easy *X-capade*

Available 2013

www.getawaygirlz.com

facebook.com/getawaygirlz

twitter.com/joanrylen

youtube.com/getawaygirlz

CPSIA information can be obtained at www.ICGtesting.com
Printed in the USA
LVOW07s1012100515

437935LV00002B/590/P